THE LONG WHISTLE

Pearl Myers

Dec. 29, 2002

Brenda - Happy Birthday!

Maybe while you're resting, you
can do a little reading. ☺

Love,
Matt, Linda & Amy

THE LONG WHISTLE

A Novel
by
P.E. Myers

Printed in Victoria, Canada

National Library of Canada Cataloguing in Publication Data

Myers, P. E. (Pearl Edith), 1929-
 The long whistle / P.E. Myers.
ISBN 1-55369-508-9
 I. Title.
PS8576.Y44L65 2002   813'.6   C2002-902008-5
PR9199.4.M93L65 2002

TRAFFORD

This book was published *on-demand* in cooperation with Trafford Publishing.
On-demand publishing is a unique process and service of making a book available for retail sale to the public taking advantage of on-demand manufacturing and Internet marketing.
On-demand publishing includes promotions, retail sales, manufacturing, order fulfilment, accounting and collecting royalties on behalf of the author.

Suite 6E, 2333 Government St., Victoria, B.C. V8T 4P4, CANADA
Phone   250-383-6864   Toll-free   1-888-232-4444 (Canada & US)
Fax   250-383-6804   E-mail   sales@trafford.com
Web site   www.trafford.com   TRAFFORD PUBLISHING IS A DIVISION OF TRAFFORD HOLDINGS LTD.
Trafford Catalogue #02-0321   www.trafford.com/robots/02-0321.html

10   9   8   7   6   5   4   3   2   1

This book is for

my father, Oscar Johnson, and

my mother, Linda Johnson

Memories are life long treasures

fOREWORD

Conor Inish, a successful Saskatchewan farmer, has a loyal, loving wife and four carefree children. For twenty years the rich prairie land had yielded abundant harvests, providing solace and security for his family. Then, a time that was tagged the *Dirty Thirties* in later years, descends upon them in all its shame and bitterness, its trauma, its devastation. Stock prices fall, USA high tariff walls shut out Canadian wheat, and the price per bushel falls from a dollar sixty to forty cents in a couple of years. The weather, too, turns against them: a ten-year drought, dust storms, sun-scorched days, endless winds blowing the soil so deep that in places only the tips of the fence posts jutted above the drifts. The economy slows, factories close, mines shut down, municipalities go bankrupt, governments muddle, jobs peter out, and then it gets worse.

This story is about those strange years—those ten long years. It is a story of life: sad times, joyful times.

Read on ...

CHAPTER 1

HE WAS A MAN of perhaps forty or fifty. He had been handsome, one could tell that easily; now the deep lines sharply etched his forehead, surrounded his eyes and mouth and seemed to cut right through his face. He was a big man, but he had been bigger, well over two hundred pounds; now on his stooped six-foot frame clothes hung as loosely as on a scarecrow. He stood, eyes downcast. He spoke softly when he told the relief officer his name. Then his gaze lifted to focus on a cardboard sign: Closed for Lunch. The relief officer slipped out back; a door slammed shut. The man behind him in the lineup offered a handshake. "I'm Forrest MacLaren," the man said.

Forrest was as small for a man as the big man was big, but he wore clothes that fit and he stood straight. One bare knee shone through his pant leg and by the look of his long, once elegant, Prince Albert coat his elbows would shine through the sleeves in a matter of days. A black fedora perched atop shoulder-length brown curls. "You're a farmer?" he asked, lowering the hand that had not received so much as a glance.

The big man nodded without turning his head.

The relief office operated out of an old dilapidated restaurant building; Coke advertisements in shreds clung to the walls; a rusty Coke machine sagged against an outside wall. An equally battered street sign would have succumbed to the pull of gravity if someone hadn't propped it upward with a tree branch after painting a happy face beside the name, Cheery Lane.

A considerable time passed before Forrest extended his hand a second time. "I'm a lawyer," he said, then corrected himself. "I was a lawyer. Now I'm applying to the government for sustenance."

The farmer slowly accepted the outstretched hand and looked up at a pair of green eyes that seemed to penetrate right through him. There was a dandy's look to the lawyer—the style of his clothes, the cut of his hair.

"It's bad all right," Forrest said, "but it's the times, my friend."

"A lawyer on the dole!" The shocking news seemed to spark life in the farmer. He turned his head to look with sad eyes at the lineup stretching two blocks behind. Most of the men were city bred; he could tell by the hats and shoes they wore—not the countryman's caps and boots.

"I'm a plumber," said the third-in-line, a tall man with strong thick hands, much like the farmer's. "And he had a garment factory," the man added, jerking an elbow at a pallid countenance who stood fourth-in-line.

"It's the times, you see," Forrest said.

"But your family," the farmer mumbled.

1

"My wife divorced me," Forrest said, matter-of-factly. "She went home to her mother when the mortgage on the house was foreclosed. We had no children."

"The bank's foreclosing my farm," the big man said, his frown deepening the lines in his forehead. "They wouldn't lower the interest. They want me to stay on the farm—work it for them—stay on *my own* farm and take orders."

"Will you?" Forrest asked.

"No siree." The farmer kicked at a lump of dirt and crushed it with the toe of his boot. "I'll go on the dole first. I'll move the family to the city."

Everyone fell silent.

Much later the third-in-line, the plumber, rubbed the back of his neck with his thick hands. "You have to live in the city a year to get relief," he said.

It appeared the farmer wasn't listening. "Anybody knows you can't pay off a loan with interest at ten percent and wheat selling at forty cents a bushel and we got to pay the shipping," he said. "Twenty-five years and they told me I'm done for."

"You have to live in the city to be eligible . . . Oh, what the hell," Forrest complained to the plumber behind him since the farmer continued to stare glassy eyed.

"One year and you can get relief," the plumber, a patient man, completed the statement.

"We're going to paint the house," the farmer said. "The lass wants white with black trim. When wheat goes back to a dollar sixty, we'll put in running water and a bathroom."

"What's your name, farmer?" Forrest asked.

"Inish, Conor Inish. Born in Canada, St. John's."

"Don't wait in line no longer," the fourth-in-line said, wagging a finger at Conor Inish. "You have to live in the city a year to get relief."

"No wheat to sell," Conor muttered. "Doesn't matter if it's forty cents or a dollar sixty if there's no wheat to sell."

"The market crashed," Forrest explained more patiently.

"Don't care about the crash," Conor said. "Don't have stocks and bonds—my cows and machinery, that's my stocks and bonds."

"The mortgagee foreclosed your land mortgage and seized your stock and machinery?" Forrest asked.

"Yessir, stock and machinery. That's what I borrowed the money for," Conor said. "Auction's Saturday. The hand bills have been out two weeks.

"Sure now, 'twas good in '28. Good crops in '28," Conor added. "She's a farm on rich land, north of the city. We always knew we'd get a crop the year after next—just didn't happen."

"Damn country, she dried up," the plumber said.

Conor looked at the ground. "Drought, grasshoppers, rust, and always that wind blowing hot and dry. Blowing my land away. Every day, blowing my land away," he said. "They say my machinery won't cover what's owing."

"*Collateral.* Did you read your contract—loan companies must not interfere with the sanctity of a contract," Forrest said.

"I'm not a lawyer," Conor said. "Can't afford a lawyer."

2

"The government created a new act, the Farmers' Creditors Arrangement Act," Forrest said. He drew a business card from his vest pocket and began to write on the back of it.

"Go north," the plumber suggested, pointing a gnarled finger in that direction. "Many farmers going up north. Government says it's better. Leave the dust storms behind; no black blizzards up there."

"The fact is, up north the best land was taken long ago," Forrest said.

"Relief camp," the garment man suggested.

"How about the goddamned hobo jungle!" Forrest said, sarcastically. "He'll provide security for his family in the hobo jungle!"

"Don't have an answer," the plumber said sadly. "But I know you got to live in the city a year before you can get relief—no use waiting here. The soup kitchen, she's right over there."

"Here," Forrest said, pressing the card in Conor Inish's palm, "give this to your banker. But don't tell him where you met me. And keep your chin up, my friend."

The big man left his place at the head of the line and shuffled off to the soup kitchen.

CHAPTER 2

"WHERE DID THE BIG MAN GO?" the relief officer asked, sliding onto his stool. He glanced indifferently at the lineup as he tapped the counter with his pencil.

"He left," Forrest said.

"Next."

"Forrest MacLaren."

"Address."

"Unknown."

"Next."

"Hold on there!" Forrest said, raising his voice. "I require an application form."

"No you don't. You need an address."

The continuous tapping of the pencil caused Forrest's nerves to cringe. "I need you to furnish money to rent a residence, and then I'll give you an address," he said, straining to regain his calm.

"I follow the rules," the relief officer said. "No address, no relief."

The man's insolence was infuriating. Forrest rose to his fullest height. "I demand to see the supervisor," he said.

"A regular will come tomorrow. Next."

"Tell me his name," Forrest demanded.

"He'll be here. Come tomorrow and wait your turn in line. Move along."

The lineup pushed forward. "Move along," the factory man said. "We won't get through today, if you don't move along."

"Furnish me an application and I'll *move along*!" Forrest said.

A flush crept up the relief officer's neck; his pencil froze. "If you don't leave, I'll report you and no one in this city of Regina will ever put you on the dole," he threatened.

Forrest reached out and grabbed him by the tie. "And I'll report you for taking a prolonged lunch break with a waiting lineup two blocks long." Forrest jerked the tie; then he waved a fist in the man's face.

The plumber tapped Forrest's shoulder. "Police," he hissed the warning.

"Hey, over here," the relief officer bellowed.

Forrest turned to see two burly police officers stride forward. "What's the trouble here?" one asked.

"I am demanding my rights," Forrest explained. "I am entitled to benefits and I am demanding an application."

"Take him away," the relief officer said aiming his pencil at Forrest. "He threatened me and he's holding up the line."

"What's the charge?" the police officer asked.

"Assault."

"An assault charge! That's preposterous!" Forrest said. "I have witnesses."

"Come along." One police officer took him by the right arm, the other by the left.

"Where are you taking me against my will?" Forrest demanded.

"To jail. The city doesn't need bums like you harassing respectable citizens."

"This is criminal," Forrest shouted. "You may not restrain me on such flimsy evidence." Forrest looked at the plumber. "Tell him what happened," he pleaded.

"Next." The relief officer's impatient voice rang clearly across the compound. The plumber stepped smartly to the front of the line. The lineup moved forward one notch. Silent men jabbed the ground with a foot and several found a sudden interest in the wind in the trees and the clear blue sky.

The officers dragged Forrest to the police car. A violent shove slid him across the seat, slamming his head against the frame, like an egg chucked against a cement wall. Forrest's body slumped and lay still.

Forrest's first awareness after he woke was the window bars. His head throbbed and his stomach retched. The world spun. Voices from other cells cut through the fog to his brain.

"The small guy, what's he in for?" a husky voice asked.

"No idea, but he looks like he could use a good meal," another said between coughs that echoed throughout the gloomy halls of the jail.

"The food ain't bad. Better'n a lotta soup kitchens. Good a place as any to winter."

"I can't wait to get out of here."

"What got you in?"

"I asked the wrong guy for a dollar."

"Beggin's agin the law," said the husky voice.

"Is it against the law to eat?"

"You better see the doc about that cough."

"Have to be on the pogey to see a doctor."

"Pogey. Ain't never bin on the pogey."

"My old man will turn in his grave if I go on the pogey. He was a proud old Scot."

"Yeah, ain't no man prouder'n an old Scot," agreed the husky voice. "I bin shut up a month. Railroad says I beat up one of their bulls. They ain't seen nothin'. So they gave me thirty days for ridin' a freight."

"Bulls—you must be talking about the railroad police."

4

"Mean, mean men. Meanest bastards on earth. I've seen men die from a few kicks by the yard bulls. They call me Jerico Joe."

Plates clattered and the conversation ceased. Forrest wanted to eat and to talk with the prisoners, but he sensed his stomach would rebel if he ate and his aching head would split if he talked; consequently, he settled back to the thin mattress and snuggled the dirty gray blanket under his chin. He thought of his father, a Scot if there ever was one. He conjured up an image of his eccentric father, clad as he'd seen him last in a century old saffron shirt fashioned of the clan tartan. Forrest chortled weakly at the ridiculous figure, barelegged and barefooted. "Weel, dinna lie there laughin' like th' slow-witted gowk ye nay doobt be!" roared his father's image. "Respect for yere forefathers is but common decency. And, aye, laddie, niver disgrace th' clan o' MacLaren by beggin'. Curse th' black knave thot takes what he's nay worked for." The Lord worked in mysterious ways, Forrest thought. The jail episode had saved him from the wrath of his father's ghost. Fitfully, Forrest slept.

Jerico Joe wasn't sure if his thirty day sentence was up tomorrow or the day after. Inside, the guards treated him well, the food tasted fine, his fellow prisoners were congenial; still, outside would be pleasant too—to breathe the fresh air, to see the countryside in late summer colors, to find his old-time friends. If the weather were cold he'd have been reluctant to leave the jail, but what he saw through the barred window was a warm sunny day.

His cell mate, Slim, had coughed and shivered all night. The guard told Slim the rule was one blanket to a prisoner, so Jerico gave him his.

Jerico had slept outdoors many nights without a blanket, and besides he always wore a lot of clothes. But there was a time in his life when he had had few clothes to wear. That was in Russia, near Leningrad, where he, his father and his mother, lived in a cabin beside a potato field belonging to a farmer who'd hired his mother. Summer and winter she cooked an early morning oatmeal breakfast before tying a red babushka over her head and hurrying across the potato field to do her chores. Just before dark she'd return with enough potatoes, corn, and beef for a stew—her pay for a day's labor. Then, one summer, his mother was let go; the potato crop had failed.

At that time Jerico was fourteen, a husky boy of average height with straw-colored hair and quick brown eyes. His name was Joseph Petrov; his parents called him Joe. His father often said that he was a boy who wouldn't amount to much, but others took a different stand, saying that he was a youth who needed encouragement and guidance to succeed in life. But Jerico never did see inside a school. His father had no respect for educated people. "Swinya! Swinya!" he called them.

His grandfather on his mother's side bought them passage to Canada, the land of opportunity. Destitute, the little family landed in Vancouver.

Jerico's father demonstrated how to make money honestly by placing a hat on its crown on the busy sidewalk and singing, or playing, a melancholy song with the harmonica. Jerico's favorite tune was "Swing Low Sweet Chariot." He found his voice trembled naturally when he came to the line about angels coming to carry him home. Jerico's new profession didn't always fare well, some days the family went without food.

It was on such a day his mother ventured across the tracks to the city dump and found enough food to carry them over. But she'd found more than food, she found an empty van, the kind in which the vegetable man delivered his produce. It wasn't much like a house, but did have walls and windows. The front seat became Jerico's bed. She salvaged half a dozen two by fours, leaned them against the roof of the van, covered them with sheets of discarded tin and boards, and nailed flattened cardboard boxes to the inside. The lean-to had no window, but the cracks let in enough light to dress and undress—his parents slept on the ground inside this room until his mother dragged in a dry mattress from a new shipment of garbage. This dwelling amongst the rats became their home, no rent to pay, for one full year.

Jerico's mother blamed the dampness for the cough she could not get rid of. She sat most of the day beside a tin heater she'd set up inside the van. The chimney poked through the ventilator in the middle of the roof as though it were a scope atop a submarine floating in a sea of garbage.

Life became routine, his mother gathering combustible material, his father wandering off to talk with buddies, Jerico himself walking up town, collecting what money people threw into his hat, buying groceries and returning home.

His mother's cough became more persistent and one day she couldn't get out of bed. Jerico went up town to fetch a doctor, but the doctor said he was far too busy to leave the office and that his mother should come to him. She wouldn't go.

One day while Jerico was sitting outside in the sun whittling a piece of cedar, a truck drove up. The driver, a boy not much older than himself, got out and lifted a lever to dump his load, and then he took a box from the seat and walked toward Jerico. "Howdy," he said. "You living here like this?"

"Yeah," Jerico said.

"Why don't your old man get a job up town?"

Jerico didn't know the answer. He couldn't remember his father ever having a job. "*I* work up town," he said.

"Guess you don't make much money. Here, take this. Then you don't have to dig for it." He held up an apple. "It's all good. Just a spot or two you can cut off."

Jerico accepted the box and placed it inside the van. When he came out the driver was still standing there.

"I whittled this," Jerico said, handing over a carved bird. "You can keep it."

After that meeting Jerico got a lift to town. The driver's name was Herbert Blake, and he lived with his parents on Main Street. He had worked for Fruit Wholesale for two years. "I don't like it," he said, "but it's a job."

Jerico told about his life in Russia and how life was much better in Vancouver.

"Really?" Herbert said.

A month later Herbert told Jerico there was an opening at Fruit Wholesale and he should apply. "When you go, wear this and ask for Mr. Charles," he said, handing Jerico a jacket.

Jerico was hesitant, but Herbert had become his best friend so one morning soon afterward Jerico put on the new jacket and headed for town.

Fruit Wholesale was a red brick building with wide steps leading to the front door. Jerico sat on the curb across the street for a good ten minutes before he slowly rose, shuffled up those steps, opened the door and peered inside. Desks crowded the room and from behind them people stared at him. He was turning to leave when the girl who sat at the front quickly rose and asked what he wanted. When Jerico told her he was looking for Mr. Charles she led him down a hallway and tapped on one of the many doors lining the walls. Mr. Charles was alone at his desk with his feet propped on top of it, and the chair in which he was sitting leaned against the wall as he puffed clouds of cigar smoke at the ceiling. He looked sharply at Jerico.

"Herbert told me you come from Russia," Mr. Charles said.

Jerico agreed that he had.

"You're a Communist, a Red. Vancouver don't hire Reds," Mr. Charles said.

Before Jerico could speak, Mr. Charles ushered him out of the office and closed the door in his face.

Mr. Charles had ruined the morning for Jerico, but the afternoon was exceptionally good on the sidewalk, and Jerico's spirits rose as he carried a slab of bacon and a dozen eggs homeward. He played a tune on his harmonica as he walked jauntily along.

It was the same day his mother died. His father told him that she'd coughed to death and that he'd buried her in the corner of a nearby cemetery when no one was nearby—he'd had no money for a service. Jerico went there that night and cried over her grave as he'd never cried before.

When he arrived home his father was out. Jerico stayed two days, waiting, then slipped an extra pair of pants over the pair he was wearing and pulled Herbert's jacket on top of his own. He wrapped the bacon in a towel. Looking back he spotted a jar of colored pebbles his mother had collected; he selected fifteen of the prettiest, one for every year of his life. He followed the railroad tracks all morning until he came to a bridge where men were idling beside a campfire. Remembering the bacon, he unwrapped it and strode up to the group with his offering.

He stayed four days, telling tales, playing cards, singing to the music of a harmonica. Jerico had left his harmonica behind—he hadn't felt like playing after his mother died. An old man by the name of Boxcar Bob took a liking to him, and Jerico soon felt right at home with his new friends. He learned to swing safely onto the freight cars, even rode the rods on a dare—but he swore he would never do *that* again.

A lad by the name of Ossified Osmond had dared him. Ossified and Jerico were both fair-haired, the same age, the same height, the same weight, but there the similarity ended: where Jerico was discerning, Ossified was heedless; where Jerico was cautious, Ossified was reckless.

"I dare you. You're scared," Ossified said.

"I ain't scared," Jerico objected.

"You're scared of riding the rods."

"What's there to be scared of?"

"You'll find out."

They hid in the shadows and watched the yard bull walk up and down, a club in his hand. Another man tapped the wheels with a hammer and stuck the spout of his oil can in here and there. Finally it came: "All aboard." The yard bull and the oil man turned and headed for the station.

"Now," Ossified hissed. He and Jerico crept forward and dived behind the wheels and under the car. The train jerked. Jerico yanked his foot out of the way and swung up beside Ossified. The train jerked again; the rails began to pound; the rods to tremble, to jump, to snap back. Face down, bellies pressed against the rods, they held on with both hands. The train picked up speed; air roared past, sand and gravel pelted their faces. Jerico squeezed his fingers tighter. Ossified had buried his face in his jacket. Jerico did the same and tried to relax his rigid grip on the rods. He wished he were on top with Boxcar Bob, looking at the stars and the moon and breathing in the clean night air. Never again would he take a dare. The noise became a thundering bedlam. He swayed and swung and cramped one leg round a rod to keep from toppling off. He imagined his body lying on the sleepers, a twisted mass of broken bone and bloody flesh, and his father standing over him looking down and saying that his son hadn't amounted to much. He thought of his mother and wondered if the pebbles had shaken out of his pocket—they were all he had for a keepsake. He should have helped her to gather the wood, helped her to make the meals when she was sick, but he hadn't thought of it—no one thought to help his mother. He didn't dare open his eyes, but he knew Ossified was still with him when a leg bumped his own. The cords in his arms felt as if they'd snap. He wanted to laugh at the craziness, the stupidity, but he was too scared. Damn it, if Ossified could do it so could he! Then the whistle blew, a faint distant sound almost blotted out by the scream of the brakes, and Jerico relaxed his hold and dared to lift his head. Ossified's eyes were white and wide in a face coated with grime and Jerico knew his own were the same. When the train stopped they got out and stood swaying and would have fallen if they hadn't reached out to steady each other. They shook out the sand imbedded in the creases of their clothes. "Better get out of here," Ossified said. They staggered toward the shadows.

For years Jerico rode the freights—on top. He saw the Pacific and the Atlantic and everything between: the mountains, the foothills, the plains, the lakes, the forests. He learned to read the hobo marks along the tracks, on a trestle, a wooden fence, a gate post: plus marks, a place that gave good handouts; two circles underlined, you can sleep safely in this man's barn; crisscross lines, a bad bull patrolling these yards; scribbled lines intersecting, the people will help if you're sick; two lines like two sticks holding a pot above a fire, a good jungle, come on in.

Then he noticed more and more men lined the roofs of the freight cars, and he learned of the crash in a place called Wall Street and these men were seeking work. Now, when Jerico knocked, householders told him there were too many hoboes and please don't knock again. Sometimes Jerico went to bed hungry—his husky figure slimmed down. When a young man approached him with a business proposition Jerico listened. Jerico had never operated in the manner the man described, but he realized to survive he had to change his ways. Almost immediately his financial position improved and after ten years was still going strong.

Slim was thanking Jerico for the blanket and saying how well he'd slept when the guard unlocked the door. "Just you," the guard barked at Jerico. Slim coughed and looked at the guard pleadingly, but when the guard ignored him, he calmly folded the two blankets to look like one and spread them to cover the mattress.

Jerico mentioned to the guard that Slim needed a doctor. "Lots of guys coughing in here," the guard said, motioning Jerico out the door.

CHAPTER 3

CONOR INISH SLIPPED THE APPLES from his overall pocket and set them on the worn leather seat beside him. The gas gauge was stuck at one quarter of a tank. It stayed there, no matter how much or how little gas the car held. The last time he'd filled the tank was at Roney's gas station in Redgarth a month ago, and he'd driven little since, only one trip from the farm to Redgarth eight miles distant. He had enough fuel to get home.

The soup at the soup kitchen hadn't been tasty, but it had been hot and nourishing and had eased the dark foreboding of disaster. He had picked up four apples for Ingrid and the children; a treat since money was scarce.

Conor's thoughts were often about his family. Ingrid, his wife, had placed her trust in his hands—he had failed that trust, but he didn't know who or what was to blame. He'd never failed his family before. He'd heard the economy slowed, but no one would tell him the cause of this frightful nightmare.

It was in the spring of the year, three years ago, the banker, Mr. Willoughby, had said, "You have a splendid year in sight, Conor. Borrow now and pay in the fall. Run livestock on that stubble. Let the cattle grow fat on the grain your new combine leaves behind." At the time the advice was sound and Conor took it. By mid-June the crop was filling, but the rain stopped and within three weeks the crop was down to nothing and there was no harvest in the fall. The amount he was able to pay barely covered the accumulating interest. Twice more Mr. Willoughby extended the loan. But there was no crop to take off the next fall and the fall after that.

To make matters worse, the livestock Conor had purchased for seventy-five dollars brought fifteen or under on the market. Mr. Willoughby said he'd done his best but the inspectors wouldn't allow another extension. Conor had seen the two hard-boiled inspectors traveling through the district; they traveled in pairs as though they were police officers in a tough neighborhood. Mr. Willoughby himself seemed to change; he wasn't the cheerful, easygoing Mr. Willoughby that Conor had once known. And when Conor handed the lawyer's card to him, Mr. Willoughby asked if he'd found it on the street. Conor had felt an uncontrollable surge of anger at the insult; he had abruptly turned his back and walked away.

Yes, he was a failure. He thought of his mother who often told him never to put the coward's name on himself. "Listen up, now," she'd say. "Show us what you can do." What could he do—find a job? He'd take any line of work he could get, but from what he'd seen in the city, jobs were nonexistent. Perhaps he could go west to harvest. There the wheat would be ripe, and he knew every aspect of harvesting. Yes, that's what he could do—go west.

The Bjornsons, Ingrid's parents, knew he was in trouble and had made a place for them all in their Winnipeg home. Winnipeg was four hundred miles to the east but the Chevy would make it. The children had much adjusting ahead, city home, city school, but true, the times were to blame and many neighbors had had to suffer the same.

By the time Conor drove the eight miles to the homestead he felt a spark of his old self returning, but when he came to the fence he'd built and the moment he opened the gate his heart ached with nostalgia. Beneath the thick clump of leafy poplars leaned the old soddie he'd built twenty-five years ago. He poked his head through the twisted frame of the caved-in doorway. Memories flooded his mind and he slumped in the grass and sobbed; eight years he'd lived in the soddie, working, improving, saving, and building up the homestead. He'd earned enough money during those eight years to build a home for his city bride.

His two Thoroughbreds trotted across the pasture, stretched their necks over the fence and waited for a neck rub or a handful of oats. Decked out in their silver-studded leather harness, the Thoroughbreds were a magnificent sight—in town all eyes turned to their beauty. Now they'd be auctioned and probably he'd never see them again.

Conor got into his '29 Chev and putted ahead on the well-packed lane, leaving behind a cloud of dust. He passed the hip-roofed barn, and slowed as he approached the house. The house was sturdy, built of fir lumber shipped from the West, and it rested on a cement foundation. The design resembled the neighborhood houses except the verandah ran half the length of the house, and from it opened the entrances to the kitchen and the living room. At Ingrid's suggestion, he meant to add on lattice trim along the roof and up the peak. On the shady, ivy-covered verandah his family would be resting, awaiting his return.

There was so much still to accomplish, so many plans gone awry. He had set his heart on surprising Ingrid with running water in the hand basin and bathtub, and a flushing toilet. One upstairs room was vacant for this eventuality. Conor roughly rubbed the moisture from his eyes and cheeks as he parked the Chevy in the shade of a poplar tree and strode to the house.

CHAPTER 4

INGRID IRATELY TOSSED HER MOP of blonde hair over her shoulders to hang down her back where it belonged. She hovered over the hot kitchen range and for the second time, jabbed a fork in the scalloped potatoes. The fork wouldn't penetrate the mass, so she jammed the lid on the pot, pushed it back inside the oven and closed the oven door. She lifted the roaster containing the roasted chicken to the warming oven at the top of the range. The wood-box was empty when she went for a stick to liven the fire. Danny had never consistently neglected his duties before, and Kathleen was no better—the empty water pail sat atop the wood-box.

Ingrid stepped to the verandah. The cool shade was a welcome relief from the kitchen's hot interior where she'd spent most of the afternoon. On the top step Danny sat staring at nothing, and Kathleen sat beside him making designs on the dusty verandah floor. Ingrid had swept the verandah twice today, but she'd sweep twice more before the day was out. She swatted at the ivy vines trailing the verandah roof and a swirl of dust settled upon her and the children.

"Mom," Kathleen complained, "do you have to do that?"

"Yes, and you have to fill the water pail," Ingrid scolded. "Danny, get up and carry in the wood. There will be no supper if the fire goes out."

Danny continued to stare and seemed not to hear his mother. Ingrid began to scold again but stopped when she saw tears in his eyes. "What is it, Danny?" she coaxed, for she'd found if she were stern, her thirteen year old would hide his feelings—he was so much his father's son she could anticipate his thoughts. "In time you'll feel better about the town," she said.

Danny placed his forehead on his arms.

"You'll find new friends," Ingrid said.

"Mutt can't come with us to town," Danny said. At Danny's words, the dog wiggled from under the step and sniffed at his face, then settled in the dust at his feet. "Mom, why don't we stay here?"

"Your father has lost the farm to the bank. That means we don't own it anymore, Danny."

"Dad shouldn't have done that," Danny said.

"It isn't his fault. Try to understand," Ingrid said. "Your father did his best but the crops failed us all."

"But if no one else lives here, we can."

"Your father thinks it's best if we move to town. The town will rent us a house and feed us and help your father find work."

"I don't see why we can't stay here," Danny said through his tears.

"The cattle and horses and machinery will be sold," Ingrid said and felt tears push at her own eyes. "Your father isn't able to farm with no machinery and he doesn't want to live here on the farm if it doesn't belong to us. Go and bring wood. Your father is coming home soon and he'll be hungry."

"But, Mom," Kathleen said, "Karen's father lost his farm and he couldn't find work in town. They had to move. I don't want to move."

"We'll live with Grandpa and Grandma if there's no other way," Ingrid said.

"Winnipeg's too far. And Grandpa won't let Danny keep Mutt," Kathleen argued. "I don't want to live with them. Grandma is always so cross."

"Don't you kids slide down the rail. Take your shoes off in the house," Danny imitated his grandmother's sharp voice.

Ingrid looked at the floor. She didn't want to live with her parents any more than the children did. Her parents had objected to Conor since the day they met him for the reason the Irish drank too much. Conor drank sparingly, but her parents wouldn't reason at the time she had tried to put them straight.

"I don't see Helga or Olaf," Ingrid said.

"They took Bossy to Old Mister Smith's bull to be bred like Dad told them," Kathleen said.

"Why do we bother when she's going to be sold?" Ingrid asked. "Her calf followed, I suppose. Kathleen, go milk. You've time before your father comes home."

"Mom, Olaf always milks," Kathleen said.

Ingrid felt her impatience rising. "You said Olaf went to Mister Smith's place. Please go milk," she said sternly.

"That cow kicks," Kathleen complained.

"If you'd cut your fingernails she wouldn't kick," Ingrid said.

Kathleen glanced at her long painted fingernails, and then looked sheepishly at her mother. She went to the kitchen, picked a milk pail from the pails atop the wood-box and headed to the corral. She walked the path to the cow corral, juggling the pail back and forth, swinging a complete circle above her head, and at the instant the pail escaped, stretched her tall slim body upward and recovered it as gracefully as a ballerina.

Ingrid watched her daughter walk across the yard. She walked like Conor and looked like Conor who had brown hair and brown eyes, unlike Olaf and Helga who had blond hair and blue eyes. She mused her family was two families: Danny and Kathleen, her husband's children, Olaf and Helga, her own.

It was seventeen years ago Olaf was born. A neighbor, Mrs. Swenson, had rushed forth at Conor's urgent plea and in under an hour had delivered the baby.

The wee boy was the spitting image of herself: same face, same hair, and same complexion. She had laughed at the sight and had apologized to Conor since it seemed the boy belonged to her alone—even the baby's infrequent cries were in a hushed voice much as her own.

But two years later, the next baby, Kathleen, was her father's daughter, and Conor apologized for fathering a girl a dead ringer of himself. The phenomenon held true for the next two pregnancies. Ingrid smiled, remembering those joyful times, prosperous times, easy times that had slipped by so swiftly. She had believed they'd go on forever—but they'd not gone on forever. No one had forecast times would come so hard that the dearth of rain and the bitter heat and the barren wind would shrivel not only the crops but also the pastures. No one had believed the family's diet to survive would consist mainly of potatoes and eggs and wild rabbits. The bank will see little profit selling the gaunt, half-starved cattle and horses; she could count their ribs beneath dingy coats. She assumed it was easier to watch them sold than to watch them starve. The baled barley and oat straw the government gave to the farmers for fodder failed to contain the food value required to keep the animals fit. She had tried cheerfulness and encouragement, but it was too much to bare knowing Conor was dying inside. Perhaps leaving was the answer; staying would be like rubbing salt into raw wounds.

"I put wood on the fire," Danny called from the kitchen.

"Open the draft," Ingrid told him. "Here come Helga and Olaf. And your father's coming up the drive."

Ingrid knew instantly the day had gone wrong—Conor's face looked more troubled than ever. She wanted to tell him not to worry, it would be all right, but the words were hollow and would offer little comfort; instead, she died a little more inside as she walked quietly by his side and waited for him to speak.

"Well, lass," he said, pressing her hand to his cheek, "tough times ahead, no relief, no jobs in town. You have to move to Winnipeg. I'm going to move on with the harvest." He sighed and hugged her to his chest.

Ingrid could think of nothing to say, and even if she had, couldn't speak for the tightness in her throat.

Olaf brought the roasted chicken to the table and cut small portions. Even stuffed with bread crumbs, the prairie chicken was scarcely enough to feed six hungry people; nevertheless, Olaf was proud since his expertise with the .22 rifle had brought it down. "There's another behind the soddie," he told his father, "but the .22 shells are gone."

"You did well, lad," Conor said. "But you won't need the shells. You'll be driving the family to Winnipeg."

"In the Chevy?" Olaf said elated. "But I'll come back," he added with quick determination.

Ingrid detected a new strength in her husband who sat at the head of the table, confronting his family. Hope filled her heart; she bowed her head and blessed the food.

"Continue your education," Conor told the children. "Do what you can to help your grandparents. I'll send money to your mother for your keep."

"What if the bank takes the Chevy?" Olaf asked.

"The bank has no right to take the Chevy. Mister Smith suggested we leave it in his barn for safekeeping. Store it there, Olaf, until you're ready to leave."

"Dad, you should drive," Danny said. "Olaf doesn't know how to drive."

"I leave in the morning to go harvesting," Conor said. "Olaf is an excellent driver."

Helga placed her hand on her father's shoulder. "Dad, don't leave. We'll have no one to look after us."

"What harvest?" Kathleen asked. "Ain't no harvest."

"You shouldn't say *ain't*," Helga scolded. "Miss Sparks said *ain't* isn't a word."

"There will be crops in other areas," Conor said. "I'll start west and then head north where the crops are later."

"I suppose you'll leave quickly. You'll want to be there when the harvest starts," Ingrid said, "but I wish you were coming with us."

"Just one more mouth for your parents to feed. Winnipeg has no job for me," Conor said.

"I'm keeping my cook stove," Ingrid said—her mouth set with determination. The stove was a good Gothic range that Conor had bought when they moved into the house—she'd no intention of parting with it.

"The cook stove, the heater, beds, table and chairs, and dishes stay," Conor said. "What you don't have room to take to Winnipeg, store in Mr. Smith's barn."

"What about my clothes?" Kathleen asked. "They're old but they're all I have."

"They won't take our clothes," Danny said.

"Why won't they?" Helga asked.

"They wouldn't fit, that's why," Danny said.

"Dad, I won't let them take Blossom," Helga said. She squeezed her father's hand. "They won't take Blossom, will they, Dad?"

"Blossom, well, I'm sorry, Honey, but Blossom will go in the auction." Conor lifted Helga in his arms. She broke into sobs. "It's not the way I want it, Helga," he said. "God willing, one day I'll get you another pony."

"Blossom kicks," Kathleen said. "She's mean. You should be glad she's going. Now Big Red, for sure Grandpa won't let us take a rooster to the city."

"We can't go," Danny said. "There's no key to lock the door."

"Someone could steal something," Helga said.

"You know we never lock the door," Conor said. "Someone passing through may need shelter."

"You can't leave, Dad," Danny persisted. "Mom's afraid of the dark, and if you leave, she'll have to go outside at night sometimes."

"We won't be here, Danny," Helga said, to put him straight. "She won't need to go out in the dark if we're not here."

"Girls, clean the table and wash the dishes," Ingrid said. "Your father and I have more to talk about. And Olaf, please water the ivy; it looks like it's drying up."

"It'll die anyway, Mom, when we're not here to water it," Olaf said, but he took two water buckets and obeyed his mother's order.

"Mom, maybe Grandpa will let me keep Mutt if I earn money for his food," Danny suggested.

13

"We'll see about Mutt," Ingrid said, noncommittally. Her father hadn't let her have a dog when she was a child; he hadn't liked dogs.

Danny couldn't let Mutt go—Mutt was his pal. Mutt went everywhere with him, protecting him—if it hadn't been for Mutt he'd probably be dead. It was just last year he'd been crossing Mr. Smith's prairie pasture on his way to join Olaf who was out hunting when he saw Mr. Smith's mean black bull had gotten out of its pen and was grazing with the cows. Danny stopped dead in his tracks. He squatted behind a small pile of rocks, but the bull turned toward him, scooping up the sod and flinging it over his back, all the while grunting and roaring deep in his throat. Danny panicked. He ran for all he was worth for the barbed wire fence he'd crawled under not long before; he didn't even slow enough to look back until his side began to ache so hard that he thought he wouldn't make it. And there was the bull; Danny could see the red in its eyes and the nostrils flaring. Danny fell. Mutt charged, and sinking his teeth into the bull's nose, hung on. The fence was near; gasping for breath, Danny hobbled to it and flung himself under. Safe on the other side he watched in horror as the bull swung his head from side to side, flinging poor Mutt far out in the grass. Mutt scurried under the fence and lay panting beside Danny.

CHAPTER 5

THE JAIL DOOR'S metallic clang woke Forrest.

"Get dressed." It was the guard and he wasn't bringing food. "You're out."

Forrest thought it incredible, but he didn't stop to argue. Within ten minutes he was in the sunshine, a free man. He was famished; he should have demanded a meal.

"Hey, you're Small Guy," a husky voice accosted him.

"Jerico Joe." Forrest recognized the man from the jail. "I'm Forrest MacLaren. Pleased to meet you on the outside."

Jerico Joe had a loud laugh—a belly laugh that erupted in short bursts.

"Join me in a free meal," Forrest invited. "Salvation Army's around the corner." Proud Scot or not, an empty stomach wasn't to be tolerated.

Jerico Joe fished in the pocket of his dirty tattered jacket—his hand came out empty. "The Sally Ann, she'd better have tobacco," he said.

On entering the soup kitchen, Forrest spotted Conor Inish, the big man who'd been waiting in line at the relief office. Conor carried a full plate and was looking for a place to sit when Forrest caught his attention and pointed to an unoccupied table. "Save a place," he called.

The line moved briskly. Forrest observed sausages, head cheese, boloney, cheese, and bread, and his mouth watered even though he was certain the food was the cheapest available.

"Got tobacco?" Jerico Joe's voice boomed at the busy attendant. She ducked under the counter and came up grasping a small bag and cigarette papers. "What, no matches?" Jerico Joe asked, peering into her eyes from beneath his pinched, bushy brows. "Ain't got no matches—hell of a Sally Ann this is," he grumbled to the crowd in general.

14

"The farmer has matches," Forrest said, employing the mollifying voice he'd perfected in the court room. He picked up tobacco and papers for himself.

They filled their plates and wound their way to the table where Conor sat. Conor hadn't touched his food; he was obviously waiting until they were seated together. Such fine manners seemed out of place in these surroundings, Forrest thought.

Jerico Joe rolled a cigarette; Conor light a match and held it for him.

Forrest noticed a change in the big man, he seemed acutely aware of his surroundings, perhaps action was what Conor Inish needed to straighten him out. Forrest felt Conor staring at his two black eyes, the cut on his chin and the rip down the leg of his pants. "Spent the night in temporary confinement," Forrest explained.

"Tell him the truth," Jerico Joe said. "Ain't no crime to spend the night in jail."

Jerico was wearing two coats and several pairs of pants; it was obvious the clothes had never seen soap and water. He'd grown an unruly red beard, which he had occasion to scratch now and then. His bedroll smelled so bad that it was spoiling Forrest's appetite. Forrest moved it under the seat in the pretense of needing more seating room.

"Farmer," Jerico nodded a greeting to Conor. "You quit farming? I'm heading west after I'm done eating."

"West?" Conor asked. "How?"

"Hop a freight," Jerico said.

"Riding the rods?" Forrest asked.

"Only if the dicks are after me for murder," Jerico said and laughed his belly laugh.

"An open boxcar?" Conor asked.

"Ain't many," Jerico said. "Maybe the branch lines. You got to get on top. You think that's easy?"

"Never had occasion to try," Forrest said.

"You don't jump on a boxcar and away you go. Gawdamighty, no!" Jerico said. "You got to get on while it's moving."

"Moving?" Conor asked. "Why moving?"

"'Cause it's leaving," Jerico said seriously.

"And the yard bulls," Forrest suggested.

"You catch on fast, Small Guy," Jerico Joe said. "Them bulls will getcha. Stay out the yard. The train is rolling."

"How fast?" Conor asked.

"You got to reckon how fast," Jerico said, loftily. "You got to run quarter as fast as the train."

Amazed, Forrest looked at Jerico—there was an art to this fiasco!

"If it's slippery, maybe sloping grade, you don't swing on if it's going more than thirty," Jerico said. "If you swing on, bump along, let go—sausage meat!"

Forrest shuddered.

"You got to travel light," Jerico continued. "A light turkey or no turkey at all. You can't swing up with a turkey in the way. Carry your stuff in your pockets."

"Your bedroll—that's a turkey?" Forrest asked.

"You catch on fast, Small Guy," Jerico Joe said with admiration. "We'd make a good team."

Forrest deliberated. "West, you say?"

"Yeah, are you headed east?" Jerico asked.

"I'm not headed anywhere," Forrest said.

"You heading west, Farmer?" Jerico asked Conor.

"Yessir," Conor said, "I'll catch the next freight."

Jerico picked up his shabby bundle. "Let's shove off," he said. He snuffed his cigarette stub against the table top and poked it inside his shirt pocket.

"Oh well, what the hell!" Forrest said. He rose, snuffed his cigarette and tucked the stub inside his hat band.

In the lead, swaggering Jerico Joe led them out the town for perhaps half a mile and onward to the rails.

The long whistle, the long call to the West, was coming down the tracks.

Jerico Joe stuffed everything in his pockets. Conor followed suit. Forrest watched—every stitch he owned he wore.

The steam engine chugged past, followed by the clatter of iron against iron, a deafening din. Conor felt his heart beating fast. Sausage meat! Sausage meat! the wheels clanged their warning.

Jerico Joe surged ahead. "Follow me fellows," he shouted over his shoulder. He let one car go by and before the next whizzed past, he jumped for the ladder and swung up. Lickety-split he went to the top and lay flat, peering down at his companions. Conor ran a good lick, grabbed, swung, and hung on. His feet fumbled for a rung and found one. Forrest scurried up behind him.

"Lie flat," Jerico ordered.

Forrest and Conor did. Conor was breathing heavily and placed his hand to his chest. "It's about all I can do," he gasped.

"For how long?" Forrest asked.

"Couple miles," Jerico said.

"Wouldn't want to try that on a slippery day," Forrest said.

"Told you it ain't easy," Jerico said.

Scores of drifters lay flat on the tops of the long line of boxcars.

The sun dipped below the horizon. A golden glow brushed the clouds; crimson streaked the western sky.

"Gawdamighty, she's a bloody mess up there," Jerico observed.

"An artist's delight," Conor said, wistfully.

"The highest to which man can attain is wonder," said Forrest.

CHAPTER 6

"GLORY BE, WHAT'VE WE HERE!" the auctioneer cried, hefting a large field stone to his shoulder. He held it there with one hand and rubbed the stubble on his whiskered chin with the other. "Where will you ever find a more serviceable foot warmer? Just heat 'er in the oven when you want to keep your tootsies warm. Give me a starting bid of a dollar on this clever invention."

The audience guffawed. "Jim, you could sell a ton of spuds a day to a country-town grocer."

"Five cents! Five cents!" a shrill female voice shouted.

"Five cents! Look, woman, I'm sick to death hearing you bid five cents. This modern invention deserves a low bid of a dollar. You're insulting science and progress alike with a measly, disgusting five-cent bid."

"Five cents! Five cents!" a group of women took up the gleeful chant.

The auctioneer reached behind his box and took a long swig from a bottle of orange pop. It dribbled down his chin.

"Drunk again," the shrill voice cut the air.

"Who wouldn't be drunk with women like youse to deal with," he boomed above the hullabaloo. "Why the hell don't you go home and mind your babies." He polished off the bottle.

"I ain't coming to any more of your auctions," the shrill voice shouted. "All you can talk is rubbish, and you don't even shave."

"Glory be! Glory be!" the auctioneer leered in her direction, winking at the crowd. "No, no, folks. I wouldn't *really* sell you this. It's a phony but this auction isn't phony, it's sound merchandise. Stick around folks. Lots here, you can see that—great stuff and going for a doh-ray-me. It's your show folks. Stick around for a square deal."

Leisurely, the colorful crowd circled the yard: women and girls in their best print dresses, men and boys in their mended and freshly ironed shirts. There was much on display: a matching chesterfield and chair, a dining room table and six chairs, a buffet, dishes, linen, and numerous household items. A score of men appraised the machinery lined at the edge of the yard: a John Deere combine and tractor, so little used that the paint was like new, a plow, disk, harrows, cultivator, wheelbarrow, hayrack, buggy, harness, and more. At the corral, farmers sized up the stock: twenty cows, as many yearlings, a dozen calves, four draft horses, and two first-class Thoroughbreds.

"Where's Mom?" Olaf asked.

"She cries all the time. Kathleen and Helga took her to Mrs. Swenson's place," Danny said. Danny had tied a length of binder twine to Mutt's collar and although the dog tugged and pulled Danny refused to let him loose. "You'll get sold if you're not careful," he warned.

"This stuff piled in the house we'll take to Mister Smith's barn," Olaf said.

"Maybe they'll come for it," Danny said.

"Nobody wants Mom's old pictures and curtains," Olaf said. "Neither the sewing machine nor the rocking chair. Hurry. Fetch the radio. Help me load this stuff in the Chevy. We'll use the back door. Prop the chicken house door open."

"What for?" Danny asked. "Big Red will get out, and we'll just have to chase after those hens again."

"Just do it!" Olaf ordered.

Danny did, then gathered Mutt in his arms and placed him on the front seat. Two loads and the boys had moved the pile—they drove the Chevy in the barn and swung the big barn doors closed.

"Come on," Olaf said. "If we run we'll see what the machinery goes for."

"I can't run a mile," Danny said. "I'll get a side-ache."

"You know the way," Olaf said. "Stop if you have to."

Olaf heard the auctioneer's droning song a half mile distant and as he drew closer he could make out the words. "This combine and tractor. It's near brand new. Top of the line. Give me a bid. You'll farm like a king."

"Like a king?" a farmer shouted. "If I'd a king's money, I'd buy it."

"That's crazy! No one wants a combine when there's nothing to cut," another said.

"I've a fifty-dollar bid, this old-timer here. Give me a hundred—calling for a hundred. Folks, you're missing the chance of a lifetime. This outfit cost the buyer near a thousand dollars; it's top of the line. Do I get a bid of a hundred? It's going, going, going, gone, to the old-timer there. Name?"

"Smith," the old man shouted.

Olaf eased through the crowd. It was Old Mister Smith. Possibly he didn't realize it wasn't kind to embarrass your neighbors by appearing at bankruptcy auction; besides, he harvested his wheat with horses pulling a binder, he'd never mentioned wanting a combine.

The crowd moved forward. "A plow. Every farmer needs a plow. Give me a bid on this plow," the auctioneer hollered.

Olaf climbed the corral fence to the top rail. He heard Old Mister Smith bid on the machinery but he always left off prior to the final bid. It was strange behavior—everyone knew Mr. Smith to be a level-headed old man. Again it happened when the auctioneer came to the stock, except Mr. Smith did buy the two Thoroughbreds. Olaf assumed the old man mistakenly bid too high and got stuck with them. On the other hand, possibly he felt that he'd made a down payment on the horses since it was his hay kept them sleek and healthy. Olaf had seen him throwing hay over the fence dividing the two farms to augment the sparse pasture grass on the Inish side. Well, he could always sell them again at the next neighborhood auction. But he didn't bid on Blossom, no one bid on the pony until the auctioneer cajoled a farmer who lived sixty miles away into shelling out two dollars for her. "I'll fatten up this piece of crow bait and feed her to my silver foxes," he said, pleased with his purchase.

Olaf looked over the crowd from his perch. He recognized a few people: a city bank teller who everyone called Little Louie because he was five feet tall, a city theater owner by the name of Farnsworth who everyone said was the wealthiest man in the city since he charged too much admission to his shows, and then there was Mr. Martin, the Redgarth butcher who probably came to the auction for the chickens. Mothers had spread their blankets beneath the poplar trees; several nursed their babies there in the shade while others distributed sandwiches to the children. It was summer holidays, school was out and children ran everywhere, playing tag round the trees and hide-and-seek in the barn. Olaf supposed Kathleen and Helga were at Mrs. Swenson's with his mother, since he couldn't see them anywhere.

Two men in a magnificent black Chrysler drove up the lane. The men, dressed in dark suits, approached the crowd and halted to watch the auction's progress. They spoke with the auctioneer and after a lengthy discussion, pushed through the crowd in Olaf's direction.

"You're Conor Inish's son?"

"Sure now. I'm Olaf Inish."

"The auctioneer told us your father is absent. Here is Mr. Willoughby's letter, advising foreclosure changes."

"What changes?" Olaf asked.

"Owing to the legalities put foreword by your father's lawyer, the land foreclosure was canceled."

"You mean we can stay?" Olaf bounced from his perch.

"That's what it means, son."

"But everything's sold. The machinery and the cattle are gone. We can't farm with no machinery."

"That's an issue your father has to face, but rest assured the land itself is unencumbered. The auction proceeds cover the outstanding lien."

Olaf accepted the letter. Still stunned at the sudden change of events, he watched the Chrysler leaving until it was merely a dot in the distance.

The crowd moved to the house, and the auctioneer went inside. In a minute he stuck his head through the doorway. "Nothing here to knock off, folks," he called. "Waste of time unless you want to run down chickens in yonder field." The crowd groaned. The sun had shone all day and the heat had been intense. The women and children were tired and ready to go home. Even the Redgarth butcher wasn't reluctant to let the auction end when he saw the chickens scattered far and wide.

"Then, that's it, folks. Gather your stuff, bring it here to me and settle up."

"Mom, don't cry. We're almost there," Kathleen said.

Ingrid wiped her eyes and blew her nose; she breathed deeply and straightened her shoulders. "I'm all right," she assured her daughters.

When they knocked on Mrs. Swenson's door, Ingrid was calm, but when Mrs. Swenson greeted them with, "Oh, my poor dears, such a terrible, terrible time," Ingrid lost her composure.

"Mom, don't cry," Kathleen pleaded. "Please, don't cry anymore."

"Do come in," Mrs. Swenson invited. "You must stay for coffee."

"Thank you," Kathleen said, "we didn't want to bother you, but Mother couldn't watch the auction any longer."

"My poor dears. You must stay here with me and rest," Mrs. Swenson said. "I'll be sorry to see you leave."

"And I'm sorry to leave," Ingrid sobbed the words, "but it's the best we can do."

"Where's Mr. Inish at this terrible time?" Mrs. Swenson asked. "A man *will* leave at the time a woman needs him most. It's not my affair, but I think a man is head of the household and that's where he should stay."

"Conor *is* head of the household, Mrs. Swenson. Harvest has started in the West. We decided together he'd go west to work," Ingrid explained.

"Men wandering far and wide. It's a curse in itself. If they come to my door asking for a meal, I tell them to go find work," Mrs. Swenson said. "And those who go on relief are a disgrace to the country. Just too lazy to work—that's what I say."

"Dad says the men are down on their luck and we ought to help them," Kathleen said.

"Oh, yes, I know what your father says, and I know he gives them food. Word like that gets around. But I say it encourages those useless people to come to our community. I forbid Mr. Swenson to have anything to do with them."

"But, Mrs. Swenson, if they don't get food, they'll starve," Kathleen pointed out.

"You're young and such a sweet girl, Kathleen. One day you'll see I'm right. Too lazy to work. Just born that way." Mrs. Swenson gulped a swallow of coffee in her haste to tell all. "Like that boy Mario in the Italian family down the road. They say his father doesn't want him around no more."

Kathleen bit her lip.

Mrs. Swenson set her coffee cup on the table with such force the liquid splashed over the side; then with her watery blue eyes she looked sternly at Kathleen. "They say he's leaving and I say good riddance to that trouble maker."

"He's leaving?" Kathleen asked anxiously. "Where's he going?"

Mrs. Swenson's scowling brows drew together. "Who knows," she said. "A boy like him."

Ingrid felt indignant. Mrs. Swenson's opinions were often testy, but this was altogether too harsh. Mario's parents were poorer than most and no doubt doing their best in these hard times. Ingrid felt no fondness for the boy either, but a girl of Kathleen's temperament, hearing such criticism, would become defensive and more enraptured. "Mrs. Swenson, I feel fine now," she said. "I just remembered I must tell Olaf something important. We must go."

"Olaf is a fine boy," Mrs. Swenson cooed. "I remember the day I brought him into this world."

"Yes, I'll always be thankful, but we must go," Ingrid said.

Helga held the door wide open—she shut it firmly behind them.

"She's a two-faced old woman and I hate her!" Kathleen blurted out as they walked homeward.

"Kathleen! That's rude!" Ingrid scolded. "She's our neighbor."

"I don't care. She's two-faced. She pretends to like Olaf and then she says terrible things about him behind his back."

"How do you know?" Ingrid asked.

"Marjorie told me. Mrs. Swenson goes to her place and sits all afternoon gossiping with her mom and dad," Kathleen said. "And Mr. Swenson, he's so henpecked he won't open his mouth unless she tells him to."

"The Swensons are on the school board and so is Mr. Black. Maybe they're discussing meetings," Ingrid said.

"Oh, Mom!" Kathleen moaned.

It was the end of the auction. As the procession of puttering cars and jingling buggies passed by, the three ran in an attempt to escape the dust. Olaf leapt from the verandah and waving a letter, came running toward them, Danny and Mutt bouncing behind. Her relatives had written, Ingrid expected, before she realized by the look on Olaf's face something exceptional had happened.

"Open it," Olaf said.

"It's from the bank," Ingrid said, looking at the envelope. "Olaf, no good news comes from the bank."

"Open it now, Mom. Don't move another step before you open the letter," Olaf said.

Kathleen took the envelope, slit it open with her fingernails, and passed it to her mother.

Ingrid read the official-looking document. "The land is unencumbered. The land foreclosure has been nullified. What does it mean?" she asked.

"It means Dad didn't lose our place," Danny said. "And Dad can come back, and I can keep Mutt."

Ingrid sniffled.

"Mom, you're crying again," Kathleen said. "This isn't something to cry about."

"I'm so happy it makes me cry," Ingrid said. "I've never been so happy." She folded the letter with care and tucked it in the bosom of her dress.

In the field Big Red crowed and strutted triumphantly among the hens. Mutt circled, barking and leaping high. The five joined their hands surrounding him, dancing, and laughing, and clapping, in their indescribable joy.

CHAPTER 7

FORREST WAS INCREDULOUS. "He's sleeping. The man's sleeping!"

"Yessir, I hear him snoring," Conor said. "I ain't had a wink myself."

"With this infernal racket, only a professional vagabond could sleep," Forrest muttered. "How is your backside, my friend?"

"Numb."

"I suppose you're famished," Forrest said.

"Those sausages I ate last night shook right down to my ankles," Conor said.

The train slowed, approaching the outskirts of a city.

"Turn round," Forrest said. "Heaven above sent a message."

Conor turned and what he saw was a makeshift sign, *Free Food*, leaning against a garage.

"Jerico," Conor said, "he's sleeping like a baby."

"Wake him," Forrest said. "There may be an art to exiting this boxcar."

Jerico's eyes peered at them from beneath coal dusted brows. He rose on an elbow and grumbled. "Could'a slept more.

"Gawdamighty! It's Mrs. Jordan's place. Hop off," he said, coming fully awake. Jerico scurried down the ladder, executed a superb jump to the sloping gravel, slid to a halt and jogged off to the garage in one smooth motion.

Conor's jump lacked similar grace. His body swung clumsily at the moment his boots hit the slope. He turned in time to see Forrest's leap—a somersault—Forrest's low-cut city shoes offered little support in slope sliding.

"Damn it to hell!" Forrest picked himself up, shook the dust out of his hair and jammed his hat back on his head.

As they came up, a chunky woman, an apron tied around her middle, greeted them. "It ain't much," she said, "just porridge, but there are raisins in it."

She stood beside a massive, ancient, cook stove, all but covered with gleaming designs and the words Royal Alexandra scrolled across the oven door. The range stood against the wall, while lined down the middle of the room rough planks served for tables and benches. A hand scrawled sign dangled from the ceiling, *Welcome*. The bowls were chipped and not one was a match to a set, but the atmosphere was charged with fellowship and all because of one little woman who looked as if she could have been the mother of any one of the many young men she served.

"Much obliged," Conor said. "I'd be pleased to help with the chores."

21

"Right kind of you. I'm Mrs. Jordan. Tell you what, when you're ready just come through the garage to the back. There are water pails to fill and wood to split."

The benches inside were occupied. Conor and Forrest took their porridge bowls to where Jerico Joe sat on the ground, arguing with a couple of men. "Look, fellows, it ain't so," Jerico was saying. "It's like this, Pete; he got killed in the Connaught Tunnel. Stupid bugger lay on top—passed out from coal smoke and fell off."

"I heard the tunnel at Field. I heard somebody pushed him off," Pete said.

"She makes no difference anywise," said the man beside Pete—"dead is dead."

"What I'm telling you boys is you got to be inside those boxcars going through a tunnel," Jerico said.

The men agreed it was the only sensible course of action.

"If you're near Calgary, the best jungle's by the Ogden Yards," Pete said.

"I been there," Jerico said. "Always got a stew pot going. All you need's salt and a spoon."

"Carrots and onions were peeking out the ground behind a house," Pete said. "Onions *make* a stew.

"Oh, hey, speaking of Calgary," Pete added, "did you hear about the dust storm that ripped the roof off a boxcar? Be damned if it didn't kill Alberta Slim."

Conor left to do the chores. The wood was knotty poplar and hard to split, but it was dry and would kindle Mrs. Jordan a quick fire. He carried the wood to the garage and piled it against the wall handy to the cook stove.

"Where's the water tap?" Forrest asked.

Conor pointed to a pump midway between the house and the garage.

Forrest worked the squeaky handle up and down until his elbows ached. "What's wrong with it?" he asked Conor. "Is it defective?"

"Prime it," Conor said.

With a cup Forrest scooped what water he could from the bottom of the reservoir and poured it in the pump with one hand as he worked the handle with the other.

"You'll need more," Conor said.

"And where do you suggest I find it? Barbaric instrument! Ought to have running water." There was some water left in Conor's water bag. "Give me a hand, will you," Forrest pleaded. "If this doesn't succeed we'll suffer thirst as vile as being lost in the Sahara." They combined their efforts and soon the pump gurgled, jerked and flowed—six strokes and the pail was full. Forrest dumped it in the Royal Alexandra's reservoir, and then he placed a full pail on the bench beside the stove. He refilled Conor's water bag before looking for Jerico Joe and his friends, but the boxcar travelers had wandered off.

"The boys mostly mutter thanks and leave," Mrs. Jordan said. "But they've been beaten down too long—one can't expect they'd think to do a chore or two. Tell you what, join me in a cup of tea."

Mrs. Jordan poured tea for three. "Why, only yesterday, a girl came," she said, "She was shy—hunger made her do it. She was such a comely little thing, no more than sixteen."

Conor pictured Kathleen sitting at that table, riding that boxcar. He pushed the unpleasant thought out of his mind; his family was safe in Winnipeg.

"It's the hard times," said Forrest.

"For too long—nearly ten years now. Some call it the Great Depression. It's taking the best years from those boys." Mrs. Jordan rose to stir what remained of the porridge and to move the pot to the stove's cool side. "Are you looking to work on the harvest?" she asked Conor.

Conor nodded. "I expect around Medicine Hat the crops are ready."

"Scattered," she said. "The men tell me north of Calgary is the place to go, but the crops ain't ready there. I know a farmer near Brooks you could try."

"Well, we're looking for work right now," Conor said.

"Hatfield is his name," Mrs. Jordan said. "He farms big and hires big if the grasshoppers ain't ate everything. He'll try to knock you down on the wages though."

"What's the rate?" Forrest asked.

"Most pay two dollars a day. Some men take less, just so they can get on."

"Go for it?" Forrest asked Conor.

Conor nodded. "There's no way but up," he said.

Swift Current Creek ran alongside the tracks. Here Conor and Forrest came upon fellow drifters sleeping in the shade of the willow bushes, or in friendly conversation, relaxing and smoking a cigarette. In a quiet spot, with the gentle sound of the brook to lull them, Conor and Forrest slept.

Jerico's belly laugh roused them. He had for sale razors, razor blades, candy bars, salted peanuts, aspirin, fountain pens, cigarette lighters, soap, shaving brushes, tobacco, and snuff.

"He steals it," a young man said.

"I ain't no thief," Jerico Joe said, insulted.

He sold the items for a dime or fifteen cents or a quarter a piece. Every item sold and every buyer was satisfied with his purchase.

"Anything you need, Small Guy?" Jerico asked. "You think I stole that stuff, don't you? Here's how you do it. Up town this guy's got a family, you see, and he wears a suit but he ain't got no money and he ain't got no job. He finds guys like me he knows has a dollar stashed somewhere. He tells me to go take a walk through the drug store and I do—me down one side and him down the other. Can't figure why but the clerk trails me step for step, and he don't even watch what the other guy's doing. We square up in the alley. I get it for a dollar."

"Handsome profit," Forrest said. "Sales total approximately five dollars. Cost one dollar. Profit four dollars—no risk involved."

Jerico Joe beamed proudly at what he supposed was praise.

"You were a willing accomplice in a robbery," Forrest said, sternly. "If convicted of a certain class of crime, a person is technically a felon."

Jerico's grin disappeared. "Awe, Small Guy," he said, "You'd turn me in, your best friend?"

"You're damned lucky I need boots, size eight," Forrest said.

"Boots are bulky. Don't know where he'll stash 'em, but we'll figure a way to fill your order," Jerico Joe said, with the air of a successful businessman. "How much money you got?"

"None," Forrest said. "No filthy lucre in my pockets."

The long whistle roused the travelers. Soon men lined the track.

The wind blew all the time—steady as a rock. Today it came out of the west. The men hunched their backs against it—to breathe was a chore—field dust swirled around the boxcars, and up into their faces. "Looks like Montana dirt to me," Conor said.

The smoke stacks blew back coal dust to choke their lungs. "How far do you think to Brooks?" Conor asked. "Much longer up here and we'll look like black men."

Forrest grinned. "Are black men hired to harvest?" he asked.

"Are white men hired to harvest?" Conor asked. "What I've seen is men looking for work."

"Medicine Hat's behind us. Two, three hours we should be there."

Conor stretched his legs. "If only I could sleep like Jerico," he said.

"If you rode the freights as long as he has, you probably could," Forrest said.

"Think he'll go harvesting?" Conor asked.

"Doubtful," Forrest said, "the body is able, but is the spirit willing? A dysfunctional personality!"

Pellets stung Forrest's back. "What? It's hail out of a clear blue sky."

Conor laughed. "It's not hail, it's grasshoppers." In seconds, layers of grasshoppers covered the boxcar roof and the men.

Forrest held one high by the long hind legs. "Repulsive rascals," he said. A piece of beer bottle glass lay in the debris on the edge of the roof. He held the glass to his eyes and looked at the sun. "I see millions, high in the sky, but I see each one individually. Here." He passed the glass to Conor.

"Terrifying," Conor said. "Nature on the loose. Hope they don't plan a stopover in Brooks."

"What's this slime splattered everywhere?" Forrest asked. He ran a finger across the edge of the roof and held the oily substance for Conor to judge.

The train slowed—the wheels had no traction—it finally slugged to a standstill. It was juice on the rails—juice of crushed grasshoppers.

Jerico Joe bolted upright. "The bulls!" he exclaimed.

"Just grasshoppers," Forrest assured him.

"You ever see the like of this—grasshoppers stopping a train?" Conor asked.

Jerico picked the insects sticking to his beard and threw them to the wind. "Slows her sometimes," he said, nonchalantly. "It'll go in a minute."

Jerico proved to be right. The grasshopper cloud dispersed and slowly the train rolled. The travelers brushed the hoppers from their clothes, scooping them over the edge.

An hour later the long whistle blew and the train slowed. Brooks came in view a mile ahead. Forrest purposely watched Jerico Joe's exit leap—perhaps he'd missed an important link in Jerico's maneuver. He wished Jerico would wait until the train slowed, but apparently he feared the railroad bulls more than he feared to disembark.

The time for his jump was now. Forrest leaned less forward than in his first effort and this time dug his heels in the gravel with all his strength. His oxfords twisted from his exertion and almost came off his feet, but he remained upright. His performance was exhilarating—perhaps he would become a successful hobo after all.

Conor walked beside a silent lad near Olaf's age. He'd seen the lad on the freight car roof, always alone, staring straight ahead at the flat prairie passing by. The lad staggered, attempting to keep up. Conor slowed his pace and soon they fell behind the group.

"Hungry?" Conor asked.

With a closed, distant face, the lad looked at Conor a long time before nodding.

Conor gave him a friendly smile. "If I know Jerico Joe, he'll lead us to the soup kitchen. I'm Conor Inish. What's your name?"

"Nick Sikorsky," the lad said, faintly.

Nick suddenly slumped to the ground, unable to go on. Conor whistled to attract the men's attention and two men came back to help. "He just ain't had a meal for a few days," one observed. They hoisted Nick's arms across their shoulders and started off. Nick gave no protest—he seemed resigned to his fate.

Conor wondered what would become of the lad; he was sympathetic since he remembered well the feeling of hopelessness.

When they arrived at the soup kitchen Conor heard considerable grumbling, nevertheless, the men ate vigorously. Conor heaped his plate to a maximum—he was hungry—he was always hungry.

Conor hadn't seen many stout men in these lean times, but he saw one now; the overweight cook was stirring an enormous pot of soup. His greasy apron covered a huge belly, and as if savoring his own soup, he rubbed it with his free hand. But he laughed a hearty laugh every time he opened his mouth, and that made up for a lot—in these hard times laughter was as scarce as food. The cook knew the Hatfield farm. "Five miles west," he said, pointing a finger in that direction.

Conor drew the lad, Nick Sikorsky, away from the foul smelling kitchen. "Done any farm work, Nick?" he asked.

Nick nodded. "Grew up on a farm," he said.

"Where at?"

"Manyberries."

"Sisters and brothers?"

"Yeah, not enough food to go round," Nick said.

"Come with us to Hatfield's place—he's hiring on," Conor said.

Nick's expression remained hopeless, but he nodded.

Jerico Joe bounded up. He dropped a gunny sack beside Forrest, waited in line for a plate of food, and then squatted beside Conor.

"How much?" Conor asked.

"Fifty cents. You ain't going to find a better deal," Jerico said. "These boots cost six times that much at a store."

Conor passed the fifty cents. "We're off to the harvest. You coming with us to Hatfield's field? It's five miles west."

"Hatfield's field?" Jerico Joe looked thoughtful. "Wal, no, Farmer," he said, "I got to meet a guy. I can't go with you this time."

Forrest approached, gunny sack in hand.

"Can't go with you, Small Guy," Jerico Joe said cheerfully. "See you 'round somewhere."

Conor was surprised at the warmth that had developed between the two men. Perhaps Forrest felt he had learned much from Jerico—a lawyer being taught by a hobo!

CHAPTER 8

"IS THIS WINDOW CLEAN?" Helga asked her mother. She was cleaning the inside window pane and Danny the outside.

Ingrid stepped to an angle out of line with the sun's glare and checked the glass. "It'll do," she said.

Danny pressed his tongue against the pane. "Danny's kissing the window," Helga shrieked. She pressed her own tongue in line with his. They giggled.

"If you play you'll never finish," Ingrid said. "See, now you have to scrub those kissing marks."

Ingrid stepped to the verandah and shook the curtains. "No point to wash these curtains before it snows," she said to the wind.

"Why?" Helga asked.

"The wind blows the dust, and the curtains get dusty in a week anyway."

"The windows get dusty," Helga said.

Mister Smith gave the *Star Weekly* magazine to Olaf after he'd read it, and there it was on the kitchen table in plain view, the funny papers left open at Li'l Abner.

"You little schemer, you finish the windows, then you can read."

"We'd be done if Kathleen were helping," Helga said. "She always has to visit Marjorie when there's work to do."

"Not fair, they discuss their school work and that's important. School starts in two weeks."

"Mom, they don't talk about school. They talk about boys." Helga giggled. "And kissing."

"Helga, don't talk like that!"

"Mario, Mario, Mario," Helga imitated Kathleen's voice.

Ingrid stroked Helga's hair. "It's only puppy love. Please, finish those windows. I want to hang these curtains."

"Kathleen loves Mario and Marjorie said Olaf has dreamy eyes. I think Marjorie loves Olaf."

"Like I said, it's *puppy love.*"

"And she gets to stay overnight," Helga pouted. "I want to stay overnight at Christine's house."

"We'll see," Ingrid said.

"There's Olaf, and he shot a rabbit. Mom, I want to go with Olaf next time," Danny said.

"Danny, you skin the rabbit after you help to move the furniture," Ingrid said.

Olaf laid the rabbit on the verandah. "Don't you touch that, Mutt," he scolded the dog. Mutt lowered his nose to the floor and looked up at Olaf with pleading eyes. Mutt had once stolen a roast of venison from the kitchen table while Ingrid's back was turned—the roast was never found. Ingrid had banished Mutt from the kitchen for two months.

"Olaf, help Danny put the old chesterfield and chair where the others used to be," Ingrid said.

"We're lucky Dad doesn't throw things out," Olaf said. "Old benches and broken chairs and all sorts of stuff in the loft."

Ingrid chuckled. "Your father is such a miser," she said. "Put the radio and rocking chair in their old places."

Olaf stepped back. "Looks fine, Mom. Not so pretty, but it's cozy."

"We'll manage," Ingrid assured him, "and if you bring home the meat, we'll do just fine."

"I'll bring home the meat, don't you worry about that," Olaf said. "But I'm worried about Dad. He doesn't even realize where we are."

"Your grandmother will forward the mail; then we'll try to reach him," Ingrid said.

"Harvesters move on with the harvest," Olaf said. "By the time we get the letter Dad could have moved on a hundred miles."

Ingrid's fear was Conor might go to Winnipeg, but there was little she could do about that. "I guess we'll just have to wait for him to come home," she said.

"We could ask the hoboes to look for him."

Ingrid was afraid of hoboes. The train tracks ran within half a mile of the house, and when a hobo came across the field and knocked at the kitchen door, she'd quickly make a sandwich or scoop leftovers onto a plate, then pass it out and hastily fasten the hook.

Conor had told her not to fear the hoboes because they were quiet men who only came for food and on receiving it would leave. But, in spite of Conor's reassurance, she could not stop the fear that came over her at the sight of a hobo.

"We could ask Jerico," Olaf said. "He knows Dad. He's the one with the scar on his forehead."

Ingrid contemplated Olaf's suggestion—her thoughts hadn't connected Conor's life to the life of a hobo. Perhaps he'll ride the freight trains the same as she'd seen hoboes do—a ghastly thought.

Ingrid hadn't looked closely at any of the strangers who came to the door, but she did recall one of the men because he was talkative. "Do you mean the fellow with hair that hangs over his forehead and the long beard?"

"Yes, it's mottled and curly. He's the one who wears a lot of clothes," Olaf said. "Mom, surely you haven't forgotten," he added, "he's the one you caught in the rain barrel." Olaf chuckled.

"He hasn't been around for a while," Ingrid said, uncomfortably. "It's late, Olaf, I'll get supper while you milk."

Indeed, how could she forget, and it was Conor's fault and he hadn't even apologized—he had laughed. It had happened shortly after one of those rare summer squalls that sometimes left water in the rain barrel. Since well water made her hair streaky, she'd taken the small metal tub and a dipper and was already around the corner of the house before she saw clothes in a heap beside the barrel. It was near supper time so it was excusable for her to think it was Conor, although he usually announced the event ahead of time. The man was ducked down, soap suds everywhere. "I want some of that water before you get it all dirty," she announced, tapping the man's shoulder with her dipper. When a straw-colored head lifted and a strange face appeared, she reeled in astonishment, tub and dipper clattered to the ground.

When she scolded Conor for allowing this to happen, he said, "Honey, he's just a man who doesn't have his own rain barrel."

27

"You shouldn't have let him," she snapped.

"Let him! I had a hell of a time convincing him to do it. He said he didn't need a bath."

Milking the cow was a slow and steady task that gave Olaf time to meditate. He wished he could at least speak to his father to ask advice, but this being impossible he had to make decisions on his own. First there was the question of food. His mother had told him she had twenty dollars, enough to keep them in flour, sugar, oatmeal and shells for his gun. The chickens, the cow and the calf would provide meat. But if the chickens were butchered there would be no eggs, and if the cow was butchered there would be no milk. That left the calf, but it was a heifer and it was needed to start a new herd. Olaf sighed. Anyway, at freeze-up he could go fishing and shoot a deer. Thank goodness the well hadn't gone dry like some of the neighbor's—he could load the water in barrels on the stone boat for the vegetable garden, if Mr. Smith would lend the Thoroughbreds. Then there was the question of firewood—winters were bitterly cold, sometimes fifty below, and his mother would burn much firewood to keep the house warm. Perhaps Old Mister Smith would let him use one of his draft horses to skid poplar poles from the bush to the house. It was customary for a group of neighborhood men to trek farm to farm cutting the logs in stove length with a circular saw outfit. To his regret he would have to miss a week of school to join them. Not that he didn't want to join this neighborly group—last fall he'd been especially joyful since Marjorie was there to help his mother and Kathleen serve the lunch. He'd be expected to take his father's place catching blocks as they fell from the spinning saw blade. His mother was always anxious at wood cutting time. Mr. Smith had lost the middle finger of his left hand to the blade, and the neighbors considered Mr. Smith to be a cautious and agile man—this was in the days before he became known as *Old* Mr. Smith. The owner, Mr. Swenson, wouldn't let a soul touch a file to the teeth of his circular saw. That was his job and his alone. Olaf had seen Mr. Swenson spend hours sharpening the blade. There were a lot of teeth, the blade's diameter was three feet, and Mr. Swenson filed until the blade cut through the blocks as though it were a knife cutting butter. Still, Olaf was sure he could handle the job safely. He'd taken careful note of how his father stood—one leg forward and one back, bracing himself against the sudden weight of the blocks as they fell from the blade. If the logs were small, the men serving them cut five or six together. It was a challenge to toss that many blocks at one time as they were often crooked; poplar trees in this country were mostly gnarled and twisted.

Bossy stood at ease contentedly chewing her cud. Olaf had no sooner settled himself on the stool than Bossy displayed her affections by nuzzling his shoulder, splattering him with slobber from her muzzle. It was a particularly large amount of slobber since she'd been chewing her cud from eating green grass by stretching her neck far between the fence wires of Mr. Smith's prairie field. Olaf wiped his head dry with his shirttail. "Tarnation, cow. Stop that!"

The tinkling sounds of milk streams on the metal pail and the soft drumming in foaming milk were music to Olaf's ears. His mind began to dream. It was Saturday night and Marjorie was snuggled in his arms as they danced to the beautiful tune "Sleepy Lagoon." He looked deeply into her eyes and what he saw there was a reflection of his own love. A slap across the back by Bossy's long tail brought him up short. "You won't do that again," he cussed, tying the long hairs of her switch around her hind leg before settling himself back to the stool. "Marjorie, will you marry me?" No, no, much too forward. "I want you to be my girl." No, not that either. What could he say that was original and loving at the same time? Ordinarily Olaf would have stayed clear of Bossy's maneuvers by quickly shrinking back out of her reach, but the weight of life's problems and the rhapsody of love had slowed his impulses. Bossy now displayed her affection with so much gusto that she knocked him off the stool and into the gutter. Fortunately, Danny had cleaned it that morning.

Ingrid sat behind the wheel of the Chevy—she was learning to drive and botching it. She felt a need to drive with Conor away harvesting. If one of the children became sick or had an accident and Olaf wasn't nearby, it would be crucial for her to drive to town to the doctor—the alternative was to ask a neighbor for help, but Ingrid wanted to handle her problems in her own way.

"Let the clutch out slower, Mom," Olaf said.

Ingrid tried again. Danny flew to and fro in the back seat. Helga giggled. The Chevy spluttered and died.

Olaf got out to crank life into the motor once more. "Take it out of gear while I crank," he said.

Ingrid was furious with herself. Countless times she'd sat beside Conor and watched him start and stop effortlessly. It had seemed so simple; she thought she'd easily jump into the driver's seat and drive away. But it wasn't that simple. She gritted her teeth, shifted to low gear, and forced the clutch pedal tight to the floor.

"Give it more gas when you let out the clutch. Listen to the motor," Olaf said.

"Don't pump the gas pedal," Danny said. "Makes it jerky."

Helga giggled and clutched the back of the driver's seat.

"You two be quiet back there," Ingrid said. She held her breath and concentrated on her left foot on the clutch, at the same time judging the motor's strength. This time the Chevy jerked less and didn't splutter as she kept her right foot steady on the gas pedal. The car rolled. Olaf had pulled out the crank and now got in the passenger seat. Ingrid looked straight ahead and gripped the wheel until her knuckles turned white. "We're going too fast," she cried. The car whizzed ahead, much faster than when Conor drove it seemed.

"Mom, it'll stop if you go any slower," Olaf said. "Speed up and shift to second."

The gears growled and shifted and carried the car smartly onward. Olaf grinned at his mother. "See, you can drive," he encouraged.

"Oh, no!" Ingrid cringed. Ahead, driving toward them was a car. "It's coming down the middle of the road."

"It'll move over when you drive closer," Olaf said.

"Mom, stop. It's the Blacks," Helga said. "Kathleen's there."

If there was one thing Ingrid had learned to do, it was how to stop; she pulled over, put her foot on the brake, and the motor died.

The Black's Ford coupe pulled alongside and Kathleen jumped out. "Mom, you're driving," she squealed in astonishment.

"Now the women drive," Mr. Black said, scowling. "What's next? A woman prime minister?"

Olaf laughed. Mr. Black believed that women belonged in the kitchen. "Well, Mr. Black, she couldn't do any worse than Mackenzie King," he pointed out.

"Next, women will drive all over the country to visit and gossip," Mr. Black said.

"There's not enough gas for that," Ingrid said.

"And what does Mr. Inish think?" Mr. Black asked. "Or is it, what he doesn't know won't hurt him!"

Mr. Black's serious attitude startled Ingrid. "I have to learn to drive to town in case the children get sick," she defended herself.

"A man can take a lot but now Conor has left," Mr. Black said.

"How is Mrs. Black?" Ingrid asked.

"Mrs. Black is at home," he said flatly.

Ingrid wondered whether that was the reason Mr. Black drove a coupe. His car had only room for two people: himself and Marjorie. Mrs. Black couldn't squeeze into one seat with Marjorie in the same fashion Kathleen did because Mrs. Black was too big.

Kathleen cast a sideways look at her mother. "Olaf will teach me to drive," she said. When her mother didn't object, she went a step further. "Mom, may Olaf drive Marjorie and me and Mario to the dance Saturday night?"

Mr. Black snorted, ordered his daughter back to the car, started the motor and nodded good-bye.

"Say thanks to Mrs. Black for having me," Kathleen called. She ran to Marjorie who hung far out the side window and gave her a hug. Soon a dust cloud in the car's wake was all the Inishes could see as the Blacks headed for home.

"Kathleen, we must be careful how we spend what little money we have. We'll use the car sparingly. Olaf can repair nearly anything that breaks, but he can't make the car run without gas," Ingrid said.

"I know, Mom," Kathleen said. "But, just this once. Olaf will park the car when we get to the hall."

"All right then, but just this once," Ingrid said. "Remember that."

Kathleen squirmed with pleasure. "Wait till I tell Marjorie. She'll be so excited."

"Let me turn around so that we can go home," Ingrid said. She looked at Olaf and then at the crank.

"You have to learn to crank it, Mom," Olaf said.

"One step at a time," Ingrid said.

This time the whole procedure went smoothly, except for the tires hitting a few bad bumps at the edge of the road.

Danny patted his mother's shoulder. "Mom, you're keen," he said. It was the highest compliment Danny could pay to anyone.

By Saturday night Olaf's mind had dwelt on the upcoming dance for long stretches at a time. As he shaved he was dancing with Marjorie, as he combed brylcream through his hair, he was holding her tight, as he polished his shoes, he was feeling their hearts beat as one. And now the time had come and the music's rhythm set Olaf's feet to tapping. He had had no chance to dance with Marjorie, every dance another man had claimed her. But he had drawn near to the place Marjorie sat between dances with Kathleen, and now he was the first. The music played "The Tennessee Waltz"; his dreams were about to become reality. He'd tell her that his feelings had grown toward her and ask did she feel the same. What words would he use to express the change from childhood friendship to adult love? "The music is beautiful," was all he could think to say.

"So many people here," Marjorie said. "I'm glad Daddy let me buy this new dress."

He wanted to tell her how attractive she looked but the words didn't come readily and before he could form them in his mind Mario cut in and whisked her away. He didn't mind other men dancing with Marjorie—except Mario. How Mario danced with all the girls suggested more than friendship. Olaf fought his jealousy but the feeling persisted. When he looked again, Mario was walking out the door with a girl he didn't know.

"Where's Mario going?" he asked Kathleen.

"To the car, I guess," Kathleen said.

"If I were you, I'd be worried that he goes outside with a girl," Olaf said.

"Oh, no," Kathleen said, "Mario's like that. He likes to be friendly with everyone."

Olaf thought Kathleen's attitude naive. He took her hand. "Let's go look," he said, drawing her outside.

"The car's gone. Did you move the car, Olaf?"

"No, I think Mario took it."

"Oh, no, please don't tell Mother," Kathleen cried. "He'll bring it back soon."

An hour later Mario returned. Olaf supposed that he'd gone to the lake where the old trapper, Andrew Sorenson, had a still. Everyone knew Andrew Sorenson made booze and sold it since he bought cull potatoes by the ton. The gossip was Andrew Sorenson shipped it to Los Angeles. Olaf had had a taste at his parent's anniversary party, and it was powerful whisky. Where Mario found the money to buy Sorenson's hooch was a puzzle—it cost seven dollars a gallon, much money in these hard times.

On the drive home the girls chatted as was their habit. Mario began to sing "Red Wing" and soon the car was lively with song and laughter. But Olaf was unusually silent.

"Hey, Olaf, old man," Mario said, "loosen up and enjoy life."

"You took the car," Olaf spat out.

Mario laughed. "I didn't take no car."

Olaf saw the episode was but a joke to Mario.

"He won't do that again," Kathleen assured her brother.

"He won't do that again," Mario mimicked. He sang the words to "Pistol Packin' Mama." "He won't do that again, babe, he won't do that again. Pistol Packin' Mama, he won't do that again."

No one joined Mario's hilarious outburst—not even Kathleen.

Arriving home, Olaf inspected the car and found the front fender dented.

"Maybe someone ran into the Chevy after you parked at the hall," Kathleen said.

"No one ran into it," Olaf said. "Mario hit something going to the lake for whisky."

"Mario wasn't really drunk. I think it happened at the hall," Kathleen insisted. "You won't tell Mom, will you?"

How could his sister be so unobservant? It was her worst trait. "Pull your head out of the sand," Olaf said. He had to rise early next morning and try to remove the dint. He was glad his mother had said they couldn't take the car a second time.

CHAPTER 9

BY THE TIME HE HAD WALKED two miles Forrest's new boots wore a blister on both heels. He had kept his old oxfords; he sat on the dusty road and changed. The afternoon was hot; hot enough Forrest wondered whether it was worth it. "If Hatfield isn't hiring I'm going to spend the afternoon cooling off in a slough," he said.

"If you can find a slough," Conor commented.

While the three had a long drink from Conor's water bag, Forrest glanced behind at an approaching dust cloud. "If that's a rig, we'll catch a ride," he said. It turned out to be a horse-drawn tank wagon, flat on the top. The driver, a young man, didn't pull in his team, but he did motion them to hop on.

"Going to Hatfield's?" the driver asked.

"Yessir," Conor said, "we want work."

"You ought to get on, I guess," the driver said. "You timed it right."

"How is that?" Conor asked.

"Three guys caught a ride back to town," the driver said. "Hatfield fired 'em."

"Fired them? Why?" Forrest asked.

"Couldn't cut it," the driver said, grinning at his own witticism.

"Country, she's drying up," Conor observed.

"Yeah, taking the water to Hatfield's. His well is going dry. He has to haul water all the way from town. Name's Jerry," he said and shook Conor's hand. Jerry, in his late teens, wore a battered straw hat the color of hay left out in the rain too long.

"We have to keep an eye on these two, Nick and Forrest," said Conor by way of introduction, "or they'll swim in your water tank to keep cool. I'm Inish."

Jerry grinned, his white teeth flashing in a darkly tanned face. "Hatfield will have a conniption," he said. "There's his outfit." He pointed to a machine threshing in a hundred and sixty acre field of ripe wheat. "And there's Hatfield." A stout man, astride a black gelding, waved his arms at the spike pitcher. "He's telling him he ain't keeping up," Jerry said. "Nobody can keep up in this heat. And here he comes to tell me I ain't driving fast enough."

Forrest could tell at a glance the black gelding could run. "Does that old man perceive he's riding a race horse?" he asked, incredulously.

"I told you those bastards were fired," Hatfield scowled at Jerry. "What you mean by bringing 'em back?"

"These men are new, Mr. Hatfield," Jerry said. "They want work."

Hatfield rode uncomfortably close to Conor and looked down at him. "What's your name?" he asked.

"Conor Inish."

"You can do a day's work?"

"I've harvested before."

Hatfield turned to Forrest.

Forrest straightened his shoulders and stood his tallest. "Forrest MacLaren," he said, defiantly.

Hatfield looked at Forrest's hands. "You ain't never seen a pitchfork," he said.

"Perseverance ensures success," said Forrest.

In the silence that followed, Hatfield looked hard at Forrest. Forrest kept his unwavering gaze fixed on Hatfield's narrow eyes.

Hatfield turned to the last of the three.

"Nick Sikorsky," Nick said.

With a quick threatening action, Hatfield reached for the tank wagon whip and raised it. "Miserable hunkies taking over this whole country. No goddam bohunk is going to work for me," he cursed. Nick slid off behind the tank wagon and stood with his eyes fixed on the ground.

"He's an experienced farm hand," Conor said. "He's young. He'll work as hard as any man."

"Damned hunkies," Hatfield said. "You take him back to town. You hear me, Jerry—no bohunk sets foot on my land."

"Are the other two hired?" Jerry asked, undisturbed, it seemed, by Hatfield's attitude.

Hatfield fastened his cold eyes on Forrest. "You figure arithmetic?" he asked.

"Mathematics at your service," Forrest said.

"I don't take no sass. That clear?" Hatfield said. "You can do my figuring, make out the men's time, and pay the dunners—if you're smart enough. Can you drive a team?"

Forrest kept his cool. He nodded; once when he was little his uncle had let him hold the reins.

"These two can sleep in the barn," Hatfield told Jerry. "They can take the team that's hitched up by the barn and get out in the field. Three hours left 'fore dark."

"We ain't talked pay," Conor said. "The going wage for harvesting is two dollars a day."

"Accounting—three dollars," Forrest stipulated.

"A dollar fifty and two," Hatfield bargained.

"No dice," Conor said.

"Mr. Hatfield, if you engage an accountant in town, cost you triple," Forrest said. He expected Hatfield was mostly bluff.

"Two fifty on the books, dollar fifty in the field," Hatfield dickered.

Forrest would have gone for that, but before he could accept, Conor spoke. "No dice! Two a day all round for harvesting," he said.

Hatfield was reluctant, but he did give in. "Get started," he said gruffly. He wheeled his black steed and galloped back to the outfit.

Conor looked at Nick, downcast and silent. "Don't take it to heart," he said.

"Hatfield needs another man," Jerry said to Conor. "I've a spare straw hat and shirt that will fit him. Next time round his name isn't Sikorsky, it's Bob Brown."

Forrest laughed. "Justice prevails," said he.

"Two dollars a day for harvesting," Conor said. "Don't let him put you down."

The Hatfield home was the typical two-story house with high-peaked roof, lacking paint, as every other house in the country was, and the barn was a faded hip-roofed building. Parked adjacent to the house was a new green '38 Ford truck. Hatfield apparently anticipated a rich harvest. Conor didn't envy the man his truck, but he did envy the man his harvest. The crop will run approximately fifteen bushels to the acre—not a bumper yield by any means, but certainly worth reaping.

The team stood hipshot in harness, resting in the shade of the big barn. Conor stroked their necks and rubbed their noses, talking softly to them all the while.

"You have to teach me horse talk, my friend," Forrest said. "I don't understand their lingo."

Conor jumped on the hayrack. Forrest followed. Conor unwrapped the reins and handed them over. Conor anticipated that Forrest could handle the job since he seemed able to adapt himself to whatever came along. "Back, boys, back," Forrest ordered, tugging at the reins. The horses immediately perked their heads and pushed the rack backward just far enough to clear the hitching rail; then they headed to the field with no prompting from the driver. Forrest leaned against the front of the hayrack and grinned proudly at Conor.

Conor didn't mind the heat; it was such a pleasure to harvest again. Activity had always kept his mind on an even keel. His arm and back muscles swelled and heaved with the lift of the sheaves on the pitchfork—those muscles would soon be as strong as ever. Fall was Conor's favorite season. The old Rumley engine's familiar chug, the whining belts rolling forward carrying the golden wheat sheaves to the very heart of the threshing machine, the spout hissing the ripe grain in a cone-shaped pile inside the granary; the exciting sounds spurred him on until he felt as if he'd jump for joy, but there was no time for such frivolity. Hatfield paid his men by the day—speed meant money. Instead of the usual eight teams, he had ten. Ten teams kept four men busy pitching into the separator. This made it necessary for the loading men to operate at top speed for the routine to run smoothly.

Forrest was a skillful driver. He edged the hayrack close to the stooks, but not too closely since Conor needed space for an ever widening swing to reach the top of the rising load. Conor pointed out the stooks he wanted loaded, he planned to arrive at the threshing machine at the time the hayrack was full. Approaching the machine, he took no risk; he held a bridle and led the team forward while the foremost hayrack pulled away. He wanted several feet of clearance between the load and the separator. Conor handed two pitchforks to Forrest atop the load before climbing the back of the hayrack.

"Old Hatfield is watching us," Forrest said.

"Ignore him," Conor said. "We're holding up our end."

"Yeah, but I dare not remove my shirt," Forrest complained. "The dastardly wheat beards are pricking through my clothes."

Conor laughed. "It's just a tickle," he said.

Forrest speared a sheaf with his large long-handled fork. "Possibly to a porcupine," he said.

Every time Forrest took a step, his boots slid off the bundle and down he went. It was necessary to thresh his arms in the prickly sheaves to return to a standing position. Conor moved to block Forrest from Hatfield's view, hurling extra bundles onto the conveyor, waiting for Forrest to get the hang of it.

"This damn Ferris Wheel! Horrible Hatfield!" Forrest wobbled up to Conor, squinting past him in Hatfield's direction. "The slave driver departed," he added, more cheerfully. Forrest peered beyond the edge of the load. The sheaves disappeared in the separator's noisy, clanking, gaping jaws, not unlike crocodile jaws, snapping, catching, and gulping their prey. "Whew," he whistled, stepping back to a safer distance, "we dare not topple into that monstrosity."

Dusk had settled over the land by the time Conor topped their third load.

Locating the stooks in the dark was becoming difficult until someone lit a straw stack so that the crew could keep working by firelight.

"How many hours in a Hatfield day?" Forrest asked.

"Probably twenty-four if the moon's full," Conor said.

May I venture to suggest we be compensated with overtime?" Forrest asked.

"Not on your life," Conor said.

"Hatfield wants this field finished." The voice announced the field pitcher who strolled in from the dark, a pitchfork over his shoulder. He was the man who'd lit the straw stack, and now he sank his pitchfork into a sheaf in Conor's stook. "Last load—I'll be glad when this day's ended," he said gruffly. "Fourteen hours. I feel I've been pole-axed."

Forrest, at the top of the load, called, "When is supper?" His last and only meal this day was twelve hours ago.

"Supper's waiting for us after the horses are stabled," the spike pitcher said.

"Damn it, I'm famished," Forrest complained.

"Lunch was brought at 3:30."

"Missed it," Conor said. "We arrived at four."

"A smoke will ease the pain," Forrest said.

"Hatfield doesn't allow rollings in the field. Only place you're allowed to light up is the bunkhouse and the eating porch. Bunkhouse ain't big enough in harvest time; you'll most likely have to sleep in the barn."

"Yessir, Hatfield told us," Conor said. "Hatfield always pays up, does he?"

The field pitcher grinned. "This crew will string him up if he didn't," he said. "I'm Jack Duncan."

"The last sheaf," Conor said, after introductions. "Let's put this load through the thresher."

While they were stabling the team in the barn, Hatfield arrived. "You got that field done, Jack?" he shouted from the doorway. "Those new guys ain't looking so good."

"It's done," Jack said. He winked at Conor. "The guys are hard workers."

Hatfield turned and walked away. The new truck sputtered to life. Spinning wheels dug up the dirt. The engine's roar faded east, toward Brooks.

"Speedy devil ain't he!" Forrest quipped.

They washed their hands and faces at the pump. Conor held his head under the spout and washed his hair while Forrest operated the handle; then Conor cupped his hand atop the rushing water and sprayed Forrest. "Fair exchange," Forrest warned, but because his arms were shorter than Conor's he couldn't even the score.

"Don't waste that water," a voice warned.

The eating room was a closed-in porch. The men had washed and were sitting at a long narrow table covered with a strawberry patterned oil cloth. They ate fried boloney, fried potatoes, fried eggs, dill pickles, and thick slices of white bread with white butter. To Conor's delight there was a huge steaming bowl of Norwegian klub.

Ingrid cooked klub whenever the luxury of pork was in the house. She made them from mashed potatoes, flour, and chopped pieces of pork, then shaped the mixture in balls and boiled them. Conor noted the men hadn't dished klub onto their plates. These men didn't realize what they were missing. There were three unoccupied chairs and before Conor sat he made certain he was next to the klub. He helped himself to four balls and smothered them with butter, ignoring the other food, except for the dill pickles. Forrest was more cautious—he took two slippery balls and waited to see what Conor did with them.

The men barely talked at the table; they were too tired. Several stabbed at the balls in the bowl and cut them in pieces on their plates after they'd seen Conor eating them so zealously; surprisingly, by meal's end not a single ball remained. Forrest himself had eaten four with a big helping of fried fare.

Forrest turned to Conor. "They're gone, my friend, and I thought we'd have a game of ball later."

From time to time a woman wearing a plain house dress and apron entered the room to remove the empty bowls. Without a word, she set the full hot bowls on the table and hastily left the room.

"Hmmm!" Forrest said. "Comely!"

"Mrs. Hatfield," Jack Duncan said, low keyed, "she never talks."

Girls' voices drifted into the room. "Who's that?" Forrest asked.

Before Jack could answer, Jerry, the tank driver, banged into the room, followed by a young man wearing clothes that resembled Jerry's.

"Where's Hatfield?" Jerry asked. "Here's the new guy he wanted. Name's Bob Brown."

Forrest jabbed Conor's ribs as he squeezed over on the bench to make room for two more fellows at the end. Two empty plates and utensils were passed down the line.

A girl in her late teens, as blonde as the woman, came carrying a coffee pot, and as she served the table, the men who wanted coffee held out their cups. Forrest held his cup in front of him so that she had to lean against his shoulder to reach it. At the moment she leaned, Forrest held the cup farther and farther from her reach. She looked puzzled before she saw the merriment in his eyes. She laughed, and then quickly covering her mouth, looked toward the kitchen.

Conor saw Jerry's displeasure with Forrest's little joke—the wide grin usually splitting his tanned face had disappeared.

"Forrest, you're stepping on Jerry's toes," Conor whispered since Forrest hadn't seemed to notice. Conor wondered what hindered Jerry; the girl looked old enough to be on her own. Was it that Hatfield expected his attractive daughter to wait on his own table all her life?

The woman appeared briefly in the doorway. "Irene," she said crisply, "start the dishes."

"She talked," Forrest said to Jack.

"First time, ain't it boys?" Jack asked the men.

"Yeah, well, Hatfield's not here," Pete Willis, the separator man said. The others nodded agreement.

"How does he keep that beauty down on the farm?" Forrest asked.

"You be careful," Jack said. "You'll get your walking ticket."

"I made her laugh. That's not a crime," Forrest said.

"By Hatfield's law it is," Jack said.

Irene went directly to the stove where a big basin of water was heating. She wasn't allowed to use soap because the slop water was fed to the pigs, so she had to scrub every dish with a cloth to clean them. Through the open doorway she could see some of the men seated in the eating room; she moved the basin far enough to the side so that she could see the man who'd made her laugh. His hair was brown and it brushed the collar of his shirt; a few shorter locks curled over his forehead like bangs. All the other men had short haircuts, shingled in the back. She liked to watch his eyes, remembering how green they were. It was odd that he wore a suit, the only man who did, and it needed fixing at the knees. He talked a lot, especially to the big man beside him. His mouth was wide and lips firm. His eyes turned toward the open doorway and she drew back, then he gathered some of the plates and brought them straight to the kitchen and passed them to her. "It was a fine meal," he said. She didn't know what to say; it was such a surprise. She tipped her head up to look at his face, then her eyes settled on his and she couldn't pull her own away. His eyes were talking to her—that was crazy, of course, but they were the most remarkable eyes she'd ever seen.

"It was a fine meal," he said again when her mother came inside the kitchen. "I'd be glad to assist with the dishes."

"No need," her mother said—she didn't smile, but her voice wasn't cold. "Irene and Isabel will do them."

He looked at her once more and then went outside with the big man.

His eyes were the deep blue green of the pine trees up north where she'd gone with her father to the races.

What would his name be, a man with eyes like that?

CHAPTER 10

THE FIRST DIFFERENCE INGRID felt concerning Conor being gone was in the night—it was darker, and the ceaseless, deranging whine of the wind was louder. During eighteen years of married life she hadn't slept one night at the farm without Conor in their bed. Noises she never noticed before, kept her awake and fearful. A brushing sound on the verandah; perhaps it was only the wind in the ivy. A tapping at the back door; was it Mutt slapping his tail against the wall? The dog would bark at prowlers, wouldn't he?

She lay for hours and could not sleep; she felt alone even though the children were close by, tucked in their beds. There had been no letter. Probably Conor had written or phoned her parents since he couldn't phone her directly—the farms had no telephones. Mr. Black had talked knowledgeably of Conor's affairs so perhaps he knew more than she did regarding Conor's feelings. Conor didn't say when he would return—was it just an easy-out, leaving his family with relatives? She hated unfaithful thoughts and in her desperate attempt to force them from her mind they became more deeply entrenched. How could she and the children survive the winter? The hot sun and drying wind were scorching the new growth, and if no rain fell there would be no feed for the cow, the calf, or the hens; furthermore, wildlife, such as deer and prairie hens, didn't stay long when there was nothing to eat.

Eventually weariness clouded her thoughts and she drowsed; then the welcome morning light disbursed her fears.

Once the children were off to school Ingrid drove to Redgarth to buy boloney, macaroni, and canned tomatoes for the woodcutters who'd arrive tomorrow, and at the same time, to save another trip to town, she decided to stock up on flour, sugar, and oatmeal to carry her family through the winter. After paying for her purchases, she tucked the three dollars left over deep inside her purse.

The grocer, Mr. Barlow, presented her with a huge bag of puffed wheat. "You're one of my best cash customers," he said. Then he carried a large box of beef bones to the Chevy and placed them with the groceries on the back seat. "For Danny's dog," he told her, but Ingrid knew he knew the bone's destination was the soup pot. He asked whether Conor found work and when she told him she hadn't heard so much as one word, he said, "Not to worry. Conor is able to take care of himself."

When Mr. Barlow mentioned he couldn't carry new charge customers, Ingrid understood what he was implying. "There's always relief if times get worse," he said. "You could get around three dollars a month."

Ingrid refused to consider that option. She'd heard farmers couldn't obtain relief unless the wife signed a nonsupport complaint. Ingrid held her head proudly. "Mr. Barlow," she said, "Conor provides."

"N-no offense," Mr. Barlow said. "You could help him by bringing extra eggs and milk to swap for groceries. I can pay you five cents a dozen for eggs. By the way, I hear the Regina Community Chest has winter clothes for children."

Ingrid thanked him and left. She drove the Chevy to the edge of town before she realized she mightn't receive money from Conor before winter set in. Conor had contributed yearly to the Chest in the City of Regina until hard times hit and they became too poorly to keep themselves properly. Danny and Helga could wear hand-me-downs, but it was imperative Olaf and Kathleen have winter coats and shoes. For herself she would not beg, but for the children she would swallow her pride. She turned the Chevy at the first wide spot on the road, bought one dollar's worth of gas at Roney's station, and headed for the city.

The Community Chest secretary was supportive and told Ingrid to go to the distributor, the Home Welfare Institution. Ingrid felt encouraged, but once again on the street she wished desperately to go home—she abhorred what she had to do and the stress wore on her nerves.

At the Home Welfare office counter, Ingrid waited uncomfortably. She was the only customer at the moment. Two clerks were delving into a large box and failed to notice her waiting.

"Betty, look at this. Wouldn't I look marvelous wearing this get-up?" The woman speaking was wearing the latest style, a loose skirt and black saddle shoes. She held a red satin gown to her body and danced elegantly. "It's such fun to come here like this," she said. "It's more fun than housework."

"Think of all the good we're doing," Betty said, flicking lint from her lacy blouse. "Look, Norma, try that dress on. No one on relief should wear a dress so fancy."

"Do you think those people need relief?" Norma asked. "My husband says there are many jobs out there."

"Your husband works for the government?" Betty said.

Norma nodded. She still held the red dress to her bosom. "He says that the poor are too lazy to find jobs."

Ingrid cleared her throat loudly.

Both women jerked to attention simultaneously as they stared at Ingrid in righteous indignation, presuming she'd willfully spied upon their conversation. "What do you want?" Betty asked irritably.

"Winter clothes for two children," Ingrid said.

"You're a farm woman," Norma said in a put-down tone. "Farmers are accommodated through the Relief Department."

"I'm not on relief," Ingrid said.

"Then what are you doing here?" Norma asked. "Farmers grow their own vegetables and have their own milk and butter." She turned to the other woman. "Jim says farmers are well off despite their complaining."

Ingrid flushed with embarrassment. "I'm not complaining," she said. "I was told to come here for children's winter clothes."

"Oh, yes, but you're from the farm. You must be from the city to get clothes here."

Betty peered at Ingrid's engagement ring. It was bright and shiny since Ingrid only wore it at times she went out.

"Why is a farm woman who wears a diamond wheedling clothes?" Norma asked bluntly.

Ingrid fought the tears pushing at her eyes. She wouldn't sell her engagement ring, and she wouldn't break down in front of these ignorant women, but knowing she couldn't check the tears, she hastily left the building. She walked up the street and sat on a bench. The passing people looked but said nothing. They know I'm a farm woman, she thought, they won't even smile at me. It was beyond her understanding why many city people and farm people were prejudiced against one another.

During the time she sat there trying to regain her composure, a man in overalls and a woman with a kerchief covering her head walked past. The couple carried several empty boxes and strode with purpose toward a single railway boxcar shunted on to a sidetrack. A crowd had gathered in front of the open car doors. Ingrid crossed the tracks to join the increasing crowd, amongst them several distant neighbors.

"What is it?" she asked the woman in the kerchief.

"Donations. The Lutheran Church sent it from Ontario," the woman said.

"Who for?" Ingrid asked.

"For the destitute Saskatchewan farm people," her husband said. "I guess that's us, aye, Annabelle."

"I need winter clothes for the children," Ingrid told the woman.

The husband helped the two women spread the clothes until they found what was suitable for their needs. Ingrid selected two warm winter coats. Her concern wasn't with the exact size as long as the coats were large enough since she'd take them apart at the seams, turn the material inside out, and cut and sew them back together to fit the children. Ingrid found boots with felt liners and since the used leather moccasins were plentiful, she took a pair for each person in her household. Satisfied, Ingrid was preparing to leave when a fellow with a long unkempt beard and matted hair approached the moccasins and in passing took two pairs and tucked them inside his coat. He should have taken a coat, Ingrid thought, since the one he wore was in tatters; after all, he had a right to the clothes the same as anyone else. Ingrid was curious—the man was familiar—he was the hobo that Olaf had called Jerico—the man who'd bathed in her water barrel. By chance he might have seen Conor, but before she could muster the courage to approach him, he left.

She said to the couple beside her, "I'm Mrs. Inish. I live north of here. I'm certain I've seen you somewhere."

"I know Conor," Mr. Custer said. "You must be his wife. Wait and we'll help you with your things."

"Conor's gone harvesting," Ingrid explained.

"I should be doing the same," Mr. Custer said, "but Annabelle, my wife here, is afraid to stay alone."

"I'm grateful for your help," Ingrid told Mrs. Custer. "I was worried—the children needed warm clothes for school."

Mrs. Custer smiled warmly, packed her things inside the empty boxes and hoisted them to her husband's arms until he could barely see above the load. She carried the last two boxes herself. Ingrid was able to carry her own after she tied the footwear by the laces.

The Custers loaded their goods in a horse-drawn car with no top. "Our Bennett buggy," Mr. Custer said. "These oat-burners are cheaper to feed than gas is to buy." He absentmindedly kicked at the heels of a heavily built roan horse while his eyes ranged freely up and down Ingrid's body.

"Are you walking?" Annabelle asked timidly.

Ingrid pointed out the Chevy. "If I'd gone harvesting like Conor we wouldn't have had to cut down the car," Mr. Custer said.

The remark warmed Ingrid inside—for the first time someone had praised Conor's decision.

"Come along for coffee. Annabelle doesn't see another woman for weeks at a stretch" Mr. Custer invited.

"I should go home. My children will be out from school," Ingrid said; also she didn't want to spend any part of the two dollars left in her purse.

"Ours too," Annabelle said.

"They'll be all right," Mr. Custer said. "They're old enough to look after themselves."

A Chinese restaurant was next to the railway tracks, and there they sat across from one another in a booth so small that their knees bumped under the table.

Mr. Custer's voice was loud. "Chinks are pretty dirty but coffee is only five cents here," he said.

Ingrid bit her lip. The Chinese cook stood nearby, waiting. His apron was no dirtier than others Ingrid had seen. He wore an expression of pained tolerance.

"Three coffees and don't take all day about it," Mr. Custer said.

Ingrid sat opposite the Custers. Mr. Custer's uncouth behavior was depressing, and she wished she'd stuck with her original decision to go home.

"Well, Annabelle," Mr. Custer said, "morning service starts at 9:30. You have to get us up early."

"Do you have far to go to church?" Ingrid asked, trying to appear interested. It seemed Mr. Custer would control the topic of conversation. Annabelle, quietly inspecting her fingernails, sat beside her husband.

"The minister comes to the school," Mr. Custer said. "It's twenty miles to the church."

"The music . . ." Annabelle said. "Yes, Annabelle," Mr. Custer interrupted, "the organ music."

"You're fortunate to have an organ," Ingrid said, half listening.

"The minister and his wife bring it with them. It ain't big so they squeeze it in the rumble seat of their old Chandler," Mr. Custer said.

Ingrid felt bored. She hoped she'd responded appropriately. Thank goodness the coffee came steaming hot and the smell pure and aromatic, not the musk odor of the burned barley she used at home. She added cream and sugar and while she sat there stirring, a man opened the back door part way and looked inside—he was the hobo she'd seen at the tracks. Ingrid watched while listening to Mr. Custer expounding on the merits of the Chandler car. The cook met the hobo. The hobo gave the cook a pair of moccasins and after much hand gesturing and quiet bartering the cook ushered him inside and pointed to the first booth beside the back door. He dropped a bundle on the ground, left it there and entered. He stood tall, as if the world were at his beck and call. The cook brought coffee and placed a plate and utensils on the table in front of him. Ingrid marveled at his face, a handsome face, if he'd only wash up. No wonder Conor had been so persistent that he bath in the water barrel.

Mr. Custer had worn down the topic of Chandler cars. "Well, Mrs. Inish, how are you making out with Conor gone?" he asked.

Ingrid didn't want to say anything more connected with Conor to Mr. Custer. The cheerful feeling she had had when he spoke well of Conor's decision had left her; besides, customers had entered, and she was certain everyone heard every word Mr. Custer was saying.

"Conor had better get back soon. A good-looker like you on the loose," he said.

"Felix, don't . . ." Annabelle began.

"It's a joke," Mr. Custer said. He winked at Ingrid. "Mrs. Inish can take a joke."

The cook set a bowl of stew and a loaf of sliced white bread on the hobo's table. The hobo heaped his plate and became absorbed with his meal. He looked up once and when his eyes met Ingrid's, rested there for a moment, then went to the bread he held and on which he'd spread a thick layer of butter.

"I should go," Ingrid said hastily. She had become conscious of Mr. Custer's roving eyes. "I'm sure my children are anxious."

She shook hands with the Custers, paid for her coffee and left. A block up the street was a pawn shop. Ingrid rolled her ring around her finger, speculating its worth. She looked in the window at rings priced from five to five hundred dollars. Who could afford a ring for five hundred dollars these days—possibly a city snob such as Betty or Norma? She caught herself—a city snob indeed—she was becoming one of those farm people who held a grudge against city people.

The Custers waved as they drove by in their Bennett buggy. Ingrid laughed at the sight of the queer contraption rolling down the street behind two horses. She quickly glanced around to see whether anyone had seen her laughter. Just a few hours ago she felt as if she wanted to cry because the city people ignored her, now she didn't want them to notice her, especially laughing to herself—she felt she was losing control and ought to go home.

She headed back to the Chevy and on the way glanced through the window of the restaurant; the hobo was still there. She hesitated a moment before opening the door and stepping inside. She wondered what she'd say—she must be going mad to even think of talking to this man—but she kept walking until she stood beside him. She had the feeling every single customer in the place was watching her and the hobo.

"I'm sorry to interrupt your meal," she said, "but I need to talk to you. My son told me your name is Jerico."

To her immense surprise, the man stood and with a graceful sweep of his arm, motioned her to sit. "Charlie," he called to the cook, "bring a coffee for the lady."

Sliding into the booth, their knees bumped. Ingrid jerked backward, recoiling against the wooden seat, straining her knees inward. As she nervously fidgeted with a paper napkin, she noticed a scar that ran along his hairline. Olaf had said the hobo called Jerico had a scar on his forehead—it was shocking.

"The bulls," he said.

Ingrid had no idea what he meant.

"The railroad bulls did it. They try to mess up my trade. Couple years ago two of 'em clubbed me and left me on the tracks to die," he said. "But they ain't so tough if you get one alone." He added a heaping spoon of sugar to the fresh coffee the cook had poured. "Maybe I'll go to jail but Small Guy, he'll get me out. He's smart, very smart man."

The last thing Ingrid had expected was to hear this man's life story and not a pleasant one at that.

"Yes, I'm Jerico Joe." He extended the grubbiest hand Ingrid had ever seen. She shook the hand. It was a firm handshake and a warm handshake.

"Do you remember me?"

"Oh, yes!" Jerico had a shy smile.

"I'm Mrs. Inish, Ingrid Inish. May I ask a favor? But the little money I have I must keep for food. I can't pay you."

Jerico Joe had nodded before she mentioned money.

"Do you remember my husband, Conor Inish? He went west to harvest," Ingrid said, "I need to send him a letter telling him to come home. By chance you've met him."

Jerico shook his head. "I come across lots of men in my trade," he said. "Don't remember all their names."

"We live near Redgarth. You stop there sometimes. He's a farmer."

"Oh, I remember Farmer. I'll give over the letter," Jerico said.

Ingrid rummaged in her purse for a pencil while Jerico reached in his pocket and pulled out a paper and smoothed the creases flat against the table.

Dear Conor,
    This is to tell you the children and I are not in Winnipeg.
    Because of some lawyer the bank did not take the farm, only the machinery.
    Please come home.
                    Love, Ingrid.

Jerico folded the paper and tucked it in the same tattered pocket where he had found it. He patted the pocket with the air of a man in full command of an important mission. "Got to go," he said. "Got to meet a guy." As he maneuvered from under the table, their knees became hopelessly tangled. Ingrid laughed and hung to the table top to keep from sliding out with him.

CHAPTER 11

HARVESTING WAS EVEN WORSE than Forrest had assumed it would be, and he had assumed it would be absolute hell. It had been tolerable before Conor pulled a back muscle. Conor had claimed he'd recover with an hour's reprieve from the pitchfork; then he elected Forrest to be his replacement at the end of that tool the devil himself invented.

Forrest kept an eye on leveling the load so that it wouldn't shift and slide to the ground. The mere thought of a repeat on the pitchfork caused Forrest to lose much time with his painstaking method of patting every sheaf until it merged with the others. He couldn't keep up—raw blisters had formed on the insides of his thumbs. He waved at the field pitcher, and was relieved to see it was Nick who came striding in.

"Nick," he said, "if Hatfield shows, I'm sacked. Assist me, will you, buddy?"

Nick looked as fresh as when he'd rolled out the hay at four in the morning. He tossed two bundles at a time if his fork happened to pick up two together. A half hour later the rack was full. Conor clucked his tongue at the team until the load rolled. He arrived at the separator in time to pull behind the rack that had unloaded. Forrest leaned against the fork handle and looked up at Conor. "You think I'll fly up there and torture myself some more?" he said. "To hell with Hatfield. Speak of the devil!" Hatfield's black gelding came trotting toward them. Hatfield drew rein so near that the gelding's nose touched Forrest's shoulder. The few times Forrest had ridden a horse, or even been near a horse, except to bet on one at the racetrack, had not prepared him for Hatfield's close encounters.

"You," Hatfield said, pointing at Nick, "get moving. Get on this rack and help this guy unload. And you," he said to Forrest, "come to the house, pronto."

Forrest was so pleased to be leaving the field that he grinned warmly at Hatfield. "Where's my conveyance?" he asked. It was pointless to walk two miles in the heat and arrive exhausted.

Hatfield looked hard at Forrest a moment before he pointed at the tank wagon; then he spun his horse and galloped off to the house.

Forrest waved both arms above his head in an effort to attract Jerry's attention— surely the man had seen him, but he didn't slow the team. Forrest ran, dived under the barbed wire fence and pulled himself up the rear of the tank. He squirmed ahead until he sat beside Jerry. "I'd enjoy a cushy position like you have," he said, displaying his blisters for Jerry to see. Jerry looked but said nothing.

"How do you fill this tank?" Forrest asked.

Jerry didn't look at him. "Hand pump," he said.

"Hmmm," Forrest said.

"I'd trade you jobs any day," Jerry said grimly. "Takes four hours to fill it."

"Four hours!"

"It's a five hundred gallon tank. What do you expect?"

Forrest didn't know what to expect, but he couldn't visualize himself working the pump handle for more than four minutes. "And you move two a day. You're a man for punishment," he said.

Jerry shrugged his shoulders.

They drove a mile in silence. Forrest didn't care for silent conversation—it wasn't his style. Years of strategically planning speeches and carrying them out orally in the court room left no room for silence; besides, it unnerved him—who could tell what the other person was scheming behind a mask of tranquility?

But it was Jerry who spoke. "Why are you going to the house?" he asked.

"Hatfield didn't say," Forrest said, "but he did mention awhile back that he needed assistance with the books."

"He don't need you on the books," Jerry scoffed. "Irene can add."

"I'll have her assist me," Forrest said, innocently.

Jerry shifted position, turning his backside to Forrest. He snapped the reins. The team speeded up.

"Careful," Forrest said, "this tank could split at the seams."

Jerry snapped the reins once more. Forrest, clinging to the swaying tank, barely kept from sliding off. A half hour later the house came in view and Forrest jumped off. Ordinarily he'd thank a man for a lift, but he didn't feel justified giving thanks for this one.

Forrest had the screened door to the eating porch half open when he heard Hatfield's voice inside. Hatfield had apparently stabled the gelding, expecting to spend the remainder of the day at the office. "I don't want you on the books," he was shouting. "Don't ask again. I've my reasons for putting this man in charge."

"What about Jerry? I thought you . . ."—it was Irene's voice.

"You thought what? If I catch you parading yourself around those men, you'll get the beating of your life. Yeah, even worse than the last," Hatfield said. Forrest heard a muffled sob and the slam of a door.

Forrest returned up the path when he heard Hatfield coming in his direction—he wanted to appear that he'd just arrived and that he hadn't heard that conversation.

"'Bout time you got here," Hatfield said. "That tank driver ain't worth his salt."

The office, a cubicle off the eating porch, was probably a pantry before being renovated. A roll-top desk occupied one end, and fronting it a wooden armchair sat ajar. Hatfield motioned Forrest to sit. Forrest sat. He contemplated the dozen cubbyholes in front of him: one with pencils and straight pens, another with rulers and erasers, the others with papers neatly placed. On the desk top were two ledgers: one brand new, the other, opened at the page most recently worked, was much the worse for wear. Forrest flipped a page.

"You don't go back in that book except to find full names. Write one name on every page," Hatfield said.

"At the top?" Forrest asked absently.

"Son-of-a-bitch," Hatfield swore. "Ain't you ever seen a book like this before?"

"Threshing is spelled wrong," Forrest said. "No *a* in threshing."

"To hell with the spelling," Hatfield grumbled, "but you better get the time right. The time's on those slips." Hatfield motioned to the largest cubbyhole stuffed with rolled papers.

The first was Rankin's time. "Rankin has thirteen hours August first," Forrest said.

Hatfield indicated the first column. "Date, August first, jot down two dollars here," he said.

"I'm able to handle that," Forrest said. "Enter two dollars regardless of how many hours worked. Right?"

"You're damn well it's right," Hatfield said. "These in this cardboard box you take away."

Forrest took a slip. "Abramson, tobacco, fifty cents; it's a payout."

Hatfield indicated the middle column. "Goes here," he said.

"Next I add the columns, subtract the payouts from wages and enter the wages payable in the right-hand column." Forrest reached for the inkwell.

"Jot this down at the top of every page," Hatfield said, "board and room, fifty cents a day."

"You didn't inform us about board and room," Forrest said. "You call sleeping in a barn a room?"

"That's the deal," Hatfield said with finality. "You bin here two weeks. That's fourteen days at fifty cents a day, take away seven dollars."

"I learned to subtract," Forrest snorted. "By the time I'm through here I'll be an expert at it. Concerning Durrand, he has no days after the fifteenth."

"He don't need pay. He's in hospital."

"What happened? He ran a pitchfork through his leg and with luck he'll die?" Forrest quipped.

"None of your business," Hatfield said, disgusted. "Gimme that page." Hatfield stuffed the paper in his hip pocket. "You've the whole month of August. Get crackin'."

"I need assistance. No one could get this *jotted down* today."

"The men get their roll when they finish tonight," Hatfield said.

Forrest snorted. "The magi and his magic wand couldn't accomplish this by tonight. Give me Bob Brown—he knows his numbers." Forrest knew perfectly well Hatfield wouldn't let the best spike pitcher he ever had leave the field.

Hatfield grumbled. "The girl can help, but you're in charge. You tell her what to jot down, hear me?"

"Loud and clear," Forrest said.

There were newspapers and magazines stacked in the corner of the cubicle. Reading was Forrest's favorite pastime, but he had had no opportunity to exercise it for the past month. "I'm going to read those newspapers in the corner," he told Hatfield.

"You can read 'em for all I care, but not on my time, you ain't."

"Not to worry. I'll take them to my r-o-o-oom."

Hatfield stepped outside the door and shouted, "Irene."

Irene came immediately—she came so immediately that Forrest wondered whether she'd been listening at the keyhole.

"I'm leaving. You jot down what this man tells you," Hatfield said in his gruff manner.

Before Irene had time to withdraw the desk's sliding leaf and wiggle a chair under, Forrest heard an engine rev, a gear shift clank, and tires scratching gravel.

"I'm Forrest MacLaren. May I call you Irene?" Forrest asked.

"If I may call you Forrest," Irene said.

It was exciting to Forrest to see he and Irene fit snugly in the narrow space. He would have to practice deep concentration to enter the figures correctly. He slid the new ledger before her. "We'll start with the names," he said.

She dipped the pen nib in the inkwell and waited, poised to write.

"You went to school in Brooks, I guess," Forrest said.

"I've been out two years," Irene said.

"Grade eight?"

"Oh, no, I finished eleven. I can do this easily."

She'd have been six when she started school—six plus eleven plus two—that made her nineteen. "Of course you can," he said. "Just wondered about small town schooling." Nineteen from his twenty-eight—nine years—hmmm.

"I could have gone another year, but Dad said I was needed on the farm," Irene said.

Forrest looked down at the soft blonde curls that touched her shoulders. He wished he'd gone to the barn and changed his sweaty shirt.

"Jerry," he said, "his last name?" Forrest looked at her, wondering.

"I'll have to look it up," she said. "So many men, you know."

She lifted her head and looked into his eyes, or more like *at* his eyes, Forrest thought. His heart skipped a beat. His bare arm brushed hers—calm! he told himself. "Enter one man's name at the top of each page," he said. "Ready! Set! Go! Joe Lewis!"

Irene laughed until she needed a handkerchief to blot the tears. Forrest, the chivalrous knight in shining armor, came to her rescue; whipping a kerchief from his breast pocket, he wiped her winsome blue eyes.

CHAPTER 12

AS CONOR PITCHED SHEAVES into the separator, he felt so anxious that he feared the worst. Two years ago, while loading stones upon a stone-boat, he had wrenched his back and had wasted a week recovering. His back was acting up again and he eased off. Nick offered to pitch all day, but Conor wouldn't accept that. Night was coming on and it was the last load—he'd endure to the day's end; also it was the finish of Hatfield's harvest, leaving here the outfit would move out to surrounding farms. He hoped he might be lucky enough to get a day's rest between jobs.

"It's payday," Nick said.

Conversation didn't disturb Nick's rhythm. Conor marveled at how Nick worked. One would think the lad had had years of experience, when he could only have had two or three. Conor marked time to the sheaves plopping the conveyor belt.

"I'll send the money home," Nick said. "They always need food."

"Keep a few dollars in your own pocket," Conor advised. Forrest had told him many a man has been jailed for vagrancy.

Conor had thought all week about payday—twenty dollars to Ingrid, eight to his own pocket. He didn't plan to spend the eight—it gave him a secure feeling just knowing he had money.

The men were waiting for Nick to pitch the last sheaf. The next step was to help Pete Willis, the separator man, clean and grease the machinery. Conor sensed a feeling of excitement; laughter echoed through the clear night air.

"Home sweet home," Jack Duncan sang. "Ain't seen the wife in a month." He danced a jig.

"Hey, cut that out. You're getting my tux dusty," Rankin said.

The men guffawed. Rankin's clothes were the most ragged of all the men—his overalls had numerous patches; they looked akin to a patchwork quilt.

Jerry returned with the second tank of water for the day and came to give them a hand. "You better come down to earth and buy yourself a pair of pants," he told Rankin.

"Hey, Jer," Rankin said, "you got all that water and you're the dirtiest."

"That ain't dirt. That's a tan," Jerry said. "You need a bath worse than I do."

"Wal, I ain't going to town like this," Pete Willis said. "Let's tie him up."

Three men grabbed Jerry, tied his hands and feet with binder twine, and left him sitting on the ground. The men stripped, two at a time, opened the tank hatch and jumped in.

"Damn it all! Where you get this water, Jer?" Rankin shouted. "It's colder than Hatfield's heart."

"Here, Conor, have a swig." Jack offered a gallon jug of moonshine. "She'll cure your back."

Conor tipped the jug to his lips. "It's pure alcohol," he gasped.

"Take a couple more. Alcohol rub on the inside," Jack said. "By grab! I should have brought more. There are a lot of us when we all get together." He went to the straw stack, dug here and there until he found two more.

"How many you got there?" Jerry asked.

"By grab, we forgot the swimming teacher," Jack said. He held the full jug to Jerry's lips.

Jerry took a swallow. "Wow," he said, "gimme some more, but not up my nose."

"You got a hollow leg or something," Jack said.

"Jack Spratt could eat no fat, but he could drink the moonshine," Pete sang, splashing until the water flowed over the top of the tank.

Conor's back definitely felt better. The truth was he felt nothing—it was powerful hooch. "Dadburn, Pete, we'll never get to the house for our pay if you don't hurry," he said.

"Here, Rankin, drink up," Jack said.

"Not me," Rankin said. "I'm leaving for home right after supper, and I'm leaving sober."

"Supper! Who cares about supper?" Pete said, accepting the jug from Rankin and tilting it back.

Jerry's speech was beginning to slur. "Untie me and lesh go," he said.

The drivers hitched their teams, the men piled onto the racks and the merry procession wound its way to the house, stopping now and then to pick up Pete and Jerry who kept falling off.

"Hey, Hatfield ain't here. His truck's gone," Jack said. "We'll eat and take a team and wagon to town."

The men filed into the eating room. Scrambled eggs, bread, wieners, and Jell-O awaited them and they made short work of it.

"If that's supper, we've had it," Pete said.

Irene served the coffee. "Your dad leave our pay?" Rankin asked.

"It's here, fellows," Forrest said, bounding into the room. Hatfield had said he didn't trust cheques and instructed Forrest to fill the envelopes with cash. Irene had written the recipient's name, the rate of pay, hours worked, and the amount of cash enclosed on the front of each envelope.

An uncomfortable silence replaced the merriment. "What in tarnation is this!" Pete exclaimed, looking at the dollar figure. "This ain't near enough money."

"The deductions," Irene said.

"Deductions? What the hell are deductions?" Pete asked.

"It's a lot of malarkey, that's what. It's that consarned Forrest MacLaren," Jerry shouted. "I don't trust him."

All eyes turned to Forrest.

Conor feared the worst—the men had polished off three gallons of potent whisky. "Sure now, wait a minute," he shouted above the clamor, "let him explain."

"There-ish no explaining to do," Jerry slurred, rising unsteadily to his feet. "He's been planning this all along. Talked Hatfield into letting him do the pay so's he could sh-skin us all. He's keeping our money for hisself."

"Look here, fellows, you must be aware of the deductions," Forrest said.

"We'll teach him a lesson he won't forget," Jerry shouted.

"Yeah, let's make him eat those fancy words," Pete said.

Jerry was the first to reach Forrest. Forrest saw the jab coming and dodged but the dodge was off—Jerry's fist landed square on his mouth. His jaw snapped; he staggered backward—Jerry was on him, pounding his head against the wall. Nick grabbed Jerry by the scruff of the neck, lifted him bodily off the floor, threw him clear across the table—coffee cups spilled their contents; plates crashed to the floor.

Conor plowed through the jumble to stand beside Nick. He fought as if he were a madman. The hates—the bankers, the politicians, the lost homestead—surfaced at once, and he struck hard to avenge them all.

Forrest sat. He'd blacked out. But now he quickly saw his chance; he bolted for the office door, banged it shut and turned the key in the lock. He jumped to the desk, leapt to the open window and pushed out the screen. Squirming through, he heard a rip—a sharp pain shot through his leg. At the instant he hit the ground, the door burst open. The night was dark, but he recalled the layout. He struck for the barn.

"Where did he go?" Jerry shouted.

"He went through the window," Pete hollered.

Pete and Jerry stampeded into the night.

"We can't get him, too dark," Pete said.

"Maybe he's in the barn. Get a lantern," Jerry said.

"Ain't no use," Pete said, swinging the lantern in all directions. The shadows were deep and the horses nervous with the men moving and shoving against them. "I got my money. I'm going off to town."

"We need more light," Jerry said. "Then we'll get him."

"Leave him alone," Rankin shouted. "I ain't having nothing to do with this."

"Hey, man, you're a jealous bastard. You kill him and you'll be the one in trouble," Jack Duncan said, moving away. "Hooch got to your brains or what! You'd better get a grip on yourself."

A moving wagon squeaked; hoof beats grew faint in the distance. Forrest leaned back on the hay to examine his wounds: one eye tooth was missing but his jaw seemed all right, the cut in his leg was deep but the bleeding had stopped.

Within minutes two men shuffled into the barn. One whistled softly.

"Up here," Forrest hissed.

"Come down," Nick said. "They left for town."

"Jerry, too?" Forrest asked. "That guy's out to kill me."

"Get your roll," Conor said. "Someone set that rack of straw afire. We'll git before Hatfield comes back. You know how to ride?"

"We'll walk. I'm not giving Hatfield a motive to jail me."

"Sure now, and he may do just that if he catches us," Conor said. "Ride and he won't catch us."

"No excuse for thievery," Forrest argued. "My conviction is only cowards steal."

"Borrow the horses," Nick said. "Turn them loose after we're a safe distance out."

Conor untied the black gelding.

"You're going to take the black horse?" Forrest said. "I forbid you to take the black horse!"

"I ain't standing here arguing with you. She's no winning with a man like Hatfield, you ought to know that. If you're so damn righteous, stay, and I wish you luck because you'll sure as hell need it," he said ominously.

"I believe in the integrity of our courts and in the jury system. Our courts are the great levelers," Forrest said.

"You can stay here and preach a blue streak all night if you want to—I'm leaving," Conor said.

The lantern hung by the door. Nick lit it. Conor saddled the black, Nick the long-legged gray.

Conor walked the black past Forrest. "I may be a coward," he said, "but I'm not stupid."

Forrest saw the rack of straw was ablaze—no doubt Jerry had set the match—but clearly he'd lost his nerve and left. If the wind fanned the flames, the barn could feasibly catch fire. The women had remained inside the house. In all likelihood they were too frightened to investigate.

The fire cast eerie streaks of shadow and light on the barn walls. A lone saddled horse stood tied to a rail at the far end of the stable. Will Irene believe that he had committed arson? What would she think if he ran? But Conor was probably right about Hatfield, and to make matters worse, Hatfield seemed to harbor feelings of resentment toward him. Another stint in jail or a prison sentence and his reputation would be shattered. Forrest gathered the newspapers and magazines and stuffed them in his roll; he freed the horse, pulled himself into the saddle, and pounded after the distant sound of hoofs.

CHAPTER 13

"YOU THINK THE BULLS around here somewhere, Boxcar?" Jerico Joe asked nervously.

Boxcar Bob squatted inside the open door while Jerico paced back and forth the full length of the empty boxcar.

"We should have got off back there apiece like I said." Jerico squeezed his brows low over his worried eyes.

"Told you I ain't walkin' first-rate," Boxcar said.

Boxcar Bob had rheumatism in his legs. Jerico maintained the old man had rheumatism throughout his whole body since he moved much too slowly for his trade.

"Cold nights coming soon. Can't take cold nights no more," Boxcar said.

Jerico knew the old man was right. His own bones rebelled against the cold fall nights, and he was a good thirty years younger than Boxcar Bob. "Wal, we'll soon be heading west," Jerico said, "but I got a mission might slow us up some."

"I need a warm coat," Boxcar said. "Look at this!" Jerico looked. What he saw was a roseate nose on a wrinkled face on an old man with a jaw covered with sharp whiskers, a worn coat that hung by threads, and a faded toque. Boxcar had never removed the toque from his head and Jerico had never seen what was underneath it, but he figured there was nothing.

Jerico perked up his head—he'd heard a crunching sound, as if someone were walking on gravel. He whirled, placing his hand across Boxcar's mouth until the sound passed by.

"Just a dog," Boxcar said after Jerico withdrew his hand. "No bulls around this time a night, and if they are, we'll just scram."

"Don't talk no more," Jerico said. "Bulls come around anytime, day or night, and you damn well know it. Shut up till we get to the jungle."

"A whole hour yet," Boxcar complained.

Jerico nodded. "You can shut up that long," he said.

When they hopped off at the Moose Jaw jungle, Boxcar could contain himself no longer. If Jerico didn't care to hear him talk, there would be plenty of men here who would, Weary Wilbur for one.

And there they were, a score of men hunched around a fire. Boxcar smelled the coffee boiling and what a welcome smell it was. He walked straight up to Weary Wilbur and tapped him on the shoulder—Weary moved his butt far enough so that Boxcar could sit.

Weary Wilbur was known to be a thoughtful man and Boxcar knew it to be true because Weary looked after him when Jerico was away trading. Weary followed within reach to be certain he didn't slip on the ladders, and warm nights he rolled up his coat for him to use as a pillow.

Jerico was talking to Ossified Osmond. Ossified had become a hardened man—hard as an iron rail and a surly man, too. Once in the jungle they called Honolulu

City, Okanagan Valley, a fellow said R.B. was the lousiest prime minister the country ever had and the other fellow said no, King was. The R.B. man pushed the King man backward and when he fell he struck his head on a sharp rock. He appeared dead. Ossified had nothing to do with it and could have backed off, but no, he took the task upon himself to clean up. A train was coming not far off. Ossified dragged the man to the tracks, and when he returned he said not to worry, just a drunk asleep on the rails. Boxcar didn't go anywhere with Ossified after that. He went with Jerico whenever possible even though Jerico didn't do little favors such as making pillows. Jerico was a first-class leader; the men listened, even Ossified, when he gave information. Jerico was the one man who said what he pleased to Ossified and got away with it. Ossified could become angry with what he took as an insult that wasn't an insult at all. His anger was easily roused because of an incident that took place in the winter some five years ago when the bulls were laying for him. He had had to cross in front of a moving train to escape, and in doing so had slipped on the ice and fallen on the rail— that was why he lacked three fingers on his left hand. He was self-conscious about that hand and usually kept it in his pocket.

"Where you bin, old man?" Weary Wilbur asked, opening his eyes as wide as his droopy eyelids would allow.

Boxcar was by far the oldest man who road the rails, but he was getting tired and wasn't able to swing up and hop off as he used to. Mostly he lived in a jungle anyway, smoking and talking to the boys. Boxcar remained seated beside Weary who'd always listen to what he had to say; strangers often moved away.

Weary rose, dished stew onto a tin plate and poured coffee for Boxcar.

Boxcar became tired after he ate. He licked a vagrant crumb off his grizzled chin, patted his stomach reflectively, stretched out where the fire warmed his back, and pulled the shreds of his coat tighter roundabout him. He heard the men humming and hawing, and he heard Jerico laughing his husky laugh as he dealt on things he carried in his pockets. Boxcar had at no time heard an argument regarding prices since Jerico was fair in his dealings. Once someone had wanted to barter over a razor strop but Jerico wouldn't; instead, he'd ignored the man and sold the strop to someone else who had gladly paid the price. It pleased Boxcar that Jerico was laughing again; no bulls came to the jungles, even those dicks were wary of jungles.

Boxcar Bob slept.

CHAPTER 14

"THERE'S NO GOPHERS HERE," Helga said. Her arm hurt as if Earl, the biggest bully in the school, were twisting it behind her back.

"There are lots of gophers here. It's a gopher colony," Danny said. "Don't spill the water."

"I can't carry this pail anymore. Why go so far?"

"We don't want to catch Herbie," Danny said.

"If we catch Herbie, we'll let him go."

"But we don't know his friends," Danny said. "These gophers are strangers."

"Maybe Old Mr. Smith doesn't want us to go here."

"Oh, yes, he does," Danny said. "He even said. He's giving me money."

51

"Why does he hate gophers?" Helga asked.

"They eat the wheat, silly. I see a place right there," Danny said, pointing to a bare patch at the edge of the field.

Danny whistled. Mutt ignored the call. He was chasing something in the poplar bluff; zigzagging, a jack rabbit struck for the open prairie.

"I need a gun," Danny said.

"You couldn't hit a rabbit," Helga giggled.

"I could."

"Could not."

Mutt hadn't seen the rabbit leave the bluff; he was sniffing helter-skelter near the edge.

Danny patted a spot by the gopher mound. "Come here, Mutt. Come on, boy. You sit right here."

Helga tipped the pail, ready to pour.

"Not there," Danny said.

"I am so," Helga said.

"Pour it in this hole, silly. It's a fresh one."

Helga mumbled to herself. She moved to where Danny pointed and tipped the pail.

"Don't pour it all," Danny said. "Save half."

Danny set his pail on the ground.

Legs taught, tail wiggling with excitement, eyes glued to the hole, Mutt stood inches above the mound. Helga poured half the contents of the pail. "See, there's nothing," she said.

"Just wait a minute," Danny said. "Stand back."

Helga looked at Danny at the time Mutt dashed at the hole. Dog, gopher and Helga whirled in a flurry of dust and dirt.

"Get away! Get away!" Danny hollered.

"I can't," Helga screamed.

Mutt gripped the gopher in his mouth; he shook it vigorously. A second gopher shot out. Mutt dropped the first and raced after the second. Danny held his foot on the gopher and stooped to pull off its tail.

"You're pulling off its tail and it isn't even dead," Helga scolded.

"I know it's not dead. If we let it go, it will grow another tail and we can catch it again," Danny said.

"I hate it when you do that," Helga cried.

Danny hated it too, but it was the only means he knew of to earn money. If he earned enough, his dad would come home—Olaf had said the reason his dad left was the family needed money. Old Mr. Smith paid a cent a tail bounty for each gopher. Olaf would let him use the .22 if he bought the shells himself. Danny made his plans: shells cost half a cent each, ten tails bought twenty shells, twenty shells were twenty more gopher tails, and by using the gun he need not carry water. Each day, after school, he'll shoot ten gophers, on Saturday, twenty. That was seventy tails in one week. Each week he'll clear thirty-five cents.

"Why do you need money?" Helga asked.

Danny snorted. "Everybody needs money." His plans were secret and he wasn't going to tell his kid sister.

Mutt wiggled up to Danny, a gopher in his mouth. Danny grinned with pleasure, five minutes, two tails.

"Put your foot here," Danny said.

"No, I ain't," Helga said. "I'm going home."

"*Ain't!* You said not to say *ain't*."

"I forgot," Helga said. "Say please."

"Pulleese!" Danny moaned.

Two holes adjoined. Helga covered both holes while Danny poured water down a third one a short distance away. Mutt waited, eyes darting foot to foot. Helga leapt aside; the gophers were pushing at the soles of her bare feet. Mutt grabbed one and killed it; then he killed the other.

Mutt's performance elated Danny so much that he rolled laughing in the dust. Helga pulled off the tails.

"Why do you need money?" she taunted, holding the tails above her head.

"Not your business," Danny said. "Give me those tails."

"Tell me first." Helga giggled, shaking the tails as she ran.

"Pulleese! Give me those tails," Danny held forth his hand.

"Tell me, tell me." Helga danced aside, away from his reach.

Danny raised his hand. "I'll tell Mom if you hit me," Helga said.

Danny sat on the ground, dejected.

Helga stopped. Danny looked sad sitting there with his chin in his hands. She laid the tails beside him.

Danny turned his back and cried. Sobs shook his whole body.

"Danny, I'm sorry," Helga said. She touched his arm. "I won't do it again."

"I want the money so Dad will come home," Danny sobbed. "That's what I want. I want my dad to come home."

CHAPTER 15

CONOR BELIEVED in the old adage *an eye for an eye and a tooth for a tooth.* It was his view that Hatfield deserved as rough a treatment from others as he gave to others. Insofar as Conor was concerned Hatfield had lied by not telling them they'd be charged room and board. He felt Hatfield owed them twenty-one dollars. He brought it up with the others.

"Prevarication," Forrest said, scowling and rubbing his jaw. He folded the newspaper he was reading and placed it beside him on the clean straw. "Hatfield's negligence has cost me more than monetary value." He looked at Conor and forced a smile, exposing a gap in his otherwise perfect set of teeth. He stretched full length on the bed of straw to expose a leg requiring medical attention.

"We ought to sell the horses," Nick suggested.

"They're branded," Conor said.

"A hanging crime?" Nick asked, rubbing the back of his neck. The ruckus had left Nick with two black eyes, one more than Conor, a split lip, swollen knuckles on both hands and the loss of one shirt sleeve.

"We've put ourselves in a vulnerable position," Forrest said.

"Turn 'em loose," Nick suggested.

"I ain't walking one step for Hatfield, vulnerable or not," Conor said.

"In that case how do you plan to maneuver out of this predicament, Mr. Conor Inish?" Forrest asked, a hint of contempt to his voice.

"You're some smart-ass of a lawyer. You figure it out," Conor retorted angrily.

"Don't get your back up, my friend," Forrest said.

"We've been here long enough," Conor said. "Let's ride."

Forrest failed to respond and Conor turned, following his gaze.

"Company?" Company was the last thing Conor expected or wanted.

"We're trespassers," Forrest said.

"It's wrong to rest in a straw stack?" Nick asked incredulously. "Maybe he'll ride on past."

But he didn't ride on past, he hailed them from the road. Conor stood and hailed him back.

The rider's eyes, peering from beneath the rim of a big black hat, roamed about the camp. "Guro," he said. "Roy Guro."

Conor saw that Guro was no bigger than Forrest, but he rode tall in the saddle and Conor wondered what manner of man was this. A wild thought flashed through his mind—for an unruly instant Conor contemplated calling him Ramrod Roy, a fanciful epithet Jerico would attach.

Forrest stood. "We're a sorry lot, I know," he apologized.

Although Nick had said little, Guro's attention was largely focused on him. Nick had given his alias, Bob Brown.

Conor assumed an explanation was due. "We've been resting, but we'll move on if you prefer," he said.

At that moment Forrest's pant leg slipped to reveal his bad leg. "Just licking our wounds," Forrest said.

"You ought to have that leg looked after," Guro said. His tone was friendly.

"When we get to a town," Forrest said. Since they rode Hatfield's horses, they'd avoided the towns.

"You all come to the house," Guro said. "My wife will mend that leg."

"Mr. Guro, we're looking to go harvesting soon as the grain ripens," Conor said, his voice pleading, for Guro's eyes were on the horses' brands.

But Guro was unconcerned. "Drop the mister. You'll most likely find ranch work," he said. "This year the grain crop is poor in this part of the country."

The change heading north hadn't gone unnoticed by Conor. The countryside was more beautiful than any he'd seen before: green bluffs of spruce and poplar caught between folding hills, creeks winding through grain fields tucked here and there wherever the land flattened enough to be worked with a plow, and above, feathery clouds scattered on the horizon. Riding into the hills, they came upon a lake where the laughing call of loons echoed across the draw. The beauty touched Conor's soul—it seemed a message—that this was the place to bring his family and start anew.

The mosquitoes swarmed. Guro put the spurs to his mount and the three men followed.

The horses loped for an hour along a worn cattle trail cutting through the grass meadows before approaching a wagon road. A half hour later a low, shake-roofed log house came in view. "Spring Meadows Ranch," Guro announced proudly. An easy walk from the house, a log barn nestled amid a poplar grove; rail corrals spread beyond the barn to a lake. Pulled off to the side of the road was an old truck. The men tied their horses to a hitch rail running the length of the porch and then clumped across the ax-hewn floor.

"Company, Mattie. Put on the coffeepot," Guro said.

Mattie stood in the doorway, a small woman dressed in worn jeans and a man's checkered shirt. Her auburn hair was combed straight back, and tied in a bun at the nape of her neck. Scrutinizing the three strangers, her expression switched beyond expectation to surprise and caution. Her eyes narrowed and came to a standstill at Nick's bruised face.

"Mattie," Guro said soothingly, "the coffeepot."

A baby's shrill cry drew Mattie back inside the house.

"Nice place you have here," Conor said. He rubbed his boots clean on a cowhide spread on the porch floor for that purpose. "I see you're a carpenter as well as a rancher."

"Came north from Rolling Hills two years ago," Guro said.

"Don't believe I've heard tell of Rolling Hills," Conor said.

"South of Brooks, fifty miles," Guro said. "We barely survived the drought of '33 and then comes the winter of '36."

"Cold?"

"Started with a chinook," Guro said. "Warm rain melted the snow on the ranges; then the wind switched to the north and coated everything with ice. Cattle couldn't break through it to get at the grass."

"Lose many?"

"Half." Guro said. "On a hunch I had put up hay that fall—saved two hundred head."

"Better here, I guess," Conor said.

Guro tossed his big hat to make a ringer on the peg on the wall. "Much better," he said. "Back to four hundred head in two years. Trouble is there's no market for beef. Government offered a cent a pound to get fifteen thousand off the market."

"Can't win for losing," Conor said.

"I'm working on a hunch," Guro said confidently. "If I keep afloat a year or two longer I'll have it made."

Conor wondered what hunch that might be, but before he could ask Guro ushered them inside to a welcome sight—four steaming coffees, buns on a platter, and butter and jam on the kitchen table.

Forrest grinned broadly. "Strawberry jam," he said.

"Mattie makes it. She has a patch out back," Guro said.

"Live off the land?" Conor asked.

"Pretty much," Guro said. "Mattie keeps a milk cow and tends the garden. Moose and deer keep us in meat."

"Do you put up hay for the animals?" Conor asked.

"Yes," Guro said, offering to refill the coffee cups. "With haying, the biggest problem is finding reliable help."

Mattie came into the room. "Nickoli finally went to sleep," she said quietly to Guro.

"He's teething," Guro told the men. "Been keeping us up for four nights."

Mattie looked uncomfortably at the three strangers.

"I hope we're not putting you out, Mrs. Guro," Conor said. "It was kind of your husband to invite us for coffee, but we'll move on as soon as Forrest here, gets his leg attended to. Your husband suggested you might look at it."

Forrest unhooked the wire pin he had fashioned. Mattie looked, drawing a sharp breath. "This leg should have had medical attention days ago," she said.

"You know what needs to be done. Just do it, Mattie," Guro said, smiling confidently at his wife.

"We've few medicines," Mattie said. "I'm afraid of gangrene."

"The nail was clean, Ma'am," Forrest said. "Shiny and clean as a baby's bum."

Mattie grinned as she felt his forehead for fever. Next she turned to Nick and tipped his chin, inspecting his split lip and bloodshot eyes. "Got my can knocked off," Nick explained. Last she glanced at Conor, who was hunched over his coffee, favoring his back.

"All right, but I want them to scrub top to bottom with soap and hot water. If you'll cook supper, Guro, I'll patch them up," Mattie said.

The men followed Guro to where a tin heater stood near the center of a small room; a large round galvanized tub leaned against the wall, empty pails and smaller tubs hung from pegs. Guro handed Forrest two pails. "Pump's out back," he said.

Forrest passed the empty pails to Nick. "Not my department," he said.

Conor laughed. "Pumps and Forrest have their ups and downs," he explained.

"Here's my department," Forrest said, eyeing the kindling stacked in a box beside the tin heater.

"Give me a hand with the horses," Guro said to Conor.

Conor waved an arm to include the entire homestead. "You build her in two years?" he asked.

Guro nodded. "Neighbors helped with the barn and house."

They unsaddled the horses at the barn and turned them loose in the fenced pasture.

"Bank took my farm," Conor said darkly. He hadn't spoken about losing the farm to anyone and he wondered why he mentioned it now. Somehow just saying it eased the hurt he felt remembering his lost homestead.

Guro was obviously a man who asked no questions, but when he came to a standstill and leaned against the corral fence, Conor took it as an invitation to say more. "Twenty-five years of my life's work gone," he went on. "Not sure I could start again and make good like you. Too old, maybe."

"Tough on the family, I suppose," Guro said softly. His manner invited confidence.

"Yes," Conor sighed, "they went to Winnipeg to live with the in-laws, while I'm making my fortune."

"No fortunes to be made for anyone, I'm thinking," Guro said. "But I'm glad I came here from Rolling Hills. Friendlier neighbors." Guro offered a cigarette to Conor, before taking one himself. His eyes turned to the horses grazing in the pasture. "Ran into a problem driving the herd up this way—down around Brooks," he said. "Five Herefords went missing. We followed the tracks to a grain farm and saw where they had crawled through the fence. We rode up to the house. The instant I told the owner my name was Gurofsky, he grabbed a whip and lashed out. Still have a scar on my arm." Guro rubbed his right forearm. "Then he ordered us off the place."

Conor looked away from those questioning eyes. He hadn't been honest with Guro. "The lad's name is Nick, Nick Sikorsky," he said to ease his guilt; the horse issue, he'd explain that later.

Guro looked through Conor and beyond him. "We'll drive your mounts to the Community Pasture. It's twenty miles—safe enough."

Forrest leaned back on the couch and closed his eyes. The pain was worth it to feel a woman's touch. It brought back memories of Irene—the feel of her closeness as they sat crammed together at the same desk. Was Irene just a sweet memory left to fade?

"It's iodine. Used all the Mercurochrome the day Guro cut his hand on the barbed wire. It'll sting," Mattie warned.

Forrest sucked in his breath and gripped her shoulder.

"Hurt?" she asked.

Forrest wiped his brow. "Oh, yes!"

"I haven't put it on yet," Mattie said, straining to keep a straight face. "I'll tell you the instant I do."

Forrest's holler carried clear to the stable. "Tarnation, what's in that concoction?"

"It comes from the sea, sea weed," Mattie explained.

"Take what's left back to the sea," Forrest said.

"This wound has to be iodized." Mattie pushed Forrest against the pillow. "Try to relax. Twice more should cover it. It's a long wound. Now!"

Forrest clenched his teeth, and clutched his leg with both hands. "Do it all. Quick," he gasped, "or you won't catch me for running."

Mattie did.

"And all this time I dreamed you were a likable lady," Forrest said.

"Mattie, better give him a brandy," Guro called from the porch.

"Too late," Mattie said. "It's finished."

Forrest brought forth a groan of woe and misery.

"All right, if you insist." Mattie poured a stiff drink in a huge glass mug. Forrest grinned at seeing "peanut butter" embossed on the glass.

Mattie handed the mug to Forrest. "To an intensely brave patient," she said. "Long may he live!"

Nick hadn't imagined the injury so severe that Forrest might die. The thought made him weak inside. He had only heard about people who died. Forrest was a pleasant companion and even though he had differences with Conor, Nick felt a deep attachment to Forrest.

Mattie smoothed salve on the cuts and bruises on Nick's face; she inspected his eyes and felt his bruised hands for breaks.

Nick judged by past experiences that he'd survive without the nursing Mattie offered, but he didn't mind after the uneasy feeling he had had at first contact subsided. He was uncomfortable when touched by a woman. His mother hadn't been a warm person—he remembered her with a hoe in her hand, not with him on her knee. The touching he did get was from his ten brothers and sisters, teasing, playing, and fighting.

Conor was the last to be doctored. He sat with an empty brandy glass in his hand; he walked tall, his back as straight as any man's. Guro caught Mattie's eye and winked.

The baby cried. On her way to the baby's room, Mattie saw that her patient number one was absorbed with the *Times* that she'd left on the end table.

CHAPTER 16

"MY FRIENDS, bow your heads. Our Father who art in Heaven, if it is your will, bestow upon us the rains that flourish the crops as in the past. We comprehend the cause is of our own making: the corrupt morals of the day clearly exposed in the revealing dress of our young women, the greed for material possessions, living beyond our means. My friends, love your enemies and pray for those who hate you. The alternative is fiery damnation. Amen."

"Amen."

Kathleen squirmed in the unyielding wooden pew. "Mom, my leg's asleep," she whispered.

Ingrid pressed her finger to her lips with a shushing sound.

Kathleen grimaced and slowly straightened her leg.

"Rub it," Danny whispered.

"They'll see me," Kathleen hissed.

The sermon ended and the congregation rose and filed slowly down the aisles, shaking the minister's hand at the church door.

Outside, Ingrid waved to Mrs. Black. To Ingrid's astonishment, Mrs. Black didn't return the greeting and without any sign of recognition, turned to follow Mr. Black to their car. Ingrid glanced around. The people rushed past, ignoring her. On the farm these days with no crop to harvest, no hay to put up, no garden to preserve or store, no one needed to rush. Quite likely the wind and heat were wearing on people's nerves.

"Mom, why do I have to love Earl?" Helga asked as they stepped into the Chevy. "He's such a bully. I hate him."

"What's form and fiction, Mom?" Danny asked.

"It's fornication, Danny," his mother corrected.

"What's fornication?"

Ingrid sighed. Always after church Conor and she faced this challenge: questions and more questions. Conor handled it with story telling and sometimes evasion, but Conor wasn't here and the explaining was her responsibility. "It's like being married illegally," she said.

Danny pondered the information. "You mean without a marriage license like you and Dad have? That's wrong?"

"Of course it's wrong, Danny. A couple shouldn't live together without being legally married."

"You mean shacked up?" Helga asked. "The Tweets are shacked up."

"Helga!" Ingrid scolded.

"Mrs. Swenson said so," Helga said. "And she told me not to talk to Bessy Tweet 'cause she's just scum."

A frown creased Ingrid's brow. "Mrs. Swenson shouldn't have told you that," she said.

"But you said it's wrong," Danny accused.

"And we're told when people are evil and sinful we should love them anyway," Olaf said. "What about a war? There's talk we'll soon be fighting the Germans. Should I tell a German I love him, then turn around and shoot him dead with a rifle?"

"You got to do it, Olaf," Danny said. "If you don't, you'll burn in hell."

"Fiery damnation," Ingrid corrected.

"Same as hell," Kathleen said. "Mom, stop the car. My leg's asleep again."

Ingrid was delighted to stop the car. She pulled over and everyone piled out. She hoped that by the time they were on the road again, the question period would be ended.

Kathleen hopped hither and yon, laughing and crying and rubbing her leg. Helga giggled. "It ain't funny," Kathleen said. She made a frightful face at her sister.

"It isn't funny, you mean. Mom, why don't you tell Kathleen not to say that word?" Helga asked.

"Many people do," Ingrid said.

"But Miss Sparks doesn't want us to say *ain't*. She says it's a sign of illness."

Olaf laughed. "A sign of illiteracy," he said.

"And she says because other people say *ain't*, is no excuse," Helga pouted. "And she's the smartest teacher we ever had!"

"Yeah, she's clever," Danny said.

"All right," Ingrid said, "if it means that much to you, we won't say *ain't* anymore."

"Ain't, ain't, ain't," Kathleen moaned. "My leg ain't stopped tingling."

Helga giggled and rubbed Kathleen's leg. "Why not go on a picnic?" Helga asked. "We never go on a picnic."

"To the lake," Kathleen added. "We can go swimming."

"We can do it, Mom," Olaf said. "It's too hot and windy to work, and anyway it's Sunday."

"Mom, will we go to fiery damnation if we work Sundays?" Danny asked.

"We'll go to the lake on one condition," Ingrid said.

All eyes turned to their mother.

"No more questions!" Ingrid said.

"We'll have a wiener roast," Kathleen said. "But I suppose there are no wieners."

"No. No wieners," Ingrid said.

Kathleen groaned her displeasure.

"If anyone complains, we won't go," Ingrid said loudly above the din of disapproval. "We shouldn't go anyway. How much gas is in the tank, Olaf?"

"Dad said the car had enough gas to go to town a few times. That's farther than going to the lake," Olaf said. "Anyway, we can buy gas at Powell's station. Mr. Smith gave me a dollar."

"He gave you a dollar!" Danny exclaimed.

"For helping *him* with the heavy hay."

"Hay? What hay?" Kathleen scorned him.

"Kathleen," Olaf said patiently, "you don't know as much as you think you know. And you don't even read."

"I read," Kathleen objected.

"Love stories isn't reading," Olaf scoffed. "Read the news. Read what's going on in the world.

"Mom, grass grew on the prairie field Mr. Smith never plowed. We cut it and stacked two stacks of hay. Dad shouldn't have worked all our land—the wind can't blow the prairie grass fields."

"Danny has money, too," Helga said. "He sold gopher tails to Mr. Smith." Danny hunched up and looked at the floor. "He doesn't want anyone to know," Helga added, not unkindly.

"Then why did you tell?" Ingrid asked. "Danny's allowed a secret if he came by the money honestly."

"He didn't steal it," Helga said in Danny's defense.

"Your father doesn't want us to steal," Ingrid said.

"Is Dad always honest?" Danny asked.

"Yes," Ingrid said, "I'm sure he is."

Olaf chuckled. Everyone looked at him, dumbfounded.

"Explain that chuckle," Ingrid ordered sternly.

"Mom, you've seen those glass gallon jugs on the south side of the car shed," Olaf said.

Ingrid looked at her feet for an instant before raising her eyes to Olaf's. "I've seen them," she said.

"There's water in them," Helga said.

"It's not water," Olaf said. "It's purple gas."

"It's not purple," Kathleen said.

"You think you know everything," Olaf accused. "It's purple gas. The sun bleached the purple out."

"Why does Dad do that?" Danny asked.

"Because it's illegal to use purple gas in the car," Olaf said.

"That's not stealing, is it, Mom?" Danny asked.

"No, it's not stealing. Your father doesn't steal."

Olaf chuckled.

"Stop it!" Ingrid ordered. "You know your father isn't a thief."

"It's called *bending the law*," said Olaf.

After a brief silence Ingrid straightened her shoulders and looked at Olaf. "If there's gas in the jug, you can keep your dollar," she said.

"Bending the law, bending the law," Danny sang the words to himself.

"What's growing on the drifts?" Kathleen wondered.

"Russian thistles—the only plant thriving on the land in the last eight years," Ingrid said bitterly.

"Miss Sparks says to drive on the right side of the road," Helga said.

"If I hit that loose gravel the Chevy will flip," Olaf said. "Everyone drives down the middle, even Miss Sparks."

"She doesn't drive down the middle," Kathleen said, "she barrels down the middle."

"Someone should tell her to drive in the right ditch," Olaf said. "She'll crash into somebody head-on one day."

"I like Miss Sparks," Danny said. "She wouldn't do that."

"We all like Miss Sparks," Ingrid said, "but it's true she drives too fast."

"I guess she's in a hurry," Helga said. "I wish I were as pretty as she is."

"Beauty is only skin deep, besides you are pretty," Ingrid said, pinching Helga's button nose.

"Her skin is nice, too, Mom," Danny said. "It's soft—I touched her cheek."

"We should ask her for supper," Helga said.

"How about next Sunday," Ingrid said.

The eight-mile drive to the lake was becoming a lung-testing ordeal. The wind puffed up black dust clouds; whirlwinds danced crazily across the road in front of the car.

"We should turn back," Ingrid said.

"No, Mom," Kathleen said, "There won't be dust at the lake."

Ingrid looked to the north. "The Simsons are gone. Their place looks vacant."

"Maybe," Helga said, "June hasn't been to school in a long time. Do you think they took those gophers with them?"

"What gophers?" Danny asked.

"The ones they salted."

"That field of dried-up thistles looks like dog puke," Danny said, and then he scrunched behind Helga, screened from his mother's threatening eyes.

"Don't drive off the road," Kathleen said. "We'll get stuck in that drift along the fence."

"Don't be ridiculous," Olaf said, "I won't drive into a three-foot wall of dirt."

Sharp gravel particles ricocheted off the windshield. Soon visibility was down to a few feet; Olaf eased the car to the right side and crawled forward at five miles an hour.

"We should stop. The wind may die down," Ingrid said.

Olaf no sooner crossed the ridge of loose gravel than an oncoming truck loomed out of the dust and roared by, missing the Chevy by inches.

"Dear lord," Ingrid said shakily, "if you hadn't pulled over, he'd have hit us."

Olaf lowered the window. "Idiot!" he shouted after the disappearing truck. "You drive like an idiot!"

The motor sputtered. "The Chevy's hot," Olaf said, looking at the gauges.

"Stay in the back seat," Ingrid told Danny and Helga when Olaf got out to inspect the radiator.

"It's plugged with dust," Olaf said. "We need a brush."

Ingrid looked at Helga; Helga looked at Danny; Danny looked at Kathleen.

"Not my hair brush," Kathleen cried.

"If you want to get to the lake, give me your brush," Olaf said.

"It's hot in here. Can't I go outside?" Danny asked.

"I'm sticking to the seat," Helga squealed.

Olaf cranked and cranked again; both times the motor sputtered and stalled. He removed the radiator cap. "It's low on water," he said.

Ingrid passed the water jug through the window.

"I had to use all the water," Olaf said, returning the empty jug. "We'll fill it at the lake. Guess we'll just sit here until the motor cools off."

"We can run to Powell's while it's cooling off," Danny said. "I need .22 shells."

"We can, I guess. It's not far," Olaf said.

Fifteen minutes later they returned.

"The wind died some," Ingrid said. "I see a car behind."

"It's a Bennett buggy," Olaf said. "I see the horses. Faith, and how doesn't he get run over?"

Helga giggled. "You talk like Dad, 'Faith, and how doesn't he get run over'." She giggled again and tossed herself back and forth in the back seat. Danny hit her.

"Danny hit me, Mom," Helga shrieked.

"You're making fun of Dad," Danny said angrily. "I'll hit you again if you don't stop that stupid laughing."

Helga's laughter turned to tears. "I wasn't making fun of Dad." She stretched her arms above the front seat and wrapped them around her mother's shoulders. "Mom, I wasn't making fun of Dad."

Ingrid felt hot tears trickle inside the back of her blouse.

Olaf turned around in the front seat. "Who's that, Mom?" he asked. The Bennett buggy was approaching at a fast clip.

"That's the buggy I saw in the city," Ingrid said.

"I haven't seen it before," Olaf said.

"The Custers," Ingrid said.

And it was, but Mr. Custer was alone. He pulled up his team in the middle of the road and hailed them. "If it ain't the Inishes having car trouble."

"The car's hot," Olaf said. "It'll go in a minute."

Mr. Custer snubbed up the reins, wound them on the steering column, and walked to Ingrid's side of the car.

Ingrid reluctantly lowered the window—her dislike for this man came upon her full force. He stuck his head inside—she recoiled against the seat.

"So you got dirt in your radiator," he said.

"Olaf brushed it clean," Ingrid said.

Mr. Custer went to his Bennett buggy and returned carrying a whisk broom. He handed it to Ingrid. "Don't need this whisk no more," he said. "You got to poke all the dirt out."

"We're going to the lake," Olaf said. "Thanks, we may need it."

"So the Inishes are off to the lake," Mr. Custer said. "The auction's at Wisefelt's place. I come back past the lake."

Ingrid was certain he was expecting an invitation to join them, but she remained silent.

"May see you then," Olaf said. He cranked the car; the Chevy was being obstinate. Mr. Custer moved to the driver's side and sat behind the wheel; his arm slid along the seat and across Ingrid's shoulders. Ingrid cringed.

"Pull the throttle," Olaf called. Mr. Custer did and the Chevy sputtered and roared.

"You drive on ahead," Mr. Custer said, and moved to his own rig.

Danny and Helga watched Mr. Custer and his horses through the rear window; Ingrid stared straight ahead.

The dust clouds thinned as they scaled a rise and there in the distance the lake shimmered in the sunshine. Soon they were at the top of a hundred foot bank, the lake and the sandy beach below.

"Not too far," Ingrid told Olaf. Deep holes scarred the beach—places people had had to dig their cars out.

Danny and Helga ran to the wild gooseberry patch. "The berries are gone," Danny called. "Somebody ate all the berries, Mom."

With their swimming trunks in hand Olaf and Danny headed to the grove of maple trees while Ingrid and the girls changed in the car. They flew to the cool wet shore, barely touching the hot sand with their bare feet.

"It's cold, Mom," Helga said, standing on tiptoe, the waves splashing up her waist.

"Dunk under," Ingrid said. "You'll soon feel warm."

They swam near the shore, and then stretched out on the wet sand, the waves rippling warm shallow water across their legs.

"It's not safe near the point," Ingrid warned. "There's a dropoff."

"All right, Mom," Helga said. "We won't go there."

"Who drowned there?" Danny asked his mother.

"You didn't know him," Ingrid said. "The accident happened long ago."

"I guess he couldn't swim," Danny said. "I can swim. So I won't drown there, right Mom?"

"The berries are gone. I'm hungry," Helga said glumly. "Olaf and Danny made a fire. It's hot enough without a fire."

"I think they have a surprise for us," Ingrid said.

Olaf cut long thin saplings and sharpened the ends. "Come and get it," he called. Soon five wiener sticks were vying for the best roasting spot.

"Your wiener is burning," Helga shrieked at Danny.

"That's the way I like it," Danny said, turning the flaming wiener with care.

Kathleen hadn't uttered a word for the past hour—her thoughts were miles away. Ingrid had noticed this occurring more frequently as time went by. Perhaps she was missing her father, or perhaps it was trouble with Mario. Whenever Kathleen looked her way Ingrid smiled warmly, but always Kathleen's eyes were sad and turned aside. Ingrid felt drained. She wished Conor were here—he had a way with Kathleen.

"The wind's still up," Olaf said. Dust clouds hovered to the east. "We have to drive through another black blizzard to get home." He filled the jug with lake water and doused the flames before refilling it to store in the car.

"Maybe the Chevy won't climb the cliff," Danny said.

"It's not a cliff," Olaf said. "It's just a bank."

Cliff or bank, bumping in and out the ruts, the Chevy did climb it and soon was on the top and back on the main road. Within minutes of rounding a curve the sun disappeared in a sinister amber haze. Olaf eased the car to the extreme right, coasting at ten miles an hour. "We can keep going," he said. "I see a few feet of road."

Approaching grain fields, they had a short reprieve since the wind couldn't readily pick up the dust as it did from the cultivated fields.

"Oh, oh, hot again," Olaf stopped the car.

"Gee!" Danny groaned, "I want to go home!"

"We all want to go home," Olaf said. "Hand me the whisk broom."

"Can't we get out?" Helga asked. "It's not dusty here."

Ingrid opened the door. The wind, even though hot, felt refreshing against her clammy skin. They stood waiting nearby the car while Olaf poked and jabbed the whisk broom into the radiator cores.

Danny ran along the ditch chasing a gopher. "There's that man again," he hollered.

Mr. Custer reined his team behind them. "You're having trouble again," he said.

"It's the radiator," Olaf said.

"We'll have the car up and running in no time," Ingrid assured him. "There's no need for you to stay."

"An extra man around the place can come in handy," Mr. Custer said. "And if Olaf don't get it to go, my team will pull you home."

"No need," Ingrid insisted, "Olaf will see us home safely."

But Mr. Custer did not take his leave. He talked to Ingrid, identifying every person he knew who attended the auction, naming who bought what, pricing every piece of merchandise sold.

"Mom, we need an air hose," Olaf said.

"Powell's station ain't got air," Mr. Custer said. "He ain't paid his power bill. I got a rope to pull you home right in my buggy."

Olaf cranked but the Chevy motor was too hot to start.

"You could ruin your motor," Mr. Custer said. He drove in front and attached the Chevy to his buggy with the rope. "Geddup, geddup there. Lean to it!" The horses obeyed the command, their hoofs spraying gravel as they got the outfit rolling.

"We're lucky Mr. Custer came along," Olaf said, steering the car. He was being careful the Chevy didn't bump into the buggy's rear end.

Ingrid was silent.

The minute the Chevy came to a stop behind Custer's Bennett buggy Ingrid jumped out and ran inside the house. She didn't care if she appeared rude; she hated how he looked at her. She'd told him plainly that Olaf would see them home safely; still he'd gone ahead, tied the Chevy to his buggy and towed them home. Olaf will have to deal with Custer; she couldn't.

And to make matters worse, there was Mr. Black filling his water tank. It wasn't his habit to arrive so late in the day—just before bed time. What'll he think—a strange man unhitching in front of her barn at this hour? She saw him looking surreptitiously around, no doubt drawing his own conclusions as to what he saw. She was beginning to understand the cold attitude of Mrs. Black and the church women—it was because of men like Black and Custer who harbor a desire to abuse women whom they consider helpless. She felt she was caught by a rope and the knot was tightening.

She lit the coal oil lamp and decided against lighting a fire in the stove since the children were tired and wanted to go straight to bed.

"Mr. Custer says it's too late for him to drive home," Olaf called through the screened door. "He wants to stay overnight."

"He'll have to sleep in the barn," Ingrid said, straining to keep her voice calm. "There's no room in the house."

"He says he won't sleep in the barn," Olaf said. "He saw a rat when we stabled the horses. Let him sleep on the couch."

"There are no rats in the barn. And if there were they'd be in the house too," Ingrid said.

"Mom, what's the matter? It's the least we can do since he towed us home."

"All right! All right! He can sleep on the couch."

His mother's behavior puzzled Olaf. Many times when his father was home, friends or travelers spent the night at the farm. But the day had been trying, the heat and the dust and the delay with the Chevy had probably unnerved his mother. He provided Mr. Custer with a blanket and a pillow and retired to the upstairs room he shared with Danny. Kathleen and Helga were already asleep in the room across the hall. He heard his mother moving about in her bedroom below as he undressed and crawled into bed. The day's events passed through his mind: the church service, the dusty trip to the lake, the swim and the wiener roast, Mr. Custer towing them home. He suddenly knelt by the bed to pray. Perhaps it was the unease he detected in his mother, or the need within himself for Marjorie, or the thought of war that had turned his mind to the Lord. He knew little about war, except it was a matter of kill the enemy or be killed by them; he felt death might come to others, but not to him. He could imagine the pain of a shot in the arm, perhaps, or shrapnel in the leg. He could imagine himself a respected man in uniform, returning home to recover, and to Marjorie—then he'd have the courage to tell her he loved her. Soon thoughts and prayers drowsily mingled as sleep overtook him.

Ingrid removed her shoes and lay fully clothed on her bed—she'd rest a few minutes before undressing. She reasoned her fears were unjustified. She was much too frightened since Conor had left—she had to learn control.

The heat woke her. The room was stuffy and hot, unusually hot for this late in the fall. She pushed the bottom pane up the tall window and stepped out on the verandah. She sat beneath the ivy, gazing at the big prairie sky riddled with blinking stars. She had no fear of the dark on a night like this; the bright moon cast shadows against the walls, the outhouse and the barn were clearly visible. She imagined Conor looking at the same stars; although it wasn't very likely, the thought gave her comfort. Since the bad times came, Conor had often risen in the night to tread softly to the verandah and sit quietly watching the sky. Sometimes she left her warm bed to sit beside him, and they'd point out the Plough and Great Bear and other constellations. She remembered how different it was when times were good, how Conor had slept through thunderstorms that shook the house. When Conor was happy he worked hard, played hard, and slept hard—it was his way. She'd not need a blanket tonight, she thought, she'd sleep in her pajamas and let the cool breeze flow through the open window.

Movement within the house caught her attention. The children rarely left their beds at night; perhaps Custer was on his way to the outhouse. Ingrid shrank behind the ivy and waited. A door squeaked, she looked, she saw no one, and then she realized it wasn't the door to the verandah she had heard—it was the door to her own bedroom. Ingrid froze. "The children are asleep," a voice whispered; Custer's voice. Ingrid stepped to the window. "Get out of my room," she said, icily.

"There you are." Custer seized her arm. "The children are asleep. Come back in."

Ingrid's voice rose hysterically, "I want you out of my room!"

"Oh, no, you don't!" he said, squeezing her arm. "You let me stay. That tells me everything."

Ingrid braced herself against the window frame. "You're hurting my arm, let go!"

"Well, if you want it in the barn that's all right by me," Custer said, stepping through the window.

"Let me go. Leave me alone!"

"Shush now," Custer said, placing his hand over her mouth. "We don't want to wake the children, do we now?"

Ingrid attempted a scream but his hand was tight on her mouth. Olaf, for God's sake, wake up. Custer was pulling her toward the barn. She dragged her feet, jerked her arms; anything to slow him, give her time to think. What can I do? Dear God, what can I do? The dog—scream, make a noise—but she couldn't scream. She twisted and squirmed and pushed against him, but his strength was more than hers and he held her, pinning her arms. The barn loomed ahead—its open door like a trap. She had to do something, anything, before he pulled her through that door. She couldn't scream but she could open her mouth; she lunged her head forward and sank her teeth into his hand.

"Bitch," he swore, tearing his hand free. She couldn't run he'd grabbed her hair, but she could reach the empty water barrels stacked atop one another — she kicked, the barrels teetered and crashed to the ground, rolling toward the house. The dog went wild; growling, hackles bristling, it charged toward them and back to the house, again toward them and back to the house. As Custer dragged her through the barn door, a barrel crashed into the verandah. She bit him again, and for the instant his hand was gone from her mouth she screamed. She fought him with her fists as he pushed her upwards on the loft ladder; suddenly, Olaf stood there in his nightshirt, a pitchfork in his hands.

"Let her go!"

Custer paused. "Nothing to worry about, son," he said. "We're fine; you just go back to the house now."

Olaf came at him. Ingrid scrambled up the ladder and in the dim light searched frantically for the pitchfork she knew was against the wall. She found it and scrambled back down.

"Son of a bitch, you stuck my hand," Custer roared at Olaf. He made a hostile move but stopped when he saw Olaf ready for another thrust.

"Leave. Leave now!" Ingrid said, poised to strike with her own fork. "Don't you ever come here again, because if you do, I'll defend myself with a gun."

Custer recoiled in horror. "Enough! Enough! I'm going," he said, clenching his bleeding hand. "Crazy people!" he muttered, his eyes taking on a wounded look. "See what you did to my hand. Crazy people!"

As Custer hurriedly harnessed his team, Ingrid and Olaf withdrew to the house.

CHAPTER 17

JUST AT THE TIME JERICO JOE decided to drift west of Medicine Hat, Boxcar Bob caught a cold and a fever. Boxcar refused to leave the warm spot by the fire he'd allotted to himself. Weary offered to stay until he was able to travel so Jerico acquired enough blankets in Medicine Hat to keep Boxcar warm, but the rest was up to Boxcar.

"I'll go with you to Brooks," Ossified told Jerico.

Jerico was hoping Ossified would stay on the train and continue traveling west. He'd told Ossified not to come to Brooks since he'd have to walk five miles in the country on a hot and dusty road. Jerico was aware that Ossified hated to walk anywhere, even on a sidewalk, so he was confident that Ossified would heed his advice, but no, here he was hopping off the train and matching Jerico's stride toward the town.

"Too early to go west," Ossified said. "They say Vancouver's wet and I hate to get wet."

Jerico wasn't certain his own decision to go to Brooks was the right one. How he'd locate Conor Inish and Small Guy was a problem. He wanted to please the fair lady, Ingrid Inish. He may even return that way to tell her he had delivered the letter to her husband—it would please him to sit in a restaurant drinking coffee with a woman who valued his knowledge and ability.

"Wal, it sure ain't wet here," Jerico said, wiping his brow.

Jerico resigned himself to the fact he had to listen to Ossified's complaints for a long time, unless he could come up with a scheme to lose him.

"But I ain't walking no five miles," Ossified said. "Ain't there a bus?"

The soup kitchen drew their attention.

After selecting his food, Jerico asked the attendant, "Where's Hatfield's field at?"

"Hatfield's? Ask the man yonder who's filling the water tank. He works for Hatfield."

While Jerico ate his meal he kept an eye on the man filling the tank.

"They ain't never learnin' to cook," Ossified complained. "The boloney is tough, the bread is stale, better soup in the jungle. This rot gut is going to ruin my stomach."

"We ought to set up an eatery in the jungle," Jerico said, and puffed his belly laugh. "We'd charge the friggin bulls and the bankers and the lawyers double."

Ossified didn't share Jerico's humor. He was sitting there staring at a grasshopper swimming awkwardly in his bowl of thin vegetable soup. Before Jerico's startled eyes, Ossified spooned the grasshopper and a carrot slice into his mouth and munched rapidly with a look of hatred on his features. Ossified often did things Jerico found odd, but this took all the prizes. Thereupon, Ossified looked at Jerico as if nothing were peculiar.

Jerico couldn't figure out why Ossified would do such a thing, unless it was that he didn't have the dexterity to fish the grasshopper out with only a pinkie and thumb on his left hand to do it with. Jerico didn't remark on the situation, since he'd felt Ossified's scorn on another occasion when he'd merely mentioned the crippled left hand.

Jerico looked at his own soup. His stomach had turned even though he'd seen men eat a variety of unusual things: gopher, skunk, coyote, snake, and porcupine. Once someone offered him roast rat and he'd enjoyed the flavor, but he hadn't known what he was eating at the time. But the black beady eyes, the long back legs, the short front ones grasping a carrot slice was altogether too much.

"Well, he won't go hungry," a fellow traveler speculated.

Jerico left. He strode toward the man who was filling the water tank. Ossified followed.

At first it seemed the man doing the pumping was going to ignore Jerico. Jerico waited until he'd filled the tank and ceased his pumping, to politely greet him. Now the man placed the lid and deliberately turned his back.

Jerico greeted the man a second time in a voice loud and clear. "It's five miles to Hatfield's field and it's a very hot day," he said, believing the man would offer a ride.

"Hatfield don't hire no bums," the man said. "He'd make me take you back to town."

"I ain't no bum," Jerico said, insulted. "I got a trade. What's your name?"

The young man snorted. "Jerry, and what's it to you—you'd end up worse off than the last three fellows who worked for Hatfield."

"What fellows?" Ossified snarled.

Jerico scowled at Ossified, and Ossified withdrew a step.

"That coward, Forrest. He won't forget who knocked out his front teeth," Jerry said.

"Forrest? You mean Small Guy? You knocked out Small Guy's front teeth?" Jerico exclaimed. Small Guy's teeth were elegant. Every time he laughed or grinned, his shiny white teeth sparkled as though they were white stones in a clear stream, and this punk had knocked them out.

"Where's Farmer?" Jerico asked gruffly. He was near the end of his patience.

"Who the hell's Farmer?" Jerry asked. "If you're talking about Conor Inish, he put his tail between his legs and ran."

"Where did he run to?"

"If Hatfield finds where they run to, he'll string 'em up. They tried to burn Hatfield's barn and they stole his horses, they did. Cowards, the whole lot."

"Small Guy ain't a coward," Jerico said hotly. "He won't hang from a tree."

Ossified appeared to have had enough of Jerry's insults. He jerked the lid off the water tank, ran to Jerry and pinned his arms to his sides. Jerico grabbed Jerry's legs and together they stuffed him in and jammed the lid in place.

Jerry's muffled screams for help alerted the soup kitchen. Men swarmed over the area. Jerico and Ossified slipped away through the crowd.

Ossified's curiosity didn't allow him to look straight ahead in the same manner as Jerico. He looked over his shoulder to see the man called Jerry sprawled on the ground with someone attempting to pump the water out of him.

Jerico heard the long whistle. "We can hop that freight if we speed up," he said and jogged in that direction

CHAPTER 18

"IS MY FACE CLEAN?" Danny asked.

"My dress, it has creases," Helga said.

"You're both fine. Just help me whip this cream and then everything is ready," Ingrid said. "Where's Kathleen?"

"She's painting her fingernails," Helga said.

"Fine, now we'll set the table and by that time Miss Sparks will be here."

"I'm hungry," Danny said.

"You have to wait," Ingrid said.

"I see her!" Danny said, rushing to the window. "She's coming fast. Just look at the dust!"

"We'll go meet her," Ingrid said, slipping off her apron.

Miss Sparks geared down her Model T Ford as she came up the lane. "Maybe her brakes don't work," Danny said, disappointed.

Out stepped a curvaceous young woman, skin darkly tanned, brown hair cut short, and dark brown eyes. Her overall appearance made Ingrid think she'd be right at home on a south sea island. How did she come by such a tan inside a school room? Then Ingrid recalled that she walked three miles, morning and afternoon, from the Mulder's place where she boarded. She didn't need to—she had the car—but she dared to be different.

Danny took a shy streak and slipped behind the ivy. Helga stepped forward and took her hand.

"We've been excited all morning about your coming," Ingrid said.

The corners of Miss Sparks mouth curved mischievously. "I do hope I'm not late," she said. "Mr. Mulder helped me change the oil in the T this morning and it took longer than we thought." She made a slight toss of her head that sent her hair back from her face.

"I couldn't wait much longer," Danny said, coming out from the ivy. "I'm really hungry."

"Don't mind him," Ingrid said. "He's always hungry. Come inside. We'll eat as soon as Olaf carves the chicken."

"You've a beautiful farm," Miss Sparks said. "In particular the house—I like the verandah, oh, what a wonderful place to lounge in the shade and read!"

Ingrid laughed. "I hate to think what the neighbors would say," she said.

Miss Sparks gave her a quizzical look. "Izaak Walton said, and wisely, *that which is everybody's business is nobody's business*," she said.

When they came inside Olaf and Kathleen greeted her, and she was made to sit at the kitchen table with a glass of freshly pumped water to sip while Olaf carved the chicken and the girls filled the bowls with vegetables.

"You know, that's the only good thing that came of this drought," Ingrid said, as they were seated around the table. "There's time to lounge. If we had a crop, we'd be harvesting sunup to sundown."

"Yes, you're right," Miss Sparks said. "Although, I must say I enjoy the endless sun."

"I hope you like your new school," Ingrid said.

"I've been here two months and it seems like two weeks," Miss Sparks said. "I like it fine. The children are delightful."

The way she said it, the expression of excitement, attracted Ingrid at once. Ingrid gave the blessing and passed the food.

"Do you get chicken to eat at the Mulder's?" Danny asked.

"Danny, what a question," Ingrid said, although she herself wondered what the Mulders served their boarder.

"Sure do, Danny," Miss Sparks said. "Sometimes beef roast. Sometimes pork chops."

"And apple pie?"

"That, too."

"Oh," Danny said. "I guess you wouldn't want to live here with us then."

Miss Sparks winked at Ingrid. Ingrid raised her eyes to the ceiling.

"Is your arm better?" Helga asked.

"What happened to your arm?" Ingrid asked.

"The children and I were playing ball," Miss Sparks said.

"And the ball hit her," Danny explained.

"We always play ball at noon hour," Helga said. "Don't we Miss Sparks?"

"Yes, Helga, not everyone approves, but, yes indeed, we do," Miss Sparks said.

Determined, Ingrid decided, and enthusiasms not easily dampened—no wonder the children were fond of their teacher.

"I heard Mr. Inish left to harvest," Miss Sparks said.

"Yes," Olaf said, "we haven't heard from Dad, but we think he found work."

"I'm sorry Mr. Inish won't be at the board meeting. I was depending on his presence," Miss Sparks said frowning slightly.

"I wish we had more chalk," Kathleen said. "It's hard to write with those little pieces. Maybe we could tell the inspector we need more."

"Mr. Mayer doesn't come again until January. I'll mention it to the school board," Miss Sparks said.

"Mom, you know Bobby, Marjorie's cousin, he throws it and it breaks even littler," Danny said.

"Tattle tail! Tattle tail!" Helga mocked.

"Now children, settle down," Ingrid scolded.

"Danny's right, Mom," Kathleen said. "He even threw one at Miss Sparks."

When all eyes turned to Miss Sparks her attention was on the chicken leg she was eating.

"Yeah, but she ducked!" Danny said proudly.

Helga giggled. Then everyone laughed, especially Miss Sparks.

Danny handed his empty plate to Kathleen. "Mom made dessert," he said. "Whipped cream."

"You don't get any unless you eat the jelly too," Kathleen said.

"Do I have to?" Danny pouted. "Let's play ball after," he added, his face brightening.

"The children tell me you sew," Miss Sparks said to Ingrid. "I've always been interested in sewing."

"She's sewing a dress for me," Helga said.

When they left the table Ingrid led the way to the corner of the living room where she kept the Singer sewing machine. "That's beautiful," Miss Sparks said, holding the dress to Helga's waist. "Oh, Helga, you'll be ever so lovely! Will you wear it to school?"

"Will I, Mom?"

"Yes, of course, dear."

"Then I'll see it when it's finished. I want to sew, but I don't know if I'm clever enough," Miss Sparks said.

"You mean my mom's clever?" Danny asked.

"Yes, Danny, she certainly is."

"Oh, well then, I guess she is," Danny said.

The ball had so many stitches that it was more oval than round, and the bat had wires holding it together. They played One-up: Ingrid, batter; Danny, catcher; Kathleen, pitcher; Helga, first base; Miss Sparks, short stop; Olaf, field. To stay *up* the batter must hit the ball and run fast enough to beat it to first and back to home or be *out*. It was underhand pitch and Kathleen moved a step forward from the pitcher's box and snapped the ball across home plate. Ingrid swung, hitting a fly that Olaf caught with one hand. Everyone moved up a notch, Danny at bat, Helga pitching. The ball bounced two times before it reached the batter's plate.

"Come closer," Danny shouted.

Helga did. Danny clamped his teeth over his tongue, drew the bat back and struck—the ball lifted over Helga's head, and to the outfield. Danny dropped the bat and ran for all he was worth—to first and half way back to home when there stood Miss Sparks holding the ball in front of her. He skidded to a stop, and there was Olaf on the other side, and every time he changed course they tossed the ball back and forth. Danny finally made a sliding dash for home and would have made it if Miss Sparks had dropped the ball—but she didn't. Danny slid under her; she lost her balance and fell on top of him just as his foot touched the plate. He was judged *out*!

A car drove past on the road, and then another and they waited for the dust to settle. When Olaf came to bat they couldn't put him out; after six tries Ingrid announced the dishes needed to be done.

There was a steady stream of chatter and laughter in the kitchen as they washed and dried the dishes and put them away, and then Miss Sparks said she had to go. The children argued there were still card games to play and crokinole to shoot, but Miss Sparks had papers to correct for Monday's classes.

"We haven't had this much fun since Conor left," Ingrid told her at the car.

Miss Sparks waved at every bend in the road.

CHAPTER 19

IT CAME TO FORREST more strongly than ever that he needed a woman in his life. Mattie's laughter was reminiscent of birds singing, of rippling streams, and it made him feel young and blithe. It brought memories of Irene, of the dimples that formed in her cheeks, and how her face changed from pensive to radiant when she smiled. He'd wanted to reach out and touch Irene, to take her out of that place and put her where she'd be free to be happy.

Two weeks ago, Guro had asked them to stay through to the end of the haying season. "You fellows have been lying around long enough," Guro said. Forrest agreed. But the two weeks of wet weather had given him time to catch up on current events. Mattie was an avid reader with plentiful material and she begrudged her patients nothing.

He absorbed reports on the possibility of war and in particular followed Chamberlain's part in the affair. Recently there had been a meeting between the two dictators, Hitler of Germany and Mussolini of Italy, and the two leaders of democratic nations, Prime Minister Chamberlain of England and Premier Daladier of France. The purpose was to settle a dispute between Germany and Czechoslovakia over a strip of land called the Sudetenland that divided the two countries. Hitler claimed the

Czechoslovak government was mistreating the Sudeten Germans and he threatened to invade the country if the territory wasn't ceded to Germany at once. Chamberlain and Daladier believed Hitler when he said it was the last time he'd demand territory in Europe and they agreed he could have the Sudetenland.

Forrest was furious. Only twenty years had passed since the last war with Germany and here was Hitler boasting his power and demanding territory with threats; the democratic powers let him, without even consulting the leaders of the threatened territories. Forrest could not restrain himself. "The rotten sons-of-bitches!" he shouted. He jumped to his feet and fired the paper clear across the room.

Mattie ran to his side. "What's the matter?" she cried. "What is it?"

"World War One! I lost two uncles in that war against Germany. Two of the most respected, intelligent, considerate people you'd ever meet. And what for—what the hell for, I ask you?"

"Calm down, Forrest," Mattie soothed. "Don't stand on that leg." Mattie guided him to the couch and eased him to a reclining position. "Calm down and tell me."

Forrest shook—he felt he might break into tears.

"I'll make you some tea," Mattie said and hurried to the kitchen.

Forrest breathed deeply and forced himself to relax. Anger never solved a thing, he told himself, don't appear the fool in front of Mattie.

Mattie passed a cup of tea. "Here, drink this. Please, tell me," she said.

"There will be war," Forrest stated flatly.

Mattie drew a sharp breath. "How do you know?"

"Mattie, just last spring Hitler sent his army to Austria, proclaiming that country a part of Germany—no opposition. Hitler claimed the Sudetenland—again, no opposition. Two years ago Hitler and Mussolini signed a treaty to provide mutual aid, and the government of Japan signed shortly after. Doesn't that tell you something?"

"But why doesn't someone stop them?" Mattie asked anxiously.

"Because they're frightened. They're not prepared. They don't *want* war."

"Oh, no, not a war! Guro would have to go," Mattie cried.

"He wouldn't have to go," Forrest assured her. "Men who raise food for the nation are granted exemption."

"But he'd go, Forrest. I'm certain he'd go."

"What's the trouble here?" Guro asked as he and Conor came inside.

"Forrest thinks there will be war," Mattie said.

"Of course there will be war," Guro said. "Just a matter of time."

"You should have told me," Mattie said.

Guro pulled Mattie to her feet and placed his arms around her. "Time enough to worry when it happens," he said. "There's good and bad to a war."

"Oh, Guro, don't say that," Mattie said.

"It's true," Forrest brightened. "We don't want war, but if it's inevitable, let's face it, and let's get at it before Hitler gets his devil's claws in more countries."

"It's been a long ten years with no jobs," Conor said wearily. "A war would solve that, but I'd hate to see my son go off to fight. He's much too young for the horrors of war."

"You fought in the first one?" Guro asked.

Conor nodded.

"You were quite young," Guro said.

72

"Twenty. Came through it without a scratch. Doubt I'd come through another, few are that lucky."

They looked at Nick who'd been standing in the doorway, listening. He looked twenty or more; although, he was only eighteen.

"I'd go to war," Nick said quietly. "Better clothes, three meals a day, smokes. No worry about police, the cold, coal dust in my skin. War can't be much worse than being swore at, stomped on—I'd show them all I'm a Canadian."

A long pause followed. For Nick that was a lengthy speech.

"I'd go to war." Forrest's voice was tense. "I'd go to war if only for the dream of personally ending that dictator's life. Revenge! Sweet revenge!"

Guro looked at Mattie. "My family, my freedom, my ranch—that's worth fighting for," he said.

Forrest wondered how Conor felt. Conor had avoided the talk of war whenever the subject arose.

"I'd go," Conor said, his face drawn and firm with knowing what war was all about. "Not for patriotism as the first time. I'd go because I've lost my farm, my home, and I've nowhere else to go. I can still put up a good fight."

"God willing there won't be a war," Mattie said, desperately. "Possibly Churchill will make England and France see sense. I read where he and many people think Hitler will grab more and more. And he is—he seized Albania and now he's after Poland. It's in the last *Times*. Forrest, I'll get it for you."

"Enough war talk," Guro said. "Time to make hay while the sun shines. We'd better get at her before Little Hawk and his Indians take off for the horse races. How is that leg, Forrest?"

Forrest recalled Hatfield's long-handled pitchfork—the devil's instrument—he rubbed his leg and grimaced.

"He should sit," Mattie said. "Let him drive a team."

"All right," Guro said, "Forrest on the hayrack. Conor and I on the two mowers, Nick and the Indians fork the hay onto the racks and build the stacks by the barn. The truck needs repairs. Until that's done we'll have to saddle the horses.

"But we've one day of harness repair," Guro added. "The Indians are all thumbs when it comes to harness repair."

"I'll do that," Conor said.

"All right. Little Hawk mows today," Guro said. He placed his big hat upon his head, eager to start.

Conor had seen the hayloft brimful on his arrival at Guro's ranch. A hoist lifted the hay inside the loft; in the field there would be a gin-pole to stack it. Since a strong back was an asset, Conor was thankful Guro had placed him driving a team.

Conor went straightaway to do his part. The workbench was piled with harness, the tools within easy reach. As he installed new rivets and replaced leather strapping, his thoughts turned to Ingrid. He wanted to send her fifty dollars by Christmas at the latest. He wouldn't ask Guro for money since the man had been kind enough to lodge and doctor them with no questions asked. He planned that after haying he'd head northwest toward Dawson Creek where the harvest was later. After the harvest he wasn't certain what he would do, except that living with his in-laws was out of the question. In his last letter to Ingrid, he told her his plans and mentioned he would quite likely be in Dawson Creek by the time she received it, and that she should write to him there care of general delivery. He didn't consider himself a first-rate letter writer and had left much unsaid. He hoped the last sentence would cover the feelings he couldn't express in a letter. "I miss you darling," he wrote, "I am doing my best, but times are hard here, too, and my one hope is to hold you in my arms again soon."

Conor was skilled at harness repair—he'd done much in his lifetime. By early afternoon he'd finished the task to his satisfaction, had placed the tools in their proper places, and had headed for the house when he looked up to see a horse lathered with white foam pounding up the wagon road. From its back a wild-eyed Indian jumped— the horse fell to its knees. The Indian plunged past him and burst through the screened door. "Come quick! Come quick, Missus!" he cried.

Conor reached the door in time to hear the Indian's words tumble over one another. "Guro, he die! He die, Missus!" he panted, pounding his chest, gasping for air.

"Calm, Tommy. Stay calm," Mattie said. Her face drained white. "Tell me. Tell me slowly."

"Guro, h-he, mower cut him bad. Bad, very bad. He die. I know he die. Blood all over. Little Hawk h-he, me, I ride like crazy man."

"Where? Where?"

"The Narrows."

"Quick, Conor, saddle three horses. Tommy, go with him. I'll get my stuff together. Hurry! Dear God, hurry!"

Conor ran for the corral, Tommy at his heels. "No saddle," Tommy said. "No time, bareback." He ran his fresh horse to the house. "I take." He grabbed two cases from Mattie's hands and leapt astride his mount. Conor followed only minutes behind with the saddled horses. Mattie brought a pillowcase stuffed with bedding for bandages; Conor tied it to his saddle. Mattie slipped a packsack across her shoulders and mounted her Arabian, Demon.

"Let's go," Conor shouted—Tommy was already out of sight.

"It's five miles," Mattie said excitedly. "Hold the horses in, to Spring Meadows— then give them their heads."

Mattie took the lead, sawing down Demon. He fought the bit for his head, gained a ground-reaching run and kept it. Conor's buckskin followed a length behind.

Curved and twisted to the land's natural contours, the rutted wagon road stretched ahead. Spruce trees whipped past, then an open gate, the entrance to Spring Meadows.

"We'll take a shortcut," Mattie yelled over her shoulder. She reined Demon on to a hard-packed trail. "Let 'em go!" Necks straining ahead the horses reached out. Through the willow brush they shot, reining in they crossed a stream with short fast steps, coming up full speed on the other side. Another meadow flashed past, another spruce grove, and soon Conor lost count. His buckskin was sweating and breathing hard and he wanted to ease him back, but Mattie kept Demon to his limit. The only ride to compare with this was during the war when he ran an emergency message to the high command; he'd carried out his errand as skillfully as any man could, but he had arrived too late. Mud, picked up by Demon's hoofs, flew up and over him. The wind swept past; horse sweat spattered his face. This must be The Narrows—the meadow closed in between two spruce groves and widened again on the far side. The teams still attached, two mowers stood apart: one at a haphazard angle, the other

74

jammed in a spruce tree. In the space between, kneeling silent men encircled a still figure lying on the ground, and Tommy Tutlack, Guro's big black hat in his hand, head bent low on his chest, stood beside his exhausted horse.

Forrest left the group and rushed to meet them.

"How is he?" Mattie cried.

Forrest held her firmly by the shoulders. "It's too late, Mattie. It's too late!"

"Oh, no, it can't be. Let me go!" Mattie begged. She flung herself away from his grasp.

"It's better not to see him," Forrest insisted. "Please, Mattie! Please! He's gone. He said for you not to see him this way."

Mattie dropped to the ground, gripped her knees and moaned, tossing side to side.

Forrest dropped to the ground beside her. "The baby, Mattie," he said, "Guro, he said to tell you to watch for his baby."

Mattie froze. She looked at Forrest, her eyes overflowing. "Oh, no," she mourned, "I forgot the baby. He's alone. He's all alone."

"We'll go back," Forrest said. "Take my hand. We'll go back *now*."

"Take these horses," Conor whispered; he seemed to have lost control of his voice. "They're rested enough to take you back if you don't push them. The baby will be fine."

CHAPTER 20

ONCE IN A WHILE Conor drew apart from his faith in God. It had happened during the war, at the times his buddies dropped one by one to die in agony, or to survive with legs or arms or half their faces blown away. He learned as a child that God was a just and loving God, but sometimes it seemed to him a contradiction to real life. He drew apart now.

Conor didn't listen to the droning sermon; he didn't sing of the green valley; he didn't look at the bowed heads. What he heard was Little Hawk's taught, shaky voice. "I drive behind in Narrows. Grouse he fly, team run. No time for gears. Guro, he fall on knife." What he saw was Guro's body, lying in a pool of blood. What he felt was the anguished heart of the black-veiled woman standing there with the baby in her arms.

Conor quietly left the graveside to gaze across the brown meadows, to the bare poplar bluffs, across the spruce groves to the hills and the cloudy sky. The mournful call of the loon echoed across the draw. He saw the ladies gather to console Mattie, and then she walked to Forrest who took the baby and guided her to the old truck where Nick waited.

Conor swung into the saddle and pointed his mount toward the ranch. It was a two-hour ride, enough time to come to task with his feelings, to strengthen himself in the hope of passing some of it on to Mattie. Riding to the ranch, Conor saw the country through Guro's eyes—eyes so often filled with wonder and excitement as they scanned the land.

When Conor rode into the yard, the old truck was parked by the porch; Nick sat on the steps, whittling a broken ax handle; Forrest stood idle, his hands on the railing. No one spoke when Conor sat. Guro's mount curved its head over the corral fence and whinnied. Two cows lingered by the barn, swishing tails at the flies. Inside, the baby cried.

All three looked up when the screened door squeaked open. "Here, please hold him," Mattie said to Forrest. "I'll make the tea."

Forrest took the baby, shushed him in his arms; still, he continued to fret. Forrest snuggled the bundle against his shoulder and awkwardly patted the tiny bum. The baby burped. "Hmmm," Forrest said, holding him at arm's length, "look what you did to my new shirt."

Nick grinned. Conor relaxed a little.

Mattie brought tea and cookies outdoors. She left Nickoli in Forrest's arms, walked to Guro's horse, rubbed his neck and scratched his ears. "I hope you fellows stay to finish the hay," she said. "We'll figure a fair wage. Guro and I put money aside for an emergency."

"We'll stay," Conor said. "We don't want pay."

But the haying went on and on, stopping and starting, dictated to by the weather and broken machinery. Nick became anxious about sending money to his parents. Conor's plans, too, were impossible since the Dawson Creek harvest was finished by now.

The middle of December found the three still at the ranch: herding the cattle from the community pasture, building additional corrals for the expanded herd, chopping holes in the ice-covered ponds, hunting deer and grouse—they were busy dawn to dusk.

It was at the supper table Mattie brought up the subject of wages. "I can pay you each forty dollars now," she said. "I'm hoping we'll agree on cattle in lieu of wages. I know you've no land but you may leave them here until the market improves."

"It may not improve," Forrest said. "The States is swamped with beef too. Their borders have been closed to Canadian cattle since '31."

"Sometimes you have to gamble," Mattie said. "Think of the men wandering aimlessly with no hope of earning money, no decent place to rest their heads. We at least have a home and something to gamble with."

"I'd go along with that," Conor said. He loved the country and wouldn't hesitate to bring his family here and start anew.

Nick nodded his agreement.

"If you'll allow me to buy a battery for your radio, I'll go with it," Forrest said in jest, although everyone knew he seriously wanted to keep up with the news and that Mattie missed her soaps, "Guiding Light" and "Ma Perkins."

With his head, Forrest rubbed Nickoli's little tummy. The baby laughed every time. Conor noticed that Forrest was learning how to hold the baby comfortably, not as though he were a stick of wood.

CHAPTER 21

OLD MR. SMITH loaned the Thoroughbreds. Olaf hitched them to the sleigh—another item missed at the auction; it had been stored in Mr. Smith's barn at the end of the winter season.

Old Mr. Smith had been young once; although, Olaf found it hard to believe, wrinkles knit his brow, creases pulled at the corners of his mouth, folds hung loose beneath his chin. He was bent in the middle and walked slower every day it seemed. Olaf understood everyone had had to be young once in his life, but to picture Mr. Smith a strapping young man was out of his reach. But Mr. Smith told how he started forty years ago with nothing but a straw hat with a hole where the crown ought to be, and how he'd plowed forty acres with a single-share plow. He had had to grip the plow handles with all his strength to cut a deep straight furrow, and at the same time shout at the obstinate oxen to for god sake keep pulling. He told how he homesteaded one quarter of land, bought a quarter every year until he had a section. Mr. Smith always ended his stories looking sad. "If I had one wish, I'd be young again," he'd say, and he'd look at Olaf in a way Olaf didn't understand.

Olaf snapped the reins and clucked his tongue. The Thoroughbreds, excited, jumped this way and that, their necks curved and heads held high. "You watch 'em," Mr. Smith had told him. "They ain't been hitched for a long time.

"Not meaning to worry you, but if your dad ain't sent word there's something dang wrong," Mr. Smith had added. Then, the next morning, Olaf saw his mother's eyes red and watery and he knew he'd better pick up the mail. There will be a letter—there had to be.

The Thoroughbreds trotted briskly, harness rustled, collar bells jingled, sleigh runners squeaked against the frozen hard-packed snow. Olaf pulled off his mitt and felt in his pocket—it was there, the ten dollars Mr. Smith had paid him, and another ten to buy Mr. Smith's groceries. His mother hadn't sent a list; she said she had no money.

Hoarfrost decorated the bare branches of the poplar trees. The sun played its rays upon the frost creating a sparkling marvel. Olaf relaxed and enjoyed the spectacle. He felt he was dreaming; he felt he was traveling a road he'd never traveled before. The day was wondrous and his spirits soared. Yesterday, he'd been walking Marjorie home from school and had lightly kissed her cheek—she had returned his kiss, full on the lips. Olaf's heart had jumped clear to the heavens. He held her hand all the way to the path that led to her house, where she put her arms around his neck. "I've feelings for you," she told him then, and at long last he found the words he wanted to say—"I love you, Marjorie."

Soon the town came in view. He planned to buy Marjorie a Christmas present; perhaps a red scarf—she favored red.

"You ain't been around for a while, Olaf," Mr. Kruger said. Mr. Kruger was the postmaster. Everyone said he was a German—no one had noticed he was a German before the talk of war. A German or not, Olaf was fond of the jovial Mr. Kruger. He'd always pass the time of day, even when meeting on the street. And something notable about him, to Olaf's amusement, was his dark hair—if a playful breeze caught Mr. Kruger with his hat off, a long thick strand of hair loosened and stretched out behind him to reveal a white bald patch at the center of his head.

"I've been working for Mr. Smith, so I've money to spend," Olaf said.

"Grand old man, Smith," Mr. Kruger said. "Here's a dollar. You buy him a bottle of wine, my present."

Olaf nodded and tucked the money with the other.

"Have some letters for you. Here are two from your papa. Winnipeg forwarded them, just came yesterday."

Olaf heaved a relieved sigh. "We've been waiting a long time for these," he said. "Dad doesn't know where we are."

"Your papa doesn't know where you are?" Mr. Kruger asked incredulously.

"And we don't know where he is either," Olaf said.

"I swear," Mr. Kruger said and clucked his tongue. "Maybe you'll know where he is once you open those letters."

"It's not easy 'cause he keeps moving," Olaf said. "He went harvesting."

Mr. Kruger looked at Olaf over his spectacles. "Long past harvest," he said.

"When Dad left he assumed we were going to Winnipeg," Olaf explained. "But we didn't go."

"I can see that," Mr. Kruger said.

"Times are bad, Mr. Kruger."

"You're right about that, Olaf. And I figured there was something fishy—those rumors about Conor, your papa, leaving and all."

"Leaving and all?" Olaf asked. "What rumors?"

"Oh, it's no cause for your concern," Mr. Kruger said. "Just Mrs. Black and those women clacking their tongues again."

"Mrs. Black? What did she say?"

"It didn't amount to much, Olaf. Let sleeping dogs lie."

"No, no, I want to know. You see, Marjorie Black and I, we, we're—" Olaf hesitated; he had said too much.

"So it's like that, is it? I'll tell you, son, if you're to be part of the Black family one day you ought to savvy what's going on. My Bessie and Mrs. Black put their heads together and came up with the news that Conor, your papa, has left your mama because she's fraternizing with other men."

"W-what other m-men?" Olaf stuttered.

"All sorts, by how they're talking."

"But that's crazy," Olaf said. "It's not true. It's not true at all." He felt pangs of guilt; he shouldn't have insisted Mr. Custer spend the night.

"Almost missed it. A letter postmarked Winnipeg," Mr. Kruger said, reading as much as he could on the outside of the envelope.

"It's from my grandparents," Olaf said.

"Your grandparents live in Winnipeg?"

"Yes, Mr. Kruger, Winnipeg—that's where Dad thought we'd gone."

Mr. Kruger removed his spectacles and leaned forward on the counter. "I told 'em to mind their own dern business but they pay no attention to me. I told 'em it's trouble they're making. Don't you worry, son. I'll tell my Bessie to lay off the Inishes or I'll start a few rumors of my own." Mr. Kruger slammed the T. Eaton catalogue on the counter. Olaf jumped.

"Sorry, son, didn't mean to scare the living daylights out of you," Mr. Kruger said.

"I don't know why they'd say that when it isn't true," Olaf said.

"Don't you worry, son. You can't tell how these things get started. But it could be your mama, Conor's wife, is the prettiest woman around. Women hate other women being prettier than they are, especially if they don't have a man of their own in the house. Maybe they're worried they'll lose their husbands." Mr. Kruger laughed as if it were the most hilarious joke he'd told in a long while.

"Here's something to keep your mama occupied these long winter evenings," Mr. Kruger said. He pushed the *T. Eaton* catalogue at Olaf. "Merry Christmas, son."

Olaf went to the grocery store. Mr. Barlow took Mr. Smith's list and money. "And how is your mother?" he asked Olaf.

"Oh, she's all right," Olaf said slowly. Maybe the whole town was gossiping about his mother. Well, he surely wasn't going to ask. Olaf straightened his shoulders and stood tall. "I've money, Mr. Barlow," he said. "May I look a spell while you're getting the list ready?" On the counter, Olaf set .22 shells, 30:30 rifle shells, two loaves of white baker's bread, Helga and Danny ate it like they ate cake, and strawberry jam for a Christmas morning treat. Then he went to the dry goods' section where he paused at a bolt of velvet material. The color was what his mother liked the best—a deep wine.

"Your mother sews?" Mr. Barlow asked.

Olaf nodded, caressing the soft fabric. "Yes, she sews dresses and coats and jackets."

"So your mother sews a fine seam," Mr. Barlow said. "She's sure to like this. The color's in style this year."

Olaf knew little about style. Probably country women didn't concern themselves with style in these hard times, but his mother would look stunning in a dress sewed of this material—that he knew positively. "She hasn't had a new dress in a while," he said.

"Four or five yards will do it. Better take five. She may tuck the waist."

"She likes long sleeves," Olaf remembered.

"Five ought to do it anyway," Mr. Barlow said. "With thread and binding to match, and fancy lace for the collar, the cost is three dollars."

For Kathleen he found a book about a family in China, written by an American woman who lived in China since she was a child, for Helga, maple buds, for Danny, hard rock Christmas candy.

Olaf looked at Mr. Barlow. "I've ten dollars," he said.

Mr. Barlow wrote the prices on his pad. "Comes to six dollars and ten cents," he said. "How is Conor? Expect you've heard by now."

"Letters came just today," Olaf said, patting his pocket. "Haven't read them yet."

"You doing all right on your own? An odd deer out your way? Or is it out of season?" Mr. Barlow asked in a low tone.

"Haven't seen deer tracks anywhere. Just horse tracks. I've been fishing with Old Mister Smith, but we don't catch many."

"Try with a net?" Mr. Barlow kept his voice low. "Must be a prairie hen or two around."

"No, there isn't and I promised Mom I'd keep meat on the table," Olaf said.

"Mr. Smith's horses must have got out," Mr. Barlow said.

"Tracks are too small to be the Thoroughbreds," Olaf said. "Just saw them behind the barn once. They're about the size of Helga's pony that was sold at the auction."

"Who bought it? Maybe it came back. Horses will do that."

"Don't know who bought it. Never saw the man before, but I remember he said he had foxes."

"Gosh, haven't heard anyone having foxes around here. You know in some parts of Europe horse meat is a delicacy." Mr. Barlow winked.

Olaf laughed. He couldn't imagine anyone eating horse meat.

"Leave your stuff here until you leave," Mr. Barlow said. "Otherwise, it's sure to freeze. I'll put in a box of bones for the dog."

"Oh, and I forgot eggs. Mom didn't say to get eggs but we need them for breakfast," Olaf said, then he remembered he hadn't bought Marjorie's gift. "Oh, no, forget it, Mr. Barlow. I've enough money left only to buy a present."

"Your hens stopped laying?"

"Sure, now. We're not able to keep the chicken house warm enough in this cold weather. Anyway, we're running out of chicken feed."

"Bank the house with snow," Mr. Barlow suggested.

"The wind just whips the snow away," Olaf said. "I'm afraid the chickens will freeze. There are only two hens left. Oh, and Mr. Kruger wants a bottle of wine for Mister Smith. He gave me a dollar."

"I'll put the bottle in his bag with a gift tag," Mr. Barlow said. "I'll put in the eggs. Is there anything else your mother needs? You may charge it since Conor probably sent money."

"Mom wouldn't want me to open her letters," Olaf said.

"That's fine, son," Mr. Barlow said. "It's Christmas. I'm sure Conor sent money along. Just pay me the next time you come to town. Ingrid will be low on flour and sugar and oatmeal by now, and she'll need yeast to make the bread dough rise."

"Thanks, Mom will appreciate that."

Olaf strode briskly up the sunny street and headed for the pawn shop that served as a jewelry store. He only meant to look in the display window but frost covered the glass so that he had to go inside to see anything. He browsed awhile, checked the prices, and since nothing had caught his eye, he turned to leave just as a clerk entered the room.

"Hello, Olaf, may I help you?"

"Just looking, Ed," Olaf said.

Ed Johnson had quit school a year ago when he got the job clerking. He carried a velvet-lined tray with two rings arranged neatly upon it.

"Those are diamond rings?" Olaf asked.

"Yes, new ones, customers ain't picked them up," Ed said. "Mr. Lewis is mad, too. Says people are real generous at Christmas, make a deposit and then back down."

"Maybe they lost their jobs."

"Could be," Ed said. "If I don't sell something soon, I could lose mine."

"That's a beauty—the one with the three small stones across the top," Olaf said.

"Mr. Lewis said it's ten dollars, and he said he's barely making cost."

"Ten dollars? I don't have ten dollars."

Mr. Lewis stood in the doorway. "You Inish's son?" he asked. Olaf nodded.

"What can you pay down?"

"Three dollars and ninety cents," Olaf said. He pulled the money from his pocket.

"You working?"

"After school for Mr. Smith."

"Give me that down and a dollar a month until it's paid."

Olaf shook his head. He knew his mother had no money and he wasn't certain his dad had sent any.

"Eight dollars. Not a cent less," Mr. Lewis said.

"But I'd want the ring for Christmas," Olaf said, "and Mr. Smith may not pay me before spring."

"Give me what you have and four dollars and ten cents in the spring. You'll have to sign the bill."

Olaf imagined Marjorie's squeal of delight. "Real diamonds!" he said.

"Most certainly they are," Mr. Lewis assured him.

What if his dad hadn't found a farmer who needed help with the harvest? Maybe the crops to the north were no better than here—if he could have only read the letter. He didn't dare to open it—his mother would be furious.

"Seven dollars, not a cent less," Mr. Lewis said, "three dollars and ten cents in the spring."

Olaf stared, dumbfounded. He hadn't dreamed the price would steadily go down. Dare he stall longer—he supposed not since Mr. Lewis turned to walk away, a disgusted look on his face.

"All right. I'll take it," Olaf said hastily. Ed placed the ring in a box and tied a red ribbon around it. Olaf put his money on the counter. Mr. Lewis wrote the bill, explained the figures, and Olaf signed it.

Olaf stepped outside to the street just as Mario was walking past.

"Hey, Olaf old man, you buying rings for the legs of your chickens?" he said.

"No," Olaf responded, "it's a nose ring for nosy people."

"I saw your sleigh at Barlow's store. I'm going to catch a ride."

"Catch a ride with someone else," Olaf said. "I'm not ready to go."

"I'll go when you're ready," Mario said, striding alongside.

"There's no telling when I'll be ready," Olaf said. "Could be late. You'd be better off to ask someone else."

Olaf entered the hardware store; his last stop, and when he returned, Mario was leaning against the door jamb, waiting.

"Where you getting the money for all this stuff you're buying?" Mario demanded.

Olaf ignored him and walked to Mr. Barlow's store. Mario matched his steps. Olaf loaded the goods into the sleigh. Mario watched.

The Thoroughbreds were frisky after the long rest. Olaf wanted to plan on the drive home about Marjorie and the ring, what he'd say, where he'd say it, but with Mario chattering aimlessly, he had no chance for that. In his anxiety, Olaf forgot to cover the groceries with the old buffalo robe kept in the sleigh for that purpose. He stopped the team to inspect the packages and to wrap them securely, and while he did Mario slid into the driver's seat.

"I'll drive," Mario said.

"If you want a ride, get over, or get out," Olaf demanded.

"Oh, come on, old man. Just let me drive."

The tugging of the reins set the Thoroughbreds to stepping nervously. When Olaf pushed Mario, he slammed into the sleigh's far side and sat there sulking. "I'd let you drive if it were my team," he said.

"It's Mr. Smith's team."

"What're you telling me—these are your dad's horses," Mario said.

81

"Mr. Smith bought them."

"How much did he pay?"

"How would I know that?"

"The old man must be loaded with money," Mario said. "I'll bet he keeps it under his bed.

"When is your dad coming home? If ever," he added, cocking his head to the side.

"He'll come home in his own good time."

"Bet you didn't even hear," Mario said.

Olaf pressed the letters to his chest. "I've letters in my pocket right now," he said.

"That's a lie," Mario said. "He didn't find no job. Well, if he did, there's money in those letters. You're loaded, too. You're rich, Olaf. Keep it in your sock, I guess."

Mario's laugh reminded Olaf of a hen's cackle after it laid an egg.

"Could be Marjorie will look at you with moony eyes," Mario went on, "I got to hand it to you, old man; you sure know what wahoos the girls. If I had money, could be Marjorie would wahoo with me, too."

Olaf looked at Mario as if he were the scum of the earth.

"I'm coming inside to get warm," Mario said when the Inish house came in view.

"I'll drive you home," Olaf offered. He didn't want Mario listening when his mother read his father's letters. It was two extra miles but would be worth it to be rid of him. Olaf kept the horses at a fast trot so that Mario wouldn't jump out.

By the time he took Mario home and delivered Mr. Smith's groceries, dusk had settled over the prairie.

His mother met him as he drove up to the house. "Did you get the mail?" she asked.

"Yes, Mom, there are two letters from Dad," Olaf said joyfully. He flung the buffalo robe to the side. "Quick, help me carry this stuff inside," he said.

Ingrid sat at the head of the table; the children waited impatiently.

"Grandmother's letter is thin. We'll open it first," Ingrid said, her cheeks flushing with excitement. She read, "I forgot to send you Conor's first letter because your father took sick. Then the second letter came and it slipped my mind again. Merry Christmas to you and the children. Have a joyful time, Mother." Ingrid passed the card so that everyone could see the picture of a decorated tree.

"Now your father's," Ingrid said.

Kathleen sliced the envelope open.

Helga giggled. "Witch's fingernails," she said.

Ingrid checked the postmark. "This was mailed at Rosebud, Alberta, three month's ago," she said. "And Grandmother forgot to send it." Ingrid shook her head in disbelief.

"Never heard of Rosebud," Olaf said.

Ingrid read, "We harvested for a Brook's farmer called Hatfield a month. I am heading north with Forrest MacLaren and a lad Olaf's age called Nick Sikorsky. Hug the children for me, Ingrid. I miss them. You are in my dreams, my love, Conor."

Helga giggled. "My love," she said.

"Now open the other letter," Danny said.

"Your father sent money," Ingrid said, showing her children the money order.

"I'll send you more money soon," she read. "I go to Dawson Creek in a few days and expect to go harvesting there. Write to me at General Delivery. I miss you darling. I am doing my best, but times are hard here, too. My one hope is to hold you in my arms again soon. I won't be in Winnipeg for Christmas. I don't want to spend my hard earned money traveling, and your parents already have a house full. Hugs for the children, Conor."

"Where was that letter written?" Olaf asked.

The postmark was illegible except for the date, October 24, 1938.

"I wish Dad would come home," Danny said, tears in his eyes. "Ain't he ever going to come home?"

"He'll come home," Olaf said. "Don't worry. No matter what anyone says, Dad is coming home. I know he is."

Ingrid sat in her room writing to Conor while the children listened to the radio. She explained why the bank didn't take the farm and why she decided to stay. She told him she'd met the hobo, Jerico, and had sent a letter. She filled four pages with what she and the children had done and still she wrote; it brought Conor near and she wished she'd never have to finish. Then she wrote on the backs of the pages and ended the letter with five x and o marks.

"I want to write to Dad," Danny said.

"Write here in the corner."

Helga wrote in another corner, and Kathleen in another and Olaf wrote at the bottom.

"Mom," Olaf said, "After we pay Mr. Barlow, we ought to save what's left of that twenty dollars for seed grain. Mr. Smith says the rains will be back next year."

"Everyone has been saying that for ten years," Ingrid said.

"Not Mr. Smith," Olaf said, "he only says what he means. He reads books on the weather and he says the drought is over. There will be a bumper crop next year—good as '28, he said."

"Mr. Smith isn't always right," Kathleen scoffed.

Ingrid believed Olaf to be earnest—he had faith in Mr. Smith's prediction. But it had been so long since the crops were prosperous that she could hardly credit such information.

"He says the government is going to distribute free seed to the farmers in the spring, and we should get all we can and buy more. He says we should sew every square inch that's cultivated."

"But we have no machinery," Ingrid said.

"He'll let us use his machinery if I seed his crop."

"There's your school work, Olaf."

"I'll study at night. It's correspondence anyway. Miss Sparks is just there to see it's done right."

"In that case we'll save all the money your father sends," Ingrid said. "Only an emergency will make us spend it."

"What's an emergency?" Danny asked.

"When you were sick with whooping cough and the doctor came—that was an emergency," Olaf explained.

Ingrid looked at Olaf in wonder. He was so young, but young people grew up fast these days.

CHAPTER 22

JERICO HAD NO IDEA what to do next, or where to go next. To find Conor Inish was proving to be a difficult mission, and no wonder, considering the man rode a horse and could travel east, west, north, or south, and points between, while Jerico, himself, rode a train and could only travel a straight line more or less. He decided to put his mission on hold. He'd keep his ears and eyes open and ask around, and by spring he'd have an idea where Conor Inish was. He wouldn't disappoint the fair lady.

"Honolulu City. Here we are," Ossified said, for the third time. Jerico covered his ears.

"Ain't nothin' wrong with Kelowna," Ossified said. "Weary and Boxcar are here and maybe Aesop."

"Aesop's in the fort," Jerico said.

"No!" Ossified stopped short in his tracks. "Where? He said he was going to keep out of them jails."

"Montana."

"How do you know?"

"How do I know anything?" Jerico said, insultingly. "I keep my eyes open and I listen, just listen! That's how I know things."

"I listen," said Ossified, defensively. "Didn't hear anyone say that."

Jerico grunted. "There it is," he said.

"What?"

"The friggin freight. You deaf or what?"

A plume of black smoke was barely visible to the east. "It ain't done whistled," Ossified said.

"Don't need to," Jerico said. "The tracks are singing."

Ossified stared at Jerico.

"You been hoppin' freights all these years and you ain't heard the track's singing," Jerico said, disgusted. "You don't listen!"

On their arrival, the first place Jerico headed was the soup kitchen.

"Not that rot gut," Ossified complained.

"Where, then? I ain't had time to trade," Jerico said.

"Acrost town. Try a handout. We've done that before."

"People are sick of those bums knocking on their doors, and you know damn well the dicks never let us alone in the city," Jerico said.

"We go acrost town where no one else goes. Six blocks, maybe."

"Six blocks? Since when do you want to walk six blocks?" Jerico asked.

"I can walk six blocks. I just don't like walking far," Ossified said.

"Don't see no dog," Ossified said, coming upon a likely house not too rich and not too poor. He walked to the back and raised his fist to knock, then quickly pulled his hand down. "Not this place," he whispered. "The cross; it's bad luck."

Jerico didn't argue.

The house next door was much the same but no cross on the door. Ossified shambled to the back and rapped listlessly—a man only clad in a pair of pants, opened the door. The man stared at them while scratching his bald head.

"H'lo," Ossified said.

"What you fellows want?"

"Could you spare a mite of food for a poor starvin' fellowman?" Ossified's pleading voice was meant to melt ice.

The man lifted his shoulders and let them down with a sigh. "My name's Raleigh, Harold Raleigh," he said.

Ossified stared at the man—it was not a usual greeting.

"Joseph Petrov," Jerico said, introducing himself. He supposed the name more deserving of alms than Jerico Joe.

Jerico kicked Ossified in the shins.

"Huh," Ossified said. "Osmond. Yeah, W-Waldorf Osmond."

"I ain't paid my taxes," Raleigh said with a hangdog look. "City wants the money tomorrow, or else."

"Oh?" Ossified said.

"Started with four houses," Raleigh said. "Dad left me money, you see. Renters kept skipping."

"Skipping?" Jerico asked.

"You know, gone in the night. Bank wants interest—that robber won't give an inch. You ever sit in a bank waiting to ask for more time?"

Ossified shook his head.

"It's like waiting for a verdict when you know the death penalty ain't changed none."

Jerico moved one foot to the other. Ossified shook his head, mouth wide open.

"See, I've sold what I can," Raleigh said. He stepped aside so that they could see into the room.

Jerico looked. He saw one table and one chair in the kitchen, and no furniture at all in the living room, and he wondered if the shirtless, barefooted Raleigh had sold his clothes too.

"You fellows might need a rocking chair. My old mother was sent to the poorhouse. You see, the city wants them taxes. They won't cut them neither."

"We'll be back," Jerico said and turned on his heel.

"Why did you say we'll be back?" Ossified asked as they left. "He ain't got no food. Why will we be back?"

Jerico was deep in thought so Ossified didn't ask again. Jerico headed for the soup kitchen. "Ugh, not that," Ossified grumbled.

The lineup was long and Jerico saw why. The selection was better than most soup kitchens: fresh buns, butter, several kinds of cheese, head cheese, mashed potatoes and meat balls floating in gravy. Their turn finally came and they lined the edge of their plates with potatoes, filling the middle as high as possible.

"You take this to Raleigh," Jerico said. "I'm going up town."

"I'm awful hungry, Jerico," Ossified said, his eyes pleading.

"Once I get back from my trading we'll get us some real food."

"But you brung good stuff," Ossified said.

"It's rot gut! You said it!" Jerico said "Go to Honolulu after you take this to Raleigh. I'll meet you there. You got any money?"

"You know I got four shinplasters," Ossified said.

"Give 'em to me," Jerico said. "I'll pay you tonight."

Ossified did, reluctantly. Not that he distrusted Jerico, Jerico never reneged on a loan, but those four shinplasters represented his worldly wealth.

Ossified walked slowly; his feet hurt. By the time he'd walked to Raleigh's house and to the jungle to find Weary Wilbur and Boxcar Bob, Jerico had arrived. Six fires burned with men cooking stew and warming cans of food around each fire. "Come on," a young man wearing a town hat invited, "there's food for all."

Jerico was puzzled at the merriment surrounding him. "We've been picking fruit and just got paid. Help yourself," another picker said.

With a good-time feeling, they dug tin plates and forks from their turkeys and filled their plates. Soon they all encircled one big fire in the center, passing tobacco, starting a singsong, and one guy brought out a mouth organ. He played and everyone hushed. The man was top-notch, and soon another guy brought one out, and another, and another, until Jerico counted a dozen.

Jerico knew this was admirable playing—the best he'd heard in a long time. The men sang along to "I'll Take You Home Again, Kathleen," "There's a Long, Long Trail A-winding," and "Mother Macree."

Ossified glanced at Jerico when they were playing "Girl of My Dreams." Did he see tears in Jerico's eyes? Impossible, he told himself, just the firelight glowing there.

An hour later the singing ceased. Jerico strode to the center and expounded on the drought, the tough times, the corrupt government; however, he explained, despite all, his fellowmen were generous, and to show his gratitude he'd sell much needed items at greatly reduced prices. Jerico had boxes full of various and unusual things, from a small accordion to a hank of yarn. There was much good humor, joshing and shoving, exclamations of delight, kidding one another as to why they needed that and what they'd use it for. Jerico approached Ossified and drew him aside.

"You sold the whole caboodle!" Ossified said.

"We're going to Raleigh's place," Jerico said.

"What? What for? Kee-ryst, not again."

"You got to come. I need protection," Jerico said.

Ossified had had no inkling Jerico thought so highly of him; he expected Jerico was toting a big sum of money.

"After we see Raleigh, we'll go for a banana split," Jerico said.

The next morning the fruit pickers warmed the leftovers, ate and began to disperse.

"Wish I were going home," a young man said, packing his turkey. "But I'm just another belly for the folks to feed."

"I hear there are jobs in Edmonton," another said.

"Not likely but I guess we keep moving on."

"We could go to war."

"What war? That ain't started yet, but if it does, I'm going. I'm tired standing around street corners."

The pickers left swinging their turkeys and singing "Coming in on a Wing and a Prayer."

"What's this say?" Ossified asked, handing Jerico a discarded newspaper. On the front page was a picture of a man with a small, square, black mustache beneath a big nose. He was dressed in a stiff military uniform.

"That's Hitler." Jerico looked closely at the paper. "He's taking Poland."

"The guy making all the trouble. And what's it say here?" Ossified pointed to a picture of several boxcars, the roofs practically covered with men.

"Knights of the Road," Jerico read.

"Knights of the Road! That's us!" Ossified said laughing.

Weary and Boxcar walked up from the toilet. It was just boards leaning against a tree and looked as if it would fall from a slight breeze.

"Hey, you guys, Hitler's taking Poland," Ossified said, knowledgeably.

Weary Wilbur opened his eyes halfway and looked at Ossified.

"Poland ain't in Canada. He can't get here," Ossified said.

"There's planes and boats, stupid," Jerico said.

"I'll shoot 'em out the sky," Boxcar offered.

"You don't own a rifle," Jerico said, scornfully.

"I could join up," Boxcar said.

They all laughed long, except Jerico. "There ain't nothing funny about a war," he said.

"A war's got naught to do with us," Ossified said. He thought he should change the subject if Jerico was going to get so hot under the collar. Jerico had been acting strangely the last month or two anyway, staring for hours into the fire, not uttering one word. All their years together, Ossified hadn't seen Jerico act that way. They'd go to Vancouver—a different town, a different jungle, the change would do wonders for Jerico.

"You going to False Creek this winter?" Ossified asked Boxcar.

"'Course," Boxcar said. "But I'm staying here as long as it's warm and dry."

Jerico left the soup kitchen.

"Everything ain't jake with Jerico," Weary said at the moment Jerico was out of hearing.

"If I didn't know better, I'd say he's in love," Boxcar said. "He'll get over it. I bin in love once."

Ossified didn't want to hear *that* story again. He started off after Jerico.

CHAPTER 23

"WANT TO TAKE THE DAY OFF, BOSS," Forrest told Mattie. Mattie offered her Arabian, Demon, because he was a joy to ride and because the truck was stored in the shed for the winter.

Forrest rode north along the wagon road. The cattle's tramping hoofs had packed the snow hard between corral and meadow. Conor had said not to feed hay but to let the cattle work their noses down to the grass through the snow that the horses pawed through. Conor was cut out for ranching, Forrest expected, since he'd settled in so easily. After Guro's death, it seemed Conor might revert to depression. Obviously he was a deep feeling man. Forrest looked at life from a less serious angle. He saw himself as a spiritual person, but never had he prayed for anything; if he wanted something, tangible or intangible, he assumed he must acquire it for himself. Guro's accident, and even his own—he rubbed his jaw, it still pained in the cold—Forrest believed predetermined and inevitable. Not that he didn't sympathize with Mattie; certainly to be left alone with a babe in arms during these hard times, and on a cattle ranch, a man's world so to speak, was a formidable challenge. He expected she'd respond to the challenge, but he missed her light laughter and camaraderie.

Forrest thoughts turned to the practical. Little Hawk's land abutted the reservation, five miles north of the community pasture. Hatfield's horses had not been herded to the ranch with the cattle. He hadn't wished to discuss this touchy subject with Conor and Nick, since it would set off an acrimonious dispute.

At the community pasture, Hatfield's three horses galloped across the field whinnying to Demon. Demon and the black gelding rubbed necks across the fence. Forrest tied the three horses by their halters and grasping the lead rope continued on his way. Summer freedom had made the horses wild and Forrest had a difficult time to control them, but he persisted, and trotting five miles through snow a foot deep subdued the animals.

He came upon a log cabin and log outbuildings in various stages of decay and collapse. Four children interrupted their play to throw sticks and stones at the dogs that came at him, yipping and howling. The black gelding let loose a swift kick that landed squarely on one dog's rear, and the terrified yelp brought Little Hawk and Tommy Tutlack at a run. They kicked the dogs to the side and swore in Cree.

Little Hawk greeted him with a handshake. "I see black horse in pasture," he said. "You sell?"

"Absolutely not," Forrest said, "you'll have another race soon, won't you?"

"I buy black horse," Little Hawk said. "How much you want?"

Tommy Tutlack ran his hand across the black's legs and pasterns. He nodded at Little Hawk.

"Money won't buy that black," Forrest said. "But I'll sell these other two."

"Could be I know who'll buy," Little Hawk said. "Why you bring black horse here?"

"He has the old brand—don't have my own. Expected you might put yours on them."

Little Hawk didn't say yes and he didn't say no, but his expressionless eyes remained glued to the black. "I use my brand, I sell two horses, you sell black to me," he said.

Forrest knew Mattie had paid the Indians recently, so recently that they probably hadn't had time to spend the money. "A horse like this black costs much money. Am I right, Little Hawk?" he asked.

"I pay you fifty tollar," Little Hawk said. "Use my brand, sell two horses. Gives you lotsa money. I pay you now, today."

Forrest held back. It wouldn't do to appear too eager. "Sixty for the black," he said. Perhaps he would sell the black if it would bring sixty dollars. The other two should bring twenty to thirty each. If he played it cagey he might come out of this deal a hundred *dollars* richer. Forrest could already see the sparkle in Conor's eyes when he handed him his share.

"Sixty," Little Hawk agreed, "but you pay me ten tollars to brand all them horses."

"All right," Forrest said. "It's a deal."

Little Hawk and Tommy straightway dug in their shirt pockets and brought forth a roll of bills—each man peeled off thirty dollars. Forrest handed a ten to Little Hawk and stuffed the remainder in his pant's pocket. "What are the other two worth?" he asked.

"No matter. I sell and I buy oats for black horse. Keep him lookin' good."

"No, no," Forrest objected.

"You say deal," Little Hawk accused.

"To hell I did!" Forrest swore. "I didn't say I'll throw in the other two horses for fifty dollars."

"Sixty tollars," Little Hawk corrected.

"What I profit is fifty," Forrest explained. Fifty split three ways wouldn't even pay for a false tooth. "Fifty is what will be in my pocket. That's not enough."

Little Hawk sighed and looked sorrowfully at the black. "Darn poor shit," he said under his breath.

Certainly the Indians wanted the black for a racer, Forrest determined; Indians understood the hind leg of a horse. Don't be too hasty selling the black, Forrest told himself. To Little Hawk he said, "Start at the beginning. Pretend I just rode up and we shook hands."

Little Hawk and Tommy walked part way to the cabin. Forrest was about to shout at them to return before he realized the direction this event had taken. He turned Demon in a tight circle, once more rode up to the Indians, and Little Hawk once again shook his hand.

"I see black horse in pasture," Little Hawk said. "You sell black horse?"

Forrest was cautious with his answer. "Absolutely not," he said. "Can you find a buyer for the other two?"

"Damn fine horse, black one," Little Hawk said. "I buy him quick, pay you now, today."

"The horses have old brands. Don't have my own. Thought you might put yours on them."

Tommy ran his hands across the black's legs and pasterns. He looked at Little Hawk and nodded.

Forrest perceived the beginning of deep frustration. He said, "You, Little Hawk, brand all three horses. I pay you ten tollars to brand, now, today." Calm, Forrest chastised himself, no need to employ Indian lingo. "When you sell the two horses, you pay me the money."

"Is good for you to pay me ten, now, today," Little Hawk said. "I buy black horse."

"No." Forrest planned to delve into that after the first deal was clear in the minds of the Indians.

Little Hawk simply couldn't get his eyes or his mind off the black horse. "You no sell, damn poor shit," he said.

Forrest laughed but he wanted to cry. How had Guro dealt with these people—but he had; therefore, there must be a method. Forrest had taken to heart his father's teaching: Always consider things from the other person's point of view. The advice was helpful now. After a pause, he opened his wallet, slipped a ten and handed the money to Little Hawk. He was precise and deliberate in his enunciation. "That ten is

for branding the three horses. When you sell the two horses you give me the money."
Both Indians nodded. Little Hawk pocketed the ten.

"Now for the black horse," Forrest said.

Little Hawk scratched his head. "I make good deal, very good deal with you on
black horse," he said.

"What's that?" Forrest asked warily.

"You leave him here. Tommy and I fix him up, feed him oats, best hay, and tell
him how to race with other horse. When he win, split money."

"Split? What do you mean, split?"

Little Hawk picked up a flat chunk of hard snow and divided it into three equal
parts, handing one part to Tommy, one to Forrest, and keeping one for himself.

"If he doesn't win, I take the black horse back. I, Forrest, own the black horse."

The Indians nodded their agreement. A handshake sealed the deal.

Forrest withdrew the money he'd received from the original deal, now canceled,
and handed the money to Little Hawk.

Little Hawk looked at it, disgusted. "I pay you thirty tollars, Tommy pay you
thirty tollars," he said.

"Yes, but I gave you ten." Forrest became aware of little hammers pounding at the
nerve ends in his brain.

"Deal was sixty tollars." Little Hawk turned to Tommy. "Poor shit," he added.

Forrest groaned. He couldn't leave Hatfield's horses in the community pasture any
longer; he couldn't take the horses to Guro's; his only hope was Little Hawk. Slowly
he reached for his wallet, pulled two five dollar bills and handed one to each Indian.

Little Hawk grinned his satisfaction. "Forrest, he like chinook come this place
when is very cold, sixty below."

"You say that!" Forrest beamed. "I'm like a warm wind on a frigid day!"

Forrest looked at his wallet, not feeling its lighter weight. With a distant and
captivated look, he closed it and slid it into his pant's pocket.

Two days later Conor broached the subject of Hatfield's horses. "There's not
enough grass on the community pasture to carry those horses through the winter," he
said.

The three were on foot hunting deer in the rough country west of the ranch. Their
mounts were half a mile behind staked in an open area where they could paw for
grass.

"I've attended to that, Conor," Forrest said. "No need for you to worry. In due
time we'll receive compensation for the hardships we suffered at Hatfield's hands."

A grouse flew up from the willows and landed fifty feet distant in the brush. "A
plentiful year for grouse," Nick noted.

"In due time? We could use the money now, I'm thinking," Conor said. He
glanced at Nick for his opinion.

"Impatience fosters defeat, my friend," Forrest said.

"Why don't you tell us? Stop pussyfooting around," Conor said.

They rounded a knoll near a drinking hole and came suddenly upon a blacktail
mother and her two fawns. All three turned their big ears and eyes full upon them.

"Mule deer," Conor said. "Bounding Blacktail!"

"Mule deer?" Forrest asked. He'd always imagined a deer having a white tail that stood straight up when approached by hunters. But on these three, the tails were streaked with black and remained down.

All at once two large dogs dashed out of the willows, yelping, leaping high above the brush and instantly it was a life and death race.

Up and away went the blacktail, mother and fawns tapping the ground and soaring to land, and tap and soar again.

"It's magnificent," Forrest said. "See how they draw up their legs in flight."

Up and away went the dogs, stretched out, straining hard.

"The dogs won't catch them," Forrest said. "They're going easily."

Conor disagreed. "They're losing time," he said. "The dogs will catch them if we don't do something."

Less than fifty feet remained between the dogs and the rearmost fawn. Conor raised his rifle and fired above the heads of the dogs to scare them and draw them back, but the dogs yelped and leapt faster at every blast of the gun. The rearmost fawn was slowing and the mother dropped back. She had but thirty feet lead on the dogs. By this time the blacktail had crossed the flat, reached a butte and striking with their toes, sailed and struck again as though they had wings to fly—arriving at the foot of the high rise the dogs were helpless and soon were left behind. The blacktail mother with her two fawns soared on till lost to view in the safety of the butte.

"I swear I'll never hunt deer again," Forrest said. "Could you take the life of a beautiful creature such as those we just saw?"

"Ranchers don't usually eat their own beef," Conor said.

"Hunt moose," Nick said. "More meat on moose and they're not pretty."

By the time the men backtracked to the horses, Nick had shot six grouse.

At the ranch, Conor and Nick scattered hay for the animals and chopped the watering holes clear of ice while Forrest skinned and gutted the grouse. Forrest placed the meat in the kitchen sink, then turned to see Mattie seated at the table, her forehead on her arms. "Mattie, what's the matter?" he asked, sliding to a chair beside her.

"Headache," Mattie said. "I'll start the supper in a few minutes."

"No you won't," Forrest said. "Come with me. I'm the doctor. You're going to the same hospital bed in which I convalesced."

Forrest guided her to the old couch in the living room, helped her stretch out, tucked a cushion under her head, and folded a blanket around her body. "There. I expect you won't allow me to rub iodine where it hurts, but I want to, to get even."

Mattie smiled up at him. "You could fetch a couple of aspirins, please," she said.

Forrest did, with a glass of water, and waited while she swallowed the pills. He affected an air of a professional doctor, placing his palm on her forehead for a while, taking her wrist and looking at his watch in deep concentration. He sat on the couch beside her, not saying a word, taking her pulse for ten minutes or more. Mattie laughed.

"Forrest," she said, "but for you and the others I'd never have pulled myself together."

Forrest, dramatic, said, "I know, we're like a chinook in this place when it's sixty below."

"I mean it," Mattie said, "and little Nickoli, I swear he thinks you're Guro."

91

"I'm so sorry, Mattie," Forrest said seriously, "for what you've had to endure. It won't be easy for you and Nickoli, I know that. But if you want to stay on at the ranch, there's always a way, and I know you'll find it."

CHAPTER 24

OLAF CIRCLED THE PASTURE a second time, cutting through the center of the poplar bluffs. It was easy walking with the snow crust frozen hard as a city sidewalk, and about the same color, too. The wind had uncovered high spots of frozen ground, and it swirled so persistently that little tufts of dust rose and settled over the whiteness of the snow; but still the sun's reflection cut at his eyes and he raised his hand to stop the glare. The icy wind cut at his cheeks and nose—his mother had warned him, if he froze his nose again he'd need a doctor. He laid the rifle on the ground and rubbed his nose with a warm bare hand until he felt a stinging tingle.

There were no deer tracks in the open, or in the bare poplar bluffs, or around the old eaten-down straw stack where he and his father had often had a successful hunt. Two days he'd walked eight miles west to the lake and back and saw no sign. Today he went east and looked since early morning. It would be sensible to give up—he knew that, but he searched the ground as he trudged homeward, still hoping, perhaps he'd missed a set of tracks since they'd not be easy to spot on the snow's hard surface.

Mutt pounced on him as he opened the kitchen door.

"You ought to take that dog along," Ingrid told him. "He'd smell the tracks."

"Mutt doesn't know how to hunt," Olaf said. "He'd scare a deer away if I did see one. Mom, he's to stay in."

"Well, all right, if you say so," Ingrid said. "But he sniffs at the door all the time you're away."

"I'm going again after I eat," Olaf said, even knowing it was foolish.

"We haven't had meat for almost a month," Ingrid reminded him. "I'd butcher that rooster except for Kathleen. Only two hens left, Olaf."

Olaf felt that his mother was accusing him of failure.

"We could butcher Bossy's calf, I guess," Ingrid said, "but it's a heifer and I wanted to keep her."

"I'll try again, Mom. There won't be any hens left, and no Big Red either, if this cold snap doesn't let up. That chicken house is freezing," Olaf said.

"We've milk and potatoes," Ingrid said.

"Scalloped potatoes, and scalloped potatoes," Olaf said, trying to sound humorous. "Not even a jack rabbit. It's just too cold, I guess. I said I'd keep meat on the table and I didn't do it. I'm sorry, Mom, but the wild animals have left."

"Coyotes are out there. I heard them singing last night," Ingrid said.

"Coyotes?" Olaf raised his voice. "Never ate a coyote."

Ingrid made a poor attempt at laughter. She patted his shoulder as he turned to leave. "You'll find a deer if you keep looking," she said.

Olaf doubted that, but he didn't say as much. "I'm going to Mr. Smith's prairie field," he said.

Olaf crossed the property line to Mr. Smith's home quarter. As he passed the barn he noticed small horse tracks among the regular sized ones of the Thoroughbreds, but no deer tracks. Every day Mr. Smith threw hay out the loft to the ground below for the Thoroughbreds, and the strange horse had obviously broken through the fence to steal the hay. Olaf headed for the prairie field. Perhaps there were a few grass spears poking through the snow, enough to tempt a wild animal or two.

The Thoroughbreds weren't in the field. Mr. Smith most likely put them inside the barn because of the extreme cold. There was snow in the air, and the wind was rising, creating a small blizzard. It was a quarter mile to the prairie patch and already Olaf's nose was feeling numb; he pulled the scarf his mother had insisted he wear to cover his face below the eyes. The scarf steamed up from his breath and froze solid, making an excellent windbreak. He stopped for a while, looking for movement other than what the wind stirred up, but what he saw was motionless prairie and rigid poplar trees. Then as Olaf drew closer, he did see something move—instantly his hopes soared. He kept to the low land and the bluffs as he moved ahead—there could be no mistake, he'd close in well under a hundred yards so there was no possibility of a poor shot. He dropped to his hands and knees and crept forward. The moaning of the wind muffled the scraping sounds of his clothes against frozen ground. Olaf came to realize it was a big deer he was stalking, bigger than any he'd hunted before. His sheathed hunting knife jabbed him in the stomach; he squirmed and wiggled until it hung from the back of his belt. His sudden movement alerted the animal; it turned to face him. Olaf was ready with the rifle, but he didn't pull the trigger—there was something drastically wrong—a deer would have bounded away, not stand facing a hunter. He waited for a break in the blowing snow and when it came all he could do was collapse to the ground in disgust. "Oh, dern!" he moaned.

The pony moved, standing broadside, an excellent target. The wind smarted at Olaf's eyes, and tugged at his scarf, and whined in his ears. In the whine he heard voices, familiar voices: "We haven't had meat for a month. Horse meat is a delicacy in Europe. Haven't heard anyone keeping foxes around here. That pony kicks. She's mean. You should be glad she's gone. I'll keep meat on the table! I'll keep meat on the table!" The gun barrel lined up just behind the shoulder blade—the pony never knew what hit him.

Danny and Helga banged into the porch, threw their mittens to the floor, shuffled to the kitchen range, and held their cold hands to the warmth. Mutt squeezed out the door before anyone could stop him. "That dog," Ingrid hollered, "Olaf wants him kept in the house."

"Why?" Danny asked. "Where's Olaf? Hunting?"

"Yes, and that's exactly why Olaf wants him kept in the house."

Helga was shivering, her face a bright red. "It was cold in school. Kathleen poked wood into the furnace all day and still we were cold. A blizzard's coming, Mom."

"I know," Ingrid said. "That wind started blowing three hours ago. And I had to go outside to get wood." She looked at Danny and scowled. "As soon as you get warm you get out there and bring in the wood."

"Shouldn't I go look for Olaf? What if he can't find his way home in the storm?"

"Honey, if you go looking for Olaf, I'll have to go looking for you. Olaf will find his way home."

"Dad always tied a rope from the barn to the house when there was a blizzard," Danny said. "You know, so that he could find his way back."

"It's all right, Danny," Helga said. "Olaf is eighteen now. He can stand on his own two feet."

"Mom," Danny said, standing directly in front of his mother. "What's respectable?"

Helga stood beside him. "What's it mean, Mom. Is it good or bad?"

"It means to be proper," Ingrid said. "Why do you ask?" She felt a chill up her spine—the knot was tightening.

"Miss Sparks," Danny said.

"What about Miss Sparks?"

"It was really Mrs. Swenson," Helga said. "She went to the front of the class and told Miss Sparks that she was worried about Danny and me."

"Worried, why?"

"She said it was a shame our mother wasn't respectable, and that something should be done about it," Helga said.

Ingrid felt a rush of heat to her face. "Where was Kathleen?" she asked.

"In the basement, putting wood on the fire."

"What did Miss Sparks say?" Ingrid asked.

"Nothing. She doesn't like Mrs. Swenson," Danny said, shaking his head.

"She did say something, Danny," Helga said. "Miss Sparks said it wasn't anyone's business."

"Oh, yes," Danny said, "and then Mrs. Swenson said she'd better make it her business. Are you respectable, Mom?"

"Yes, Danny, I am respectable. Don't listen to gossip."

"But why does she say it?" Danny asked.

"I don't know," Ingrid said. "But you—all of us—have to have faith in one another."

"You mean like faith in God?" Helga asked.

"Yes, Sweetheart, exactly. Now get started on your chores. When anyone talks like that, don't let it bother you. I love all my children and I will do nothing to hurt them."

Danny smiled and kissed her cheek.

"We love you, too, Mom," Helga said.

Kathleen went straight to the chicken house to feed the chickens and gather the eggs—of course, there wouldn't be any eggs, but she always looked because her mother always asked. There was only one hen on the roost when she went inside. This being unusual she looked under the roost and to her horror saw Big Red and the other hen lying on the straw apparently dead. Big Red uttered a weak croak when she lifted him. Quickly she carried him to the house. "Mom, Red's sick. May I put him by the stove where it's warm?" she called from the porch.

"What happened?" Ingrid asked.

Kathleen brought the rooster in and laid it on the warm floor close to the stove. "He's almost frozen," Kathleen said. "I think he's going to die."

"Olaf said it was too cold in the chicken house," Ingrid said. They looked closely at Big Red who had by now scrambled awkwardly to his feet. "Are the hens all right?"

"One's on the roost and the other looks dead," Kathleen said. "I'll bring them in."

"If they're alive, bring them in," Ingrid said. "We'll have to keep them inside until it warms up. Put straw in that big box in the porch. Helga, Danny, help her. They may live if you hurry."

They quickly stuffed the big box with straw, placed it beside the warm range, and placed Big Red inside. A minute later Kathleen returned with one hen. "The other hen didn't make it," she said sadly. "It's dead under the roost."

"Give it to Mutt," Danny said. "He's too skinny. He needs more to eat."

"We'll see," Ingrid said, "just leave it for now." She might have plans for that hen—frozen it would keep until she had time to think about it.

Danny and Helga filled the wood box and every time they opened the kitchen door a blast of cold air flowed into the room. Kathleen sat beside Big Red stroking his long tail feathers.

"It's dark, Mom," Danny said, nudging the door closed with his foot on his final armful of wood. "Olaf ought to be back."

A barking and whining and scratching came at the door. Danny flung the door wide and there stood Olaf holding a piece of liver wrapped in a burlap bag. He stomped into the room, placed the liver on the table, and hugged the warmth of the stove. "Mutt led me home. Couldn't see a thing," he said.

"Faith, son, your father will be proud of you. I said you'd find a deer if you kept trying. I suppose you left it in Mr. Smith's barn," Ingrid said.

Olaf's face was so cold and stiff that it pained him to smile, but he managed a wide one that made words unnecessary.

Ingrid worried all week about the board meeting scheduled for Friday. Monday she decided not to go—it was too cold to walk to the school; Tuesday she was going—she'd never gone before, but she felt she had every right to go in Conor's place; Wednesday, she could see no reason to torment herself like this—she'd stay home.

Thursday, Helga and Danny burst into the house. "Mom, Kathleen—she's hurt," Danny shouted.

"Where is she? What happened?"

"Bobby threw a rock," Helga said.

"Mom, what's a hooker?" Danny asked.

"Where's Kathleen?"

"In the chicken house."

Ingrid found Kathleen with her face buried in Big Red's feathers.

"I'm not going to school—never again!" Kathleen cried, lifting her swollen face— the rock had narrowly missed her eye.

"You're cold. Come in the house," Ingrid said, placing her arm around Kathleen's shoulders.

Helga cleared off the couch and tucked a blanket around Kathleen; Danny fetched a chunk of ice from outdoors and Ingrid wrapped it in a towel and held it to Kathleen's eye.

Olaf came in from the barn. "What's wrong?" he asked.

"Bobby hit her with a rock," Danny said.

"Why did he do that? I'll wring his bloody neck!"

Strangely, Ingrid felt calm; she'd go to that meeting.

Mr. Wiggins, chairman of the school board, wiggled his wiry body into the student's desk and spread his papers. The desks had been drawn in a semicircle close to the heat register and the board members, Mrs. Swenson, Mr. Black, and Mr. Swenson, had picked the warmest place they could find. An unexpected guest, Mr. Mayer, the school inspector, sat next to Mr. Wiggins. There was one vacant seat; apparently the school board had forgotten they'd not yet found a replacement for Conor Inish. In a chair beside it, and to the side of the semi circle, sat Miss Sparks.

Mr. Black had recently recovered from the flu; the rings around his eyes were quite dark and he often wiped them with a handkerchief that he kept in his vest pocket. Mrs. Swenson did not remain in her seat. She walked about the room, her thin lips pressed in a straight line as she read the lessons on the blackboard and inspected the papers stacked on the teacher's desk.

The minutes of the last meeting were about to be read, when Old Mr. Smith slowly opened the basement door and peered inside. "Mighty cold down there," he said.

"It's mighty cold up here," Mrs. Swenson said. "Why didn't you come earlier?"

"What's this?" Mr. Mayer asked.

"We asked the old man to stoke the furnace," Mr. Wiggins said. "Couldn't meet in here without a fire."

"Let him sit, certainly," Mr. Mayer said.

Mr. Smith walked in, followed by Ingrid. "Mrs. Inish caught a ride," he said, "too cold to walk."

"This is a board meeting," Mrs. Swenson said, crossing her arms on her ample bosom. "It isn't open to anyone who happens to be passing by."

"With no proper introductions, "Mr. Mayer said, "I must ask if you're the wife of Conor Inish, the absent member of the board."

"Recent member," Mrs. Swenson corrected.

"I think it's quite proper for Mrs. Inish to sit in as proxy for her husband. You do not as yet have a replacement," Mr. Mayer said.

"With all due respect," Mrs. Swenson said, "you don't understand the problems of this community."

Mr. Mayer glanced around. "Perhaps someone should enlighten me. Mr. Swenson?"

Mr. Swenson's round eyes settled on his wife; he seemed to shrink inside his coat as he opened his mouth. He closed it quickly when Mr. Wiggins suggested the meeting begin.

"There's a lot of stuff to work through," Mr. Wiggins said, "and unless it warms up in here...."

"All right," Mr. Mayer said, motioning Ingrid to take the vacant seat.

The problem of the leaky roof came up and was disposed of with the suggestion the board supply the replacement shingles and look for volunteers to put them in place. The suggestion that the school was in dire need of a paint job was shelved for lack of money.

"Now the toilets," Mrs. Swenson said. "They aren't pumped out as promised by volunteers. Mr. Baker should be made to take his turn."

"How are you going to make anyone take their turn?" Mr. Wiggins asked. "It ain't a pleasant job, you know."

"Nevertheless, you, Mr. Wiggins, must discuss it with him and insist that he keep his promise. You'll assist him if necessary," Mrs. Swenson said.

Mr. Wiggins was smoking a cigarette—Ingrid saw him lean on his elbow, take a quick breath and blow a smoke ring—he watched it float to the ceiling. "Now, regrettably," he cleared his throat, "it's been drawn to my attention by a member of the board that corrections need to be made to the conduct of our teacher, Miss Sparks."

"Be specific. Which member?" Mr. Mayer asked.

"No disrespect, Mr. Mayer, but I thought everyone would know without being told."

Mr. Mayer shrugged his shoulders slightly and glanced at Mrs. Swenson over the rim of his glasses.

"It's the time spent on nonsense such as softball in the summer and snowball in the winter," Mr. Black said. "It's not right. A teacher should teach the three R's." Mrs. Swenson looked at Mr. Black with a smile of encouragement. "And that ain't all," Mr. Black went on, "this is a God fearing community. Miss Sparks is blaspheming against God—she was seen playing ball on the Sabbath with an uninvited woman right in this room."

Ingrid cast a glance at Miss Sparks who sat with her head tipped back and her frank eyes on Mr. Black.

Mr. Black wiped the sweat from his forehead.

"Too hot in here?" Old Mr. Smith asked.

"No, no," Mr. Black said, "go down and put more wood on the fire."

Mr. Wiggins took a deep draw on his cigarette. "Yet another complaint," he said. "This one's about the room and board provided by the Mulders."

Ingrid noticed Miss Sparks' astonished expression.

"I understand your mother-in-law passed on," Mr. Mayer said, addressing himself to Mr. Black. "Sincerest regrets. That leaves an empty room I suppose."

Mr. Black chose to ignore the remark. "It's been brought to my attention that hoboes are becoming a problem in this community," he said.

"Not exactly a problem of the school board," Mr. Wiggins objected.

"We should all be concerned," Mrs. Swenson spoke sharply. "It's always been my contention that those people, for their own good, should be sent on their way."

"You mean refused food?" Mr. Wiggins asked.

"It encourages them to stay in the area. They're another bad influence. There's a constant fear of crime in the community."

"There is?" Mr. Wiggins sat upright. "They sleep in my barn and ain't stole so much as a pitchfork. What crime are you talking about?"

Mrs. Swenson glanced at Ingrid. "Decent women are afraid of their advances," she said. "Other women encourage them."

Ingrid felt her knees go weak. How could she stand against this formidable woman? But she had to—for Kathleen, for all of her children. She gathered all her courage and rose from her desk. "Mr. Chairman," Ingrid said, surprised that her voice wasn't cracking, "am I allowed to comment on that insinuation?"

Mr. Wiggins' eyebrows arched. "Go ahead," he said.

"Mrs. Swenson, Mr. Black, I could ignore your callousness except for my children. First of all, I'll always give food to a hungry person, regardless of what you think or anyone else thinks. Then, perhaps you'll put this in the minutes of this meeting, Mr. Chairman: I've never been unfaithful to my husband, and I'm proud to say that I've held my family together in spite of the malice, the suspicion." Ingrid felt her knees again; she quickly sat back.

Mr. Wiggins moved sideways in his desk. He leaned forward with his hands pushing his knees as if he were an excited fan at the fights.

Miss Sparks rose. "Mr. Chairman, Board Members, Mr. Mayer, perhaps you haven't noticed as I have that a happy child makes a better student—good concentration, less fidgeting, no chalk throwing. But what makes a child happy? Is it being forbidden to play, forced to conform, not allowed the freedom to develop his or her own individuality? I think not. Children need to know that their families, their teacher, their community, support them. When I play with the children there is a purpose—it creates a bond, a trust. I think it makes me a better teacher. That's all I have to say on that subject. Regarding the question of fidelity—I feel free to comment since Mrs. Swenson chose to make it the board's business—I would suggest Mr. Black that you and the widow, Mrs. Charles, make your entrance to the Grande Hotel later in the evening when you are less likely to be seen." Miss Sparks let the shocked silence endure for a moment before she went on. "Regarding the Mulders, I have never been treated better or been more comfortable. However, constant agitation from Mrs. Swenson has made my stay at Redgarth impossible. I resign."

Miss Sparks smiled at Ingrid, buttoned her coat, picked up her hat and gloves and went out the door.

Mrs. Swenson stood; her voice was piercing. "I've never been so humiliated in my life. That—that creature, who does she think she is? You—you let her go," she said, pointing a finger at Mr. Wiggins, "She's good riddance."

"Come," she turned to her husband. "I've endured enough."

"Sit. Sit down," said Mr. Mayer. "The meeting has yet to be adjourned."

"Sparks goes, or I go," threatened Mrs. Swenson.

A drop of sweat dripped off Mr. Black's nose. "You mean—you mean you'd go? You start her, and then you go?"

"I didn't start her—ah, start anything. It was you and your hen-pecked wife," Mrs. Swenson said.

"It's men that's hen-pecked, not women," Mr. Swenson corrected.

Mrs. Swenson lost her composure. She turned toward the door.

"She's going," said Mr. Wiggins, ruffling his pages—he'd lost his place.

"Seconded," said Mr. Mayer.

All eyes watched Mrs. Swenson's lofty back as she went out the door.

"Now how do you do that?" Mr. Mayer asked the chairman. "Try as I might, I cannot blow a smoke ring."

"It's easy, sir. It's all in the way you hold your tongue."

98

CHAPTER 25

"WAL, THE INDIANS DONE IT," Weary Wilbur mumbled more to himself than to anyone else. The smoke curled down and to the sides to spread thickly through every square inch of the tin hovel. The hole in the roof, instead of sucking the smoke out, blocked it, until Weary flung the makeshift door to the side, and hunching at the stomach, retching at the mouth, came stumbling out.

Jerico sat outside yarning with the boys. He was telling the story of how he'd defended a friend named Double Track from the wrath of two railroad bulls and how he'd almost lost his own life in the skirmish. At the height of the story he stood and swung his fists at imaginary adversaries. "Just one more blow, but I tripped, and they both bashed me with their clubs till I was near dead. Got the scars to prove it." He pushed up his tangled hair to reveal his forehead. "Never let those bulls corner you," Jerico said. The boys nodded respectfully.

They sat beside a fire from which a thin smoke stream rose straight up to spread and push at the bottom of the bridge twenty feet above their heads. Boxcar sat so close that steam rose from his damp coat. "If he catches fire, all he has to do is run into the rain," Jerico said when Boxcar refused to move.

Jerico was simmering a stew in a large tin can that had at one time contained lard. Years ago he'd found the can in an alley behind a restaurant and since it was the correct size for a jungle stew, had coveted it ever since. At the times he left Vancouver for summer travel across the land, he hid the can in the bridge supports and over the years had always found it there on his return. The smell was mouthwatering if you got a whiff, but most whiffs were the rank stink of Boxcar's steaming coat.

"Well, old man," Weary addressed Boxcar, "we got to get a heater. S'pose one of those tin ones will do and a few chunks of stove pipe."

No one acknowledged his statement, so Weary raised his voice. "Fellows, we got to get a heater or this old man will die."

As if to support Weary's observation, Boxcar shivered, coughed, and gurgled in his throat.

Six men had a deck of cards and were playing poker; tiny stones represented money. "If you all chipped in we could buy one of them there tin heaters. They're only a couple a bucks," Weary said.

"Got no money," a player said between bets. "He won't die. Doc here will fix him up."

The man called Doc placed his cards face down, stooped by Boxcar and looked inside his mouth, then he took Boxcar's hand in his and felt the wrist for a pulse. "Better do something," Doc said, taking up the cards he'd just left.

"It'll be like a hospital," Weary said in an effort to capture more interest. "Those who get sick will stay in there until he gets well."

That statement aroused a few chuckles.

"It's just a rat trap," a player said.

"I saw a heater on a junk pile by the tracks," a youth said. "Rusty though."

"Where at?"

The youth reflected awhile. "Just south of Red Deer," he said.

That statement aroused a few more chuckles.

"That old man ought to be in an old folk's home. They'd look after him."

Weary grunted in disgust. "He's free as the wind. He wouldn't last a minute locked up inside a place like that," he said.

"We need ketchup," Jerico said.

The man who won most poker games and who claimed to be a finance consultant, scrimmaged in his turkey until he found a bottle.

Everyone gathered on all sides of Jerico's stew pot. The consultant had a head of lettuce that he broke into many chunks, Doc brought forth a loaf of bread, stale but edible, and the Red Deer youth set a squished sponge cake on the rickety board structure they called a table.

Weary dished a plateful for Boxcar. Boxcar shivered and shook his head. "I ought to have some chicken soup," he said.

"Old man," Weary said, "we got to do something."

"We got to do something," Weary told Jerico after they'd eaten their meal. "Maybe Ossified knows where we can get a heater."

"No idea where he is."

"Aesop—he's out of the fort. Could be he knows."

"No idea where he is either."

Jerico saw Weary's eyes were wide open. He suddenly realized this was an emergency; however, a heater being a bulky item, he had no connections.

The rain became a drizzle, the sun showed weakly, and by threes and fours the jungle emptied, except for Boxcar who stayed to hug the fire. He pulled his blanket up to his chin. "Don't remember Vancouver being this cold," he said.

"By gosh, the old man's dead," the Red Deer youth exclaimed, staring down at the lump that looked like a soggy old dog. He carried an empty oil drum, and his companion came behind with arms piled high with empty jam pails and lard pails the circumference of a stovepipe.

"Get Doc."

Doc felt for a pulse. "He's alive," he said.

They cut a hole in the top of the drum, using a chisel and a rock and a rusty hacksaw blade. Next they cut a door at the front, large enough to swallow wood chunks. This done, they cut out the ends of the tins and fitted them together so tightly that they couldn't twist and fall apart. This contrivance they carried inside the hovel and set against the wall. With wire twisted here and there to hold the chimney firm and the end forced up through a hole where the sheets joined in the roof, the project was finished.

Many years this spot under the bridge had been a jungle. The men, not having much to occupy their time, hunted for combustible material: broken wooden sidewalks, old railway ties, tree branches, fences of unwary homeowners. The Red Deer youth gathered dried chips and moss and with the loan of a few matches built a fire in the heater. Doc employed several companions and together they carried the old man, blanket and all, into the warm hovel.

An hour later Weary returned bearing a jar of chicken soup. He looked with awe at the heater. "Angels in heaven," he said breathlessly, "you're pretty nice fellows."

CHAPTER 26

OLAF WAS SO ABSORBED by thoughts of Marjorie that he tipped the sack of wheat too abruptly and the hopper overflowed. Carefully he scooped the spilled wheat with his cupped hands, blew the dust and dirt aside, and tossed it into the hopper. Marjorie wasn't attending school and Olaf couldn't figure out why. He'd kept the ring in his room since he'd come to the conclusion that he should pay for it before he gave it to her. There had been no harsh words—the last time he'd seen her, in the warmth that flowed between them he'd nearly mentioned the ring. Olaf closed the hopper lid and climbed onto the metal seat. The four draft horses leaned into their collars, the harness squeaked, the tugs rattled, and the seeder rolled. Olaf checked that every spout dropped a thin stream of wheat into the soil.

Danny relieved after school and the seeder sewed early morning till late night. Mr. Smith had been careful that the grain seed didn't get damp so that the flow would be steady and even. Every night he helped Olaf unhook the horses, feed them grain, and turn them loose in the pasture. The hot sun shone every day—the same as all the other springs Olaf remembered, but he didn't lose hope.

It was the middle of June before the last oat kernel was planted and Ingrid and Olaf walked across the fields to view Olaf's labors. "Your father couldn't do better," she said, smiling. "Now, the rains must come."

"It'll rain. Mr. Smith hasn't changed his mind about that," Olaf said.

"How wonderful to dream," Ingrid said with a whimsical expression. "How surprised your father will be. Same as '28—tall, thick wheat fields, waving in the wind like golden waves on a golden ocean."

"I was only seven, Mom. I don't remember."

The rain did come. Not a week went by before a thunder cloud passed overhead and dropped its precious cargo. Helga, Danny and Kathleen arrived home from school, their clothes dripping to form little pools on the verandah floor. Mutt shook himself and sprayed them all, yet none complained. Helga stuck out her tongue to feel the drops and insisted Kathleen do the same—Kathleen became carefree and cheerful as she used to be.

"Miss Sparks wants us to take wheat to school so that we can see how seeds sprout," Helga said.

"She's catching rain water," Danny said. "She says it's better than well water."

"I saw Marjorie," Helga said.

"You saw Marjorie?" Olaf asked anxiously.

"In the Black's yard. I waved but I guess she didn't see me," Helga said.

"When I go there, Mrs. Black tells me I can't see her," Kathleen said.

"Does she say why?" Olaf asked.

"Once she said Marjorie was sick, next time she'd gone for a walk, but Mrs. Black wouldn't say where, next time she'd gone to see her aunt."

"She doesn't come to school," Helga said.

"Maybe she doesn't want to," Danny said.

"It's the same when I go to the Black's place," Olaf said. "Mr. Black is always too busy to talk."

Ingrid said nothing. The Blacks had rejected her and she hardly considered them friends anymore, but she missed Marjorie's visits. The girl was always considerate and friendly.

"And I saw Mario, too," Helga said. "He was drunk."

"He wasn't drunk!" Kathleen said. "People are always saying that!"

"He walked like this," Helga said, wobbling side to side. "Mrs. Swenson says he's on-the-bottle."

Danny laughed.

"It appears he has a problem," Ingrid said soberly.

"Oh, Mom," Kathleen cried, "you're all against him."

Ingrid said no more, but she wished fervently Kathleen had set her heart on a different boy.

Olaf spoke up. "Mr. Smith says . . ."

"I hate what Mr. Smith says," Kathleen cried. She broke into tears and ran inside the house.

"I only wanted to say Mr. Smith asked me to check over the combines with him," Olaf said.

"He's counting his chickens before they're hatched," Ingrid said, "but, on the other hand, everything is growing fine, even the garden."

Two drenches within two weeks and the radio announced the expectation of a bumper crop.

But Ingrid had heard that before, many times during the last ten years. At the time the crop was ready to fill, the rains stopped, or hail pounded it into the ground, or rust withered it, or hoppers swarmed and devoured it. Last year gulls by the thousands flew upon the hordes of grasshoppers and glutted themselves to a point they could barely get off the ground. However, Mr. Smith wasn't one to talk idly and her hopes soared. The hopes of every farmer left within the southern grain belt soared.

The rains kept coming at regular intervals, and by August the fields were thick with ripe, well-filled grain heads waiting for the harvest.

Ingrid found her happiness overshadowed by Kathleen's despair. Now, Olaf too, became despondent since Marjorie had dropped out of his life. Her troubled mind saw Conor's return as the only solution to the family's happiness. It was a year since he left, and she could think of no way to bring him home.

CHAPTER 27

CONOR HAD NO IDEA that Forrest was an avid fan of the race horse; for the past week horse racing was the topic of the day. He pretended to be horrified. "So you're a gambler," he said. "You had a long stretch of bad luck."

"If I'd had real betting money on that last ten-to-one-shot, I probably wouldn't be here today, but I'm not an incorrigible gambler," Forrest said.

Spring Meadow was aglow with spring flowers when the glorified day arrived, daisies and buttercups tossed their blossoms to the breezes and the sun stirred the crocuses to life. Conor bounced the truck through the meadows and along the wagon trail that led to the main road. Nick and Forrest squeezed in the front seat beside him, with Mattie and Nickoli perched on Forrest's knee.

"We should have arrived yesterday and camped," Forrest said, impatiently eyeing the multitude of tents, wagons, and horses surrounding the track. "I hear Indians arrive days in advance.

"Who wants to bet on the races?" he added as Conor pulled up the truck.

Nick didn't want to bet, but he did want to watch, and Mattie said she and the baby would wait with Nick.

The betting ground was cluttered with horses, saddles, guns, beaded jackets and moccasins, blankets, and various other wagers. Two sturdy Indians stood guard at the betting post where the people put their money down.

Little Hawk had decked the black with war paint. "Bet on the painted black," Forrest urged.

Conor looked at the black's competition, an Arabian, and he recalled how Demon could run. "The Arabian's a winner," he said.

"No, no," Forrest insisted, "look at the black's form. He'll beat the Arabian by a mile."

Conor looked—the shiny black gelding had the makings of an outstanding runner—he even looked familiar.

Little Hawk, handsome in a beaded doeskin jacket and white Stetson, mounted the black and rode out to an earsplitting whoop from the Indians. It was a pretty sight—the black rearing high to come down prancing, foam flying. Then a white man called Jones rode out, pulled his hat low to almost touch the tip of his nose. His Arabian was quiet, well trained, a veteran. The cowboys, the ranchers, the farmers cheered as he pushed daintily through the crowd.

"I'll bet on the Arabian," Conor said.

Forrest groaned his displeasure. "You'll burn your fingers," he warned.

They went back to the others and moved ahead to a spot where the spectators thinned and where they had a clear view to the finish line.

"Little Hawk always paints his horse for war," Mattie said. "He claims it brings him good luck in the races."

"Paints his own face, too, I see," Conor observed. "He rides a fine black gelding," he added—and then it hit him. "My lord! That's Hat . . ." He turned and stared at Forrest.

Forrest's green eyes stared back.

The gun cracked and all eyes shot ahead to the starting.

The Arabian flashed out, a full length ahead, to the white's robust shouts and Forrest's groan of alarm. Little Hawk whipped side to side, and the black crept up, the Indians whooping to see it. He eased ahead, through the heel dust, to the tail, to the flank, to the stirrups. Forrest danced foot to foot, the excitement excruciating; Nickoli jounced and laughed at every step. They came like the wind, the black only holding when Little Hawk leaned far forward and gave a sharp war cry into the horse's ear. The black exploded in a burst of fright, and low to the ground, flew ahead, coming up neck and neck. The crowd erupted, screaming and yelling and shouting for their own. Little Hawk cut the black with the butt of his quirt and drew ahead by a length. Jones, a superb horseman, put the leather to his mount, but too late—the black was past the finish line. Little Hawk drew him in, to the cheers of the Indians and every horse lover there.

Forrest patted the baby bundle. "Nickoli, the best horse won! My winnings," Forrest said happily, "I'm off to collect my win . . ." His voice broke. Conor looked to see why—across the track, wending his way to the betting ground, was Hatfield.

Conor turned aside. "He hasn't seen us," he said. "Nick, get back to the truck."

"What is it?" Mattie asked.

"A guy who owes Guro five Hereford cows," Conor said.

"What do you mean?"

"Guro didn't tell you?" Conor asked. Mattie shook her head. "When Guro drove his herd here from Rolling Hills, five Herefords went missing. He tracked them to Hatfield's farm. Hatfield wouldn't let him on the place," Conor said.

"But that has nothing to do with you," Mattie said.

"Perhaps Forrest should explain," Conor said.

"Why the hell didn't you tell me?" Forrest asked Conor, then turning to Mattie he said, "It's a long story, Mattie. Please leave it till we're back at the ranch."

Nickoli began to fuss and cry for his bottle. By the time his mother located it, they'd returned to watching Hatfield collecting his bet.

Forrest chuckled. "He knows a runner when he sees one," he said.

Conor didn't think the situation humorous.

At the edge of the crowd the jockeys talked while their horses stood swishing their tales.

"We're in for it," Conor said. "Hatfield's on his way to the horses."

Hatfield looked at the black horse, stepped around him and looked again, then stepped up to Little Hawk.

Conor drew in his breath.

"Nothing to fret about," Forrest assured him. "No evidence—not one iota."

Hatfield walked close to Little Hawk, talking in his face. Little Hawk apparently didn't like what he heard, since he stepped back and waved a fist at Hatfield. Little Hawk was a small man, no equal to Hatfield. "Aw, damn!" Forrest said, and before he could get there, Little Hawk was lying in the dust. Forrest pulled him to his feet.

"You!" Hatfield said. "What the hell you doing here?"

"I'm a spectator at the races," Forrest said.

"So you're in this. I ought to have known," Hatfield said, his lip curling in disgust.

"Don't hit him!" It was Irene standing between them.

"Get out of here. You get in the way and you'll get hit too," Hatfield shouted. "Goddam, betray your own father!"

"Calm down, Hatfield!" Forrest said. "If you have a gripe, settle it by the law."

"Have a gripe! You bet I have a gripe—that black horse belongs to me." Hatfield swatted Irene out of his way and strode toward the horse.

The Indian crowd moved in. Littler Hawk, Tommy Tutlack and the guards angrily milled about. "It's all right, let him alone," Forrest shouted. He caught up to Hatfield. "There's another matter you should be concerned about," he said, matching Hatfield's steps. "What does the name Roy Gurofsky mean to you?"

"Not a damn thing. Never heard of him," Hatfield said.

"Two years ago? Five Hereford cows? That may run against you in court."

Irene ran up and looked imploringly at Forrest. He held her firmly by the arm.

Hatfield turned, lifting his head he sneered with haughty denial. "To hell with all of you!" he shouted at the crowd. "And you—" he shook his fist at Forrest, "you'll hate the day you were born before I'm through with you." He turned on his heel, stomped to his truck and drove off.

"What will I do?" Irene whispered to Forrest. "I've nowhere to go."

It was calving time at the ranch. Mattie rode Demon through the meadows in search of those few cows that couldn't easily give birth; Conor was then called upon to perform the doctoring necessary to save both mother and calf. From the hundred or so new calves now born, he'd lost one, a record that even Guro couldn't have topped.

With Irene taking care of Nickoli and preparing the meals, Mattie was free to ride the range, and she did joyfully from morning till dusk.

Irene was crooning and rocking Nickoli in his cradle when Mattie entered the kitchen. Irene had shaped the bread dough in loaves and had set them near the stove to rise. "You're doing too much," Mattie said.

"You took me in," Irene said. "I don't know what I'd have done if you hadn't."

"That doesn't mean you have to work day and night. Forrest is going to Lacombe to pick up batteries. Go with him and get this list of groceries," Mattie said. "I can bake the bread. I did before you came, you know."

Irene had one dress, the print she'd worn to the races. "Wear slacks," Mattie told her and handed over a pair of her own. They were too big in the waist. "We can cut down one of Guro's belts," Mattie said.

"I'm sorry about your husband," Irene said. "Forrest told me what happened."

Mattie lost her happy look. "It was dreadful," she said. "I don't think I'll ever forget." Tears came to her eyes. Irene reached out to her and they clung like two lost souls. Mattie was the first to recover. "You go now. I've little Nickoli to think of," she said.

When Forrest drove past the house he saw Mattie through the window, a sad look on her face.

"I mentioned her husband and I shouldn't have," Irene said. "I made her cry."

Forrest saw that Irene had been crying too. Sympathetic, he decided; a quality inherited from her mother no doubt. Irene had been at the ranch seven days, but he'd seen little of her—meal times and evenings were short since Conor insisted on a constant vigil of the cows.

Forrest wore a new pair of jeans and shirt that he'd bought in Lacombe last winter. He had gotten rid of his old suit and coat along with his past life. He felt he could never go back to the confines of an office after experiencing the wide open spaces.

"Irene, I hope you like it here," Forrest said.

"Oh, yes, I do," Irene said, turning to face him. Forrest again felt the tug at his heart that her look had given him before. He began to drive along the wagon trail through the meadows. Tiger lilies swayed in the wind, and sweet clover swept the air with a sweet fragrance. On impulse Forrest stopped the truck, got out and picked a bouquet. Irene held the flowers to her face to smell the sweet scent—lovely, Forrest thought.

"The ranchers don't graze their animals here until summer," he said as they came to the community pasture. "Gives the grass time to grow." Farther on, Little Hawk's dogs raced out to chase after the truck.

105

"There's the black horse that won the race," Irene said. "It certainly does look like Dad's horse."

"It was," Forrest said. "But he traded three horses for five cattle—a fair trade, don't you think?"

Irene agreed. "But I don't know what Dad would think," she said.

"Don't you?" Forrest asked.

"Always of himself, Mom says. Dad isn't so fierce as he pretends to be. It's only since the hard times that he's so cross. I can remember when he played games with Isabel and me—catch and hide-and-seek, games like that."

"Really?"

"Yes, Mom says he just won't face reality."

"It's a mean trick to leave you behind."

"I don't mind now that Mattie took me in, but I think I should look for work in Lacombe," Irene said.

"But why?" Forrest asked, alarmed. "Mattie needs assistance with Nickoli, and you said that you like it here."

"Oh, oh!" Irene said, looking at the gauges. "It's the rad."

"Those hills we just climbed."

Irene looked through the back window. "There's a bucket, now all we need is water."

In a few minutes they came across a slough in a field. Forrest stopped at the side of the road, climbed in the back and handed down the bucket. Irene took off her shoes and rolled up her pant legs. That seemed to be a good idea, so Forrest did the same. "Race you!" he said.

Irene crawled through the barbed wire fence, and then struck in a straight line for the slough. The field was newly seeded; little spurts of dust burst up from the soles of her bare feet. Forrest was nearly up to her when he stubbed his big toe on a rock; it stung so dreadfully that he sat down right there and gave it a close inspection, then he watched Irene running, pail bobbing in her hand. When she turned, he waved; she dropped the pail and came back to him.

"My toe!" he said, still holding his foot in his hand.

"Sliver?"

"Stubbed it—could be broken," Forrest said. "Sliver, too, maybe. Help me to the slough. A soaking will be helpful."

Irene lifted on his arms until he stood. Forrest placed his arm across her shoulders and they hobbled forward. "Sometimes little things can be painful," Forrest said, grinning shamelessly. He leaned against her—Irene staggered under his weight.

The land had been tilled close to the edge of the slough. "There's no place to sit," Irene said.

"There." Forrest indicated a mound of grass near the middle.

Irene tested the mud with the ball of her foot. Forrest started toward the mound and Irene quickly stepped forward to steady him. The mud sucked like a live thing. "I can't lift my feet," Irene said.

"Try lifting one at a time," Forrest said with an impish grin.

"If you'll stand . . ." Forrest shifted as Irene spoke and his feet slipped from under him.

106

Irene laughed. "Oh, I'm sorry," she said, "but I couldn't help it. You look so funny, half in the water."

She tried to lift him but unexpectedly landed in Forrest's lap. "So there now, the other half's wet," Forrest said, joining in her laughter.

"Oh, dear," Irene said, "I can't go looking for a job like this."

"No, you can't," Forrest said; his features composed.

Irene leaned her head against his shoulder—the only comfortable position she could find.

"We can talk awhile. We haven't had much of a chance to get to know each other at the ranch," Forrest said.

Irene giggled. "Talk in a slough?" she asked.

"Mind?"

"No, not really," Irene said. She was looking at his eyes again. There were tiny freckles across the bridge of her nose. "I hope no one sees us," she said. "They'd think we're crazy."

"We are," Forrest said. "Anyway, there's no more than one car a week travels on this road."

"The farmer might come to look at his crop," Irene said.

"And find two monkeys in his slough," Forrest said. "He'd probably invite us for dinner."

"Forrest . . ."

"Aren't you comfortable? We could move to that mound of grass and dry off."

"Oh, no, I'm comfortable," Irene said. "I was wondering, do you think I could ride Black Blizzard in a race?"

"The black horse?" he asked.

Irene nodded her head against his shoulder. "I always wanted to ride him, but Dad wouldn't allow it. You know how he is," she said.

Forrest chuckled. "Yes, I know how Hatfield is. Could you win the race?"

Irene nodded.

"Just like that, aye? We'll have to talk to Little Hawk on the return trip," Forrest said. "Black Blizzard—that name suits him to a T."

"It's my name for him," Irene said. "He's like a black dust cloud speeding across the prairie. Dad couldn't catch him without chasing him into a corner, but he'd come right up to me and rub his nose against my neck."

Forrest gave her a squeeze. "For sure we'll talk to Little Hawk," he said. Forrest had nothing to lean against. "We're going to have to move, Honey," he said. Irene wiggled from his lap. She hadn't resented his word off endearment, Forrest noticed; that was encouraging.

Hand in hand they plodded through the water and walked across the field to the truck where they put their shoes on. Forrest's toe had made a remarkable recovery. He topped up the radiator, then checked underneath for leaks and noticed the muffler was loose; a few more bumps would surely knock it off. Guro obviously had been used to his truck failing to function properly; in the back Forrest found a roll of wire, a spare tire, tubes, tire pump and other paraphernalia. "What's this?" he asked, holding high an odd shaped part.

"It's a carburetor," Irene said.

Forrest secured the muffler as best he could with the wire. It should suffice, he thought, since the main road was smooth gravel. "Are you dry enough to travel?" he asked.

"We'll dry off in the breeze," Irene said. The floor boards had half inch spaces between them, allowing the air to travel freely throughout the cab.

"We'll talk when we get to Lacombe," Forrest said above the noise of the motor. The countryside passed by: small lakes, pine groves, cultivated fields. Ducks swam in the ditches and flew up so close that it seemed they'd be run down, but they banked at the last instant and whizzed off. Crows swooped low over the land, watching for a bird nest they could rob. Hawks perched on fence posts with an ear cocked to the sound of an unwary mouse or perhaps a gopher. Orange and yellow orioles flitted among the bushes. Forrest had seen it all before but now it was different—he was sharing it with Irene.

He parked on the main street of Lacombe and together they shopped, then hand in hand they explored the main street. In a knickknack place Forrest bought a broach carved in the shape of a bird in flight. "Beautiful," he described it, "for a beautiful lady."

"Next stop, oil and gas, then we're off for home," Forrest said. He recalled that he'd planned to price the cost of a false tooth, but it had become unimportant.

They stopped at Little Hawk's cabin but he had not returned. Black Blizzard trotted to the fence and stretched his neck for the apple that Irene had brought from the grocery box. He ate it from her hand while she stroked his neck. "He knows me after all that time," she said.

"We'll come back in a few days," Forrest promised. "We'd better go. The truck has no headlights."

They were a scant five miles from the ranch when the motor spluttered, threatening to die. Forrest pumped the gas pedal to no avail; a few jerks and the motor stopped. "The gauges are fine," Forrest noted. "It can't be out of gas unless the tank leaks or this gauge isn't accurate."

They got out, one on each side, and crawled under. "No leaks here," Forrest said. "How about your side?" He squirmed under until he could see both sides.

Irene knocked the tank with her knuckles. "Seems full," she said.

Forrest's arm touched the hot muffler. "Ouch!" When he jerked away, his elbow hit Irene in the eye. "Oh, Sweetheart, I'm so sorry," he whispered. He pulled her toward him and kissed her eye. "Kisses make it better," he mumbled. Irene moved her lips in line with his and slid her arms around his shoulders.

"Trouble under there?" It was Little Hawk's face peering under the truck and it had a worried look. "You, Forrest? You all right?"

"Little Hawk, just the man I wanted to see," Forrest said with misgivings. They squirmed from under the truck and dusted off their clothes.

"It's soon dark. I give you ride home," Little Hawk said.

CHAPTER 28

HAYING STARTED EARLY; Mattie put Conor in charge. Conor contracted Little Hawk and his Indians. The contract went smoothly, no injuries to speak of; Conor often pondered the means Guro's accident could have been averted.

Conor felt comfortable with the ranching business. He began to conceive plans to start his own ranch and to bring his family together again, but the one thing most needed was what he failed to have: money. His share from the sale of the two horses had been ten dollars, and the black gelding had put fifty dollars into his pocket even though he hadn't bet on it. The fifty he had sent to Ingrid last week.

Conor spotted the advertisement in the newspaper that Forrest had brought from town: Fifty Herefords wanted, best quality, four cents a pound on the hoof.

Conor pointed out to Mattie that with the spring calves her herd was too large for the hay available for stacking; consequently, if she had to feed early in the winter, part of the herd would starve before spring. Mattie understood—she had watched cattle starve at Rolling Hills.

"Four cents a pound is unusually high," Conor said. "He'll probably want to pick his own stock."

Mattie decided hastily; taxes were unpaid, welding bills were due, and the grocery bill was high.

They arranged the deal: fifty cattle to be driven to Cochrane, a week's slow drive, since the buyer, Mr. Bradford, expected the cattle to arrive in the same tiptop shape that he'd selected them. He sketched the safest route, keeping in mind grass and water.

"Ease 'em along," Conor told the men. The Herefords strung out following Conor and the big bay he called King, as though they were goslings following the mother goose. Forrest and Nick rode the drags; Forrest astride Demon, and Nick, a mare called Cupid. Nick led the pack horse, a small Indian paint.

At noon, they brought the herd to a standstill and let them graze while they ate the venison sandwiches Mattie had packed.

"We'll attend the theater in Cochrane," Forrest said.

"I plan to buy riding boots," Conor said. "These farm boots aren't the best for riding a horse."

"They were the best for riding the rods," Forrest recalled.

"Seems a long time ago," Conor said.

"This isn't a trail drive. It's more like a holiday," Nick said, grinning.

"Bandits could charge out of those bushes, kill us all and make off with the herd," Forrest drawled.

"You ever been on a trail drive?" Nick asked.

"No," Forrest said. "I'm a white-collar man. Never rubbed elbows with cowboys."

"My great-grandpa came over the Western Trail."

"I expect he'd savvy concerning bandits," Forrest said.

"He trailed to Dakota from down Texas way."

"Did the Indians trouble him?"

"Yeah, kept stealing the cattle. Gramps says the Indians were hungry."

"Your great-grandfather alive?" Forrest asked.

"He's alive, he's eighty."

"I'll bet he has interesting stories to tell," Conor said.

"Once he starts, he doesn't stop. It's wolves, wild rivers, lightning, stampedes," Nick said.

"And bandits," Conor added. "I heard tell there were two or three thousand cattle in one trail herd."

Forrest whistled his astonishment. "You aren't pulling my leg now."

"And only ten or twelve cowboys," Conor added.

Forrest looked at Conor and at Nick and at the fifty Herefords grazing peacefully. "We can't possibly succeed," he quipped.

As the herd wound across the green prairies and through the foothills, the men basked in a relaxation that recently had been lacking in their lives. There was time to comment on the feathery clouds at the peaks of the mountains, on how the valleys opened to steep-walled coulees, on why the foothills appeared purple in the distance. At night, to the soft sounds of the creek and the crackle of the campfire, they confided their past and their hopes for the future and spoke of many things until it was time to call it a day. When they arrived at Cochrane, Nick was reluctant to end the drive. "I just might trail 'em all the way to the Rio Grande," he joked.

Mr. Bradford and his cowhands arrived and assisted in driving the cattle to the scales at the railway tracks, weighed them, brought forth a chequebook and wrote in the figures. "We'll take 'em from here," he said. "You fellows come to the ranch, go back in the morning."

"Much obliged," Conor said, "but we don't get to a town often. We plan to shop."

"Ride due west until you find us," Mr. Bradford said. "You're welcome day or night." He rode off to follow his cowhands, who by now had headed the herd toward his ranch.

"Tie the horses here at the tracks until we find a place to spend the night," Forrest suggested.

"I'll bring the pack," Nick said.

"Leave it. It's safe enough," Conor said. "That Indian pony will kick a stranger to death if he tries to approach."

The three men strode through the bright lights, sizing up the town. While Conor and Nick looked for boots, Forrest excused himself; a shop across the street had caught his eye. Shopping done, they stopped at a restaurant and consumed three large steaks. They reserved a room at a hotel where saddled horses stood hipshot, tied to a rail, then they filed into the gent's section for a drink.

A sudden whoop and crash caught the attention of patrons and staff alike. "It's war you say?" someone shouted. "How do you know that?"

"On the radio. Jake heard it," the waiter said.

"Well, go to hell! It's war. Canada declared war!"

"Poland, I'll bet the damn Germans advanced on Poland," the waiter said.

"Germans are inside Warsaw right now," Jake said, keeping one ear to the radio.

"God bless Churchill!" Forrest said.

"We've nothing to fight with," someone snorted.

"Who cares?" a youth exclaimed excitedly. "We've finally somewhere to go. Where's the recruiting office?"

"You'll find out soon enough," said a disgruntled old-timer with a three-day beard and a loud voice. "You young fry, you can get swallowed up by a war, you know."

The hotel owner rushed into the room. "What we have here, Jake? A rebellion?"

"It's war, boss," Jake said. "Canada declared war!"

"War!" The owner shouted above the din. "Drinks to Mackenzie King. Son of a gun! Drinks on the house!"

"We'll make the next round," Forrest said to Conor. "I'll put up five." He'd spent the black gelding's winnings in the little shop across the street—spending five now would leave five in his pocket.

Conor shook his head doubtfully. "Here's two dollars in change," he said. "*You* told me what happens to vagrants."

Nick offered five.

Forrest figured twelve ought to do it. He felt inspired. Staggering slightly, he wound around the tables to the bar. "A round," he shouted to the bartender. He took a step up onto the platform reserved for entertainers, the bar stools and tables below. "In the name of God we'll do our duty! We'll knock the stuffing out of Hitler!" The cheers set the glasses to rattling. "No country, no country in this world deserves a beating more than Germany. I lost two precious uncles to Germany not twenty years ago. I say, here's to them!" He raised his glass and down the hatch.

"We'll drink to that. Splendid cause. Bravo! Bravo!"

"I was telling my friends here, come up here, Conor, Nick," Forrest said, beckoning emphatically.

Conor and Nick weren't comfortable in the limelight, but the whisky and the excitement took precedence, and they, too, staggered slightly, standing above the crowd.

"My buddies," Forrest told the crowd, "we'll fight. Won't we fellows?" Conor and Nick raised their fisted arms in the spirit of the gathering. "We've numerous reasons to go to war: to get that guy," Forrest pounded a table, "to honor our country, our flag, our Queen, for a decent meal and clothes that aren't lousy."

"To get away from my nagging wife," spoke up a short stout fellow, flinging his hat to sail across the room.

"A shyster of a boss," his companion said, looking around cautiously.

"My girl, she . . ." a youth shouted.

"She'll love you twice as much!"

The crowd milled with excitement. A patron waved a chair above his head. Jake and the boss stood side by side. "Easy men. Easy now," the boss soothed. "Coffee on the house. You all sit down now. You're welcome to sit and we'll discuss this like rational men. Coffee's on the house."

Conor, Forrest and Nick squared up with the bartender.

"You may stable at the rear. If you come late and the front door's locked, use the rear entrance. Remember, men, we're going to win this war, we got to stay calm," the boss said, anticipating the worst from their flushed faces. "Smashing a hotel ain't going to win a war."

The cool evening air had a calming effect on the three men staggering to the tracks to pick up their horses. The hoot of an owl hushed the yards. The streetlights waned. "Where in tarnation did we leave them!" Conor said, stumbling over a rail.

In the deep shadows Nick came face to face with a freight car. "Which way?" he asked.

"Shush," Forrest hissed. From somewhere in the maze, sounds came as if someone were clubbing a dog—take that! And that! And that! "What the hell's going on!"

They waited. There was no sound whatsoever—even the owl kept still.

"Ossified, get that bastard," a deep voice hissed, followed by the slow crunch of boots on cinders. "There he is. His club, get that friggin club." The boots ran this way and that way—heavy breathing, sporadic curses, wrenching, jerking, twisting, and the cinders grinding beneath their feet. On and on it came, louder, more violent—the thud of a club, the curse on contact. "Get it. The club. Over there," the husky voice gasped. A scramble, a sickening sound, again and again the club struck its mark. "Enough! Enough!"

"You're friggin right about that," the man called Ossified said. "One more kick will do it."

After the last thud, the night became still, deathly still. Forrest placed a hand on Conor's shoulder telling him not to move. "Sounds like Jerico," he whispered.

"Boxcar's dead." It was the voice called Ossified. "What now, leave him here?"

There was the sound of two men struggling with a burden.

"We'll get him out on one of them horses."

"By gad, they mean to steal our horses," Conor hissed. The three moved in that direction.

"Put him acrost the bay, Jerico. We'd better git fast."

"Jerico!" Forrest ran forward. "Jerico Joe!"

Jerico lowered his end of the burden to the ground. "Small Guy?" he said, peering into the dimness. "Where you come from? You just come now?"

"We've been here a spell, looking for our horses," Forrest said.

Jerico became uneasy, so uneasy that beads of sweat broke out on his forehead. It had happened too quickly; they should have left Boxcar where he died.

Forrest looked at the bruised and beaten body there on the ground.

"The bull killed him," Jerico explained. "Old man couldn't get away fast enough."

"Yeah," the man called Ossified said. "Get him out. I'll take him."

Jerico looked nervously at Forrest. "Bring the horse right back. Can't leave the old man on the tracks."

"Hello, Farmer," Jerico recognized Conor.

Conor nodded. "Leave the horse at the hotel," he said.

Ossified untied Conor's bay and clumsily swung aboard. Jerico boosted the body and Ossified draped it across the horse in back of the saddle. Ossified nodded at the three men and rode into the night.

"I got to get out," Jerico said. "Another bull could come along."

"Follow us," Forrest said. They led the horses through the dark streets to the rear of the hotel and stabled them before clumping up the back stairs to their room.

Jerico stood by the door while the others took off their boots. The room was airless and smelled stale, much as a jail. "Sit," Forrest said and with a socked foot pushed a chair toward him. Jerico sat. He was too nervous to talk, too nervous to do anything but sit.

"Wish we had coffee," Conor said.

Forrest handed Nick a quarter. "Go see if the restaurant's open. Bring back a pot," Forrest said.

Slowly Jerico relaxed; could be it wasn't as bad as he'd supposed. He wondered why Forrest hadn't asked questions, and why everyone was so calm

Nick returned with a pot of coffee, four cups, sugar and cream on a tray.

"Canada declared war," Forrest told Jerico.

"Lots of people get killed in a war," Jerico said. His own observation made him feel better, loosened his tongue. He was certain the bull was dead. Ossified savvied what parts of a man to club and kick. If anyone could get him off, Small Guy could. "Had it coming," Jerico defended himself.

Forrest nodded. "But the law may not agree. What do you think, Conor?"

Then Jerico remembered the letter—Conor Inish's letter. He dug in an inside shirt pocket and brought forth the paper creased so deeply that it had torn at the folds. Tenderly he opened it and spread the paper flat against his knee, then handed it to Conor.

Conor held it beneath the one light bulb in the room and read. It was Ingrid's handwriting, it was the only letter he'd received since he left. A flood of emotion gripped him. "How did you get it?" he asked.

Jerico became dreamy eyed. He was thinking of himself and the fair lady having coffee in a restaurant, a picture he'd brought to mind many times. "She gave it to me, almost a year ago," he said.

"Trouble, Conor?" Forrest asked.

Conor handed Forrest the letter, walked to a chair and collapsed upon it.

Forrest read aloud, "The children and I are not in Winnipeg. Because of some lawyer the bank did not take the farm, only the machinery. Please come home. Love, Ingrid."

Forrest folded the letter neatly and handed it to Conor. "Justice prevails," he said. He chuckled, a pleasant chuckle starting deep within the chest and bubbling upward until his eyes ran tears. He clapped Conor's shoulder. "Justice prevails!"

CHAPTER 29

JERICO CLEANED UP. Forrest saw to it—he sensed he would throw up from the smell permeating the small hotel room. To complicate the proceedings, Jerico came up with the assumption he didn't need a shower, although everyone else tripped up the hall. Forrest, however, hadn't missed the expression of fondness on Jerico's features as he'd unfolded the letter. "Ladies adore the smell of soap," Forrest said. "It's something I've never totally grasped, but a soapy smell will draw a woman every time."

While Jerico was showering, Forrest sneaked in, removed everything from Jerico's pockets and got rid of his clothes. Conor gave a shirt, Nick, pants, Forrest, underwear and socks. Forrest placed these items in exactly the same place Jerico's clothes had been.

The following morning Jerico went to a barber and came out with his hair cut the length of Forrest's and with his beard trimmed.

113

The new Jerico rode north with the three men, starting before the birds waked and arriving at the ranch in time for supper. Forrest had picked up a smoked ham, and that's what they ate at the kitchen table, along with boiled potatoes and carrots from Mattie's garden. The talk was of the trip, of Conor's newly won farm, and the latest on the war.

Forrest was restless; he wanted to talk to Irene in private. When the meal was finally finished, Conor offered to help with the dishes. "Are you feeling all right?" Forrest asked.

"Just thought you and Irene might have something to say to each other," Conor said.

"For a dumb farmer, you're awfully observant," Forrest remarked.

Conor playfully punched him in the ribs and pushed him out the door.

Forrest thought Irene looked pensive as she sat on the porch steps. He was uncertain as to what to say or do. The war had been looming over their heads for so long it had become a myth, then suddenly there it was, a driving force in their lives. He gave Irene a hand up. Neither spoke as they walked along the wagon road. They hardly noticed the splash of color the early fall flowers gave to the countryside. They stopped and Irene lifted her face to him; he kissed her deeply. He hadn't wanted to rush her decision but now he felt he had no choice. "Irene," he said softly, "I want you to know I love you and no matter your answer I always will. It's not fair to you, I know, we've known each other for so short a time." Forrest had to look away from her eyes when the question formed in his mind. "Would you ever marry me?" he asked.

"I'll marry you, Forrest. I love you," Irene said.

"Conor wants to leave in a few days."

"I'll wait for you here. Mattie asked me to stay on and help her with the ranch."

"Are you sure? I want you to be sure," Forrest said.

"I'm sure," Irene said. "I've never been surer of anything in my life."

"I bought a ring." Forrest patted every pocket before he found it. The ring was a gold band imbedded with small diamonds, and Forrest knew he'd made the right choice by her expression. "You'll pull me through this war, Irene," he said. "I'll have more than a fighting chance with you to fight for."

"Look!" Irene said when they came to the creek. The ripples shone with rainbow colors catching the last rays of the sun. It seemed a good omen for their plans. "When you come back, we'll get our own ranch," she said.

"We will, Sweetheart. That's exactly what we'll do."

"Do you think Mattie and I can keep the ranch going by ourselves?" Irene asked.

"Mattie knows the ranching business thoroughly. You're familiar with farm life, not much different from ranching. Conor says he'll be able to help at calving time and Mattie can depend on Little Hawk. Then, there are my furloughs."

"What will you do?"

"I always wanted to try my hand at flying. I'll try for the air force."

"The others?"

"Nick says the army. Jerico says he'll go where I go."

"He's such a strange man," Irene said.

"Yes and no. We're all strange now and then," Forrest said. "Remember the slough?" Forrest saw the dimples form in her cheeks and he drew her close.

They married in the court house. That evening Mattie held a party at the ranch. Conor, Nick, and Jerico supplied several bottles of wine; Little Hawk, Tommy Tutlack and their wives brought venison stew; two neighboring ranchers, Larson and Scott and their wives brought home-baked bread and pies. They talked war—everyone, everywhere, talked war. They discussed ranching with Forrest, wheat farming with Conor, horse racing with Little Hawk, and the fine art of baking homemade bread with Irene and Mattie. They danced to records until they discovered Jerico played the mouth organ. Mattie brought Guro's harmonica and insisted Jerico play. To Forrest's amazement Jerico played exceedingly well, harmonizing "Sleepy Lagoon," "There's a Long, Long Trail A-Winding," "Girl of My Dreams."

"Captain Joe, where did you learn to play the harmonica so cleverly?" Forrest asked.

Jerico grinned and kept on playing, but he flatly refused to dance.

The party came to an end at three in the morning. The Scotts had invited Mattie and Nickoli for the weekend—Forrest and Irene had free run of the house. The guests cheered and hugged and kissed the newlyweds—and then they were alone. Forrest stretched full length on the couch, pretending he was going to spend the night right there. Irene, dressed in her nightgown, stood in the bedroom doorway watching, then she slipped back inside and latched the door.

Forrest looked up. He saw no one, and he saw the bedroom door closed. He tiptoed over there and turned the knob—the door was locked. He'd been buffaloed—caught in his own trap! He couldn't let a woman outwit him, even if it was Irene. He sneaked outdoors and crept around the house until he was at the foot of the bedroom window. He pushed upward on the frame, no luck; he pushed to the right and to the left—at that moment someone attacked him, threw a blanket over his head and held it tight around his arms.

"It's me! It's me!," Forrest shouted, trying to thresh his way free. Then he heard laughter—Irene's laughter. Forrest grabbed her and together they rolled over and over. When the rolling stopped they kissed a kiss of hope, and love, and passion.

"What in tarnation is going on out there? You two get to bed!" It was Conor's voice coming from the bunkhouse.

CHAPTER 30

OLAF WAS YOUNG, only eighteen, but he was big and he was strong. Broad across the shoulders, arms tight with muscles, he could work from dawn to dark, and he did. But he was sick at heart, and the work didn't get his mind off Marjorie—the many hours driving the combine, scooping the grain with the shovel—but it helped.

And then the news broke, Canada declared war against Germany. He would have dropped everything and rushed to the recruiting office, except for the crop. He felt a need to leave here, and then there was the war—a godsend!

The weather was perfect for harvesting and every hour counted. Despite Mr. Smith's caution, a cutter knife broke. Olaf should have had a spare knife for such an emergency, but he didn't. If he hurried to town he could be back on the combine in an hour.

His mother saw him headed for the Chevy.

"I'm in a hurry," Olaf said.

"Kathleen can buy the groceries while you get the repairs. It won't take extra time," his mother said.

Olaf drove fast.

The two had their respective tasks completed and were loading the car when Mario stepped up beside Olaf. "Give me a ride home," he said.

"You'll have to sit with this stuff in the back seat. Get in. I'm in a hurry," Olaf said.

"You ought to let me drive," Mario said. "You're bloody slow."

Kathleen sat sideways in the front seat so that she could look at Mario and talk to him. "Olaf's in a hurry," she said, "the combine broke."

"If he's in such a hurry, he should let me drive." Mario wrapped an arm around Olaf's neck and squeezed. "Come on, old man," he said, "you ain't so high and mighty you can't let a fellow take the wheel."

"Cut that out, Mario!" Olaf shouted.

"Don't do that Mario," Kathleen said. "We'll drive in the ditch."

"Don't do that!" Mario mocked. "You girls are all alike. Don't do that, Mario! And Marjorie ain't no different. Don't do that Mario!"

"You've seen Marjorie?" Kathleen asked. "She's supposed to be at her aunt's place."

"I ain't seen her lately," Mario said.

Olaf stopped the car and turned to look at Mario. "When did you see her?" he demanded.

"While ago. What do you care, she's just a slut," Mario said.

"Marjorie isn't like *that*. Why do you say *that*?" Kathleen cried.

"You don't know anything about Marjorie. She ain't what you think she is," Mario said with a knowing smile.

"You don't call a girl a slut without something to back it up," Olaf said sharply. "Exactly what do you mean?"

"A girl that acts friendly and warms a guy up, that's what I mean, and says no when he wants some, what kind of girl is that if she ain't a slut. Anyway, if she wasn't, she is now," Mario said smugly.

"You did that to Marjorie!" Olaf's voice cracked with shock.

"You would too, old man, if you'd been there. Let me drive," Mario said, stepping out.

Olaf leapt out. "You son-of-a-bitch! I'll kill you!"

Mario grabbed the cutter blade, and holding it in his fist he swung, slicing Olaf's forehead. He swung again—blood flowed down Olaf's arm. But Mario hadn't bargained on Olaf's fury—a fist to the stomach doubled him up, a fist to the head sent him reeling. Savagely Olaf grabbed his hair, threw him against the car, beating him unmercifully.

Kathleen grabbed Olaf's arm and hung on. "You're killing him, Olaf. Stop it. Now!" She threw herself across Mario's body as it sprawled on the gravel road.

Olaf ached for that final kick, but he couldn't; Kathleen blocked the way.

Olaf sat and placed his bloody forehead on his arms—his body shook with broken sobs. Kathleen sat beside him, her hand on his shoulder.

"It's Mario's dad," Kathleen said softly. Olaf hadn't even heard the buggy drive up and he didn't care. By the time he had the strength to check the sobs and raise his head to glance around, Mario was gone.

At the house Kathleen washed Olaf's wounds at the kitchen sink, spread the cuts with Mercurochrome, wrapped his arm in a towel, and tied a bandage to cover his forehead. Soon afterward they drove to the field where Olaf replaced the broken blade, climbed on the combine and went back to work.

Kathleen sat in the car and watched the combine circle the field until the hopper was full. She drove to the granary, and taking the extra shovel matched Olaf scoop for scoop.

Olaf's wounds shocked Ingrid. She refused to stop asking questions before her children had given her a complete account.

"I'll enlist," Olaf told his mother, "when the harvest is finished."

Ingrid was heartsick—her son off to war, taking with him so grave a memory. She excused herself, saying that the day was long and she needed fresh air and she would go for a drive and return in an hour.

At the Black's farm, the dog welcomed Ingrid. Tail wagging, it led her to the back door. Ingrid supposed the door to slam shut in her face by Mrs. Black's look.

"Who is it?" Mr. Black called. No one answered, so he came to see for himself.

Ingrid remained outside the door. "I've come here, not for myself, but for my son," she said. "There's a bond between my son Olaf and your daughter Marjorie."

"Our daughter," Mr. Black snorted, "she ain't our daughter."

"Our children can't always control their own destiny," Ingrid said. "Olaf is going to war with a wounded heart. I ask you to tell me, where is Marjorie?"

"She ain't our daughter." Mr. Black turned abruptly and left the room.

"Mrs. Black, I know you disapprove of me. I accept that," Ingrid said. "But that has nothing to do with our children. We have to give them hope if we expect them to survive. In the name of God, please tell me, where is Marjorie?"

Mrs. Black stared at the doorway through which her husband had left the room. She appeared to be making a choice. Slowly she pulled a drawer from the kitchen table and wrote on a paper she found there.

"God bless you," Ingrid said as she left.

CHAPTER 31

WHERE CONOR SAT on top of the freight car he could see the Brook's soup kitchen.

"Wonder whether Hatfield's in town," he said.

"I won't hop off to find out," Forrest said.

"No grasshoppers like the time we came," Nick said. "Remember how the train stopped on the slippery goo."

Conor laughed. He laughed easily these days. With a contented smile he sat for hours watching the golden grain fields slide past.

"Perhaps you'll have a crop the same as that," Forrest said.

"No such luck. The machinery and the horses are sold. No way anyone could put the crop in."

"That's a shame," said Nick. "First crop in ten years. I hope my pa had seed."

"There will be many harvest jobs," Conor said. He felt satisfied that he could hire on within a day or two's travel from home.

"My *wife* packed sandwiches," Forrest said.

"Your *wife*," Conor said grinning. "Ain't you the smug one. I saw you wearing your heart on your sleeve, and you won her in less than a year."

"How long were you acquainted with your wife prior to your marriage?" Forrest asked.

"Eight years."

"Eight years! Those were eight wasted years, Conor," Forrest said seriously. "I've been told that farmers are slow—but that's not slow—that's asleep at the switch."

Jerico laughed.

"Why the humor?" Forrest asked.

"Asleep at the switch." Jerico laughed again. "We ought to get to Mrs. Jordan's tomorrow," he added, more seriously.

"For breakfast," Conor said.

"For breakfast!" Forrest exclaimed. "You mean we ride nonstop?"

"Have to get home."

"Eight years. Eight wasted years," Forrest said, shaking his head.

Mrs. Jordan's huge Royal Alexandra cook stove stood in the same place. The welcome sign hung above the same plank tables, but only a few men sat there. Mrs. Jordan said that she remembered Conor and Forrest doing her chores. "Did you find Hatfield's place last fall?" she asked.

"You were right. He tried to gyp us on wages," Forrest said. "He proved to be a scoundrel."

"Shouldn't have suggested him," Mrs. Jordan apologized.

"No, not at all," Forrest said, "in a fashion he financed our gold mine."

Mrs. Jordan didn't ask what he meant, since Jerico had caught her eye. She touched his shoulder. "Jerico, I'd know you anywhere, but, my, how you've changed."

Jerico recalled a broach in his shirt pocket that hadn't sold. "For all those meals I et," he said and handed it to her.

The men unpacked the last sandwiches, washed them down with Mrs. Jordan's hot tea, and resumed their journey.

It was eight o'clock the next morning the freight pulled into Redgarth.

"Man, oh, man," Forrest complained, "I'll never become a Sergeant in the Royal Canadian Air Force shook up like this." They were so sore and stiff that they made a comical sight hopping off the freight, but by the time they walked to Redgarth the kinks had worked out.

"There's my car," Conor said, walking up the street. "I wonder who this is in town so early."

Olaf stepped beyond the doctor's office. His arm was in a sling and a bandage ran across the top of his head.

Conor walked straight up to him. "Faith, son, what happened to you?"

A slow smile spread across Olaf's face, like the morning sun breaking across the horizon. "You're back, Dad. I knew you'd come back," he said.

Conor gently placed a hand on Olaf's shoulder. "Is your mother in town?" he asked.

"No. She made me go to the doctor or else I'd be combining," Olaf said. "We've a *bumper* crop, Dad."

Conor felt hands covering his eyes; he twisted and caught Kathleen in his arms. She hugged him unmercifully. "Dad, you came home—Olaf said you'd come home."

"Of course I came home. Did anyone think I wouldn't?"

"Conor Inish," Mr. Kruger shouted from the post office. Strand of hair flying, Mr. Kruger hurried across the street to shake Conor's hand. "I told 'em you'd come back. Them women ought to be rolled up and stuffed in a mail box."

Conor introduced his companions. Forrest uttered a feeble excuse to go somewhere, and Jerico mentioned he had to meet a guy.

"You're coming to the farm. I want you to meet my wife," Conor spoke proudly. He'd show this Forrest why waiting eight years was worthwhile.

"I feel I've been gone for years and years," Conor confided. "Faith, it feels good to be home."

"No dust, no dust anywhere," Nick said, as if it were a miracle.

There was the old faded barn, the house, and the ivy-covered verandah on which stood a trim woman with a mop of blonde hair curling down her back.

Conor stopped the car, honked the horn, and stepped out. A tide of joy swept over him when he saw that radiant smile she kept for him alone. Heart leaping he caught her in his arms.

"Conor, is it you?" she cried, touching his eyes and his lips with her fingertips. "You look so tall. Have you grown?"

"Darling, such a silly question," Conor said and chuckled.

"But, but you look so much younger. Is it really you? Have you come back?"

"It's no dream, Sweetheart. You bet I've come back," he said and kissed her. "And if I ever leave again, you're coming with me.

"Sweet darling, I've missed you so much," he whispered. He saw her face flush with happiness and he kissed her again, he felt he'd never get enough of her kisses.

"The others," Ingrid said breathlessly. "Who are the others?"

Helga, with a jubilant shriek, ran to his side. Danny shyly slipped his hand inside his own.

Olaf and Nick toured the works of the combine while Forrest waited impatiently to meet Conor's wife. Jerico, out of his element, sat on the car's running board, fidgeting.

"Mrs. Inish, you're better known to me than my own wife," Forrest said, a twinkle in his eye, "but Conor has kept the best part secret."

Ingrid giggled like a schoolgirl.

"Conor said his wife was so unattractive that it took eight years to muster the courage to marry her."

Conor snorted. "This fellow here has only once in his entire life done anything right. Because of a lawyer, Forrest here, the farm is *saved*."

"You are *that* lawyer?" Ingrid asked, incredulously. "And who is he?"

"Captain Jerico Joe," Forrest said, with a flourish in Jerico's direction.

The scene in the coffee shop flashed through Ingrid's mind—the friendly, confident hobo, his matted hair covering an ugly scar, his clothes filthy. She'd thought how handsome he'd be if he'd clean up, and here he was, cleaned up.

Ingrid approached him. "Jerico, remember me? Ingrid Inish," she said.

Jerico at once recovered his *savoir-faire*. He removed his cap, bowed a deep bow, and offered his arm. Gracefully Ingrid accepted, and together they entered the house.

"I'll be damned," Forrest said to Conor.

CHAPTER 32

"I'VE BEEN HERE BEFORE," Conor said.

"It's familiar all right. It's Cheery Lane," Forrest said. The street sign with the happy face had been straightened and pounded into the ground.

"And the old Coke machine is leaning against the wall in the same place," Forrest added, "but those aren't relief clerks behind that counter. I wouldn't have believed we'd line up to risk our lives in a year's time."

A sergeant marched up and down the lines of waiting men. "No need for haste, boys," he shouted. "We'll get you all in."

Conor looked at the waiting lines stretching clear to the old soup kitchen. The lines were every class: jungle men in ragged clothes, businessmen in slick suits, farmers in overalls, youths just out of college, and veterans from the First World War.

Jerico sat on the curb, and Nick and Olaf followed suit. It appeared they had a long wait ahead.

"Conor Inish, you're the one who has to provide for us all," Forrest said, extending his hand for a handshake. "You better get back driving that combine."

Conor was hesitant to leave his four companions—they were so much a part of him—but he knew that all there was to say was said, and all there was to do was done. Silently he shook their hands, one by one, and then hugged his son good-bye.

He forced his thoughts to Ingrid. She'd be waiting on the shady verandah for his return.

ISBN 1553695089

9 781553 695080